T0269721

Cry
Wolf

Also available by Lark O. Jensen

Alaska Untamed Mysteries

Bear Witness

Writing as Linda O. Johnston

Kendra Ballantine Series

Feline Fatale
Howl Deadly
Never Say Sty
Double Dog Dare
The Fright of the Iguana
Meow Is for Murder
Fine-Feathered Death
Nothing to Fear but Ferrets
Sit, Stay, Slay

Alpha Force Series

Visionary Wolf
Protector Wolf
Canadian Wolf
Loyal Wolf
Untamed Wolf
Undercover Wolf
Hawk's Challenge
Cougar's Conquest
Guardian Wolf
Alaskan Wolf
Claws of the Lynx
Alpha Wolf

Pet Rescue Mysteries

Chihuahua Chaos
Teacup Turbulence
Oodles of Poodles
Hounds Abound
The More the Terrier
Beagle Mania

Superstition Mysteries

Unlucky Charms
Knock on Wood
Lost Under a Ladder

Barkery & Biscuits Mysteries

For a Good Paws
Pick & Chews
Bad to the Bone
To Catch a Treat
Bite the Biscuit

K-9 Ranch Rescue Series

Trained to Protect
Second Chance Soldier

Shelter of Secrets Series

Her Undercover Refuge
Guardian K-9 on Call
Undercover Cowboy Defender

Other Books

Covert Alliance
Alias Mommy
Tommy's Mom
Covert Attraction
Undercover Soldier
Back to Life
Not a Moment Too Soon
Tommy's Mum
Operation: Reunited
Marriage: Classified
Alias Mummy
The Ballad of Jack O'Dair
Once a Cavalier
Stranger on the Mountain
Point in Time
A Glimpse of Forever

Cry
Wolf

AN ALASKA
UNTAMED MYSTERY

Lark O. Jensen

CROOKED
LANE

NEW YORK

This is a work of fiction. All of the names, characters, organizations, places and events portrayed in this novel are either products of the author's imagination or are used fictitiously. Any resemblance to real or actual events, locales, or persons, living or dead, is entirely coincidental.

Copyright © 2023 by Linda O. Johnston

All rights reserved.

Published in the United States by Crooked Lane Books, an imprint of The Quick Brown Fox & Company LLC.

Crooked Lane Books and its logo are trademarks of The Quick Brown Fox & Company LLC.

Library of Congress Catalog-in-Publication data available upon request.

ISBN (hardcover): 978-1-63910-455-0
ISBN (ebook): 978-1-63910-456-7

Cover illustration by Ben Perini

Printed in the United States.

www.crookedlanebooks.com

Crooked Lane Books
34 West 27th St., 10th Floor
New York, NY 10001

First Edition: November 2023

10 9 8 7 6 5 4 3 2 1

This is another book dedicated to Fred Johnston, Linda O. Johnston's husband. Yes, he's still a buddy of Lark O. Jensen too.

Chapter One

"I can't wait till next week!" I exclaimed to Wayne Deerfield, executive director of Juneau Wildlife World. His surname was highly appropriate considering where he worked, although the fifty-something man resembled a bear more than a deer. He was large and muscular enough to help wrangle the animals when necessary, a good thing.

"Yep, it'll start a valuable time for all of us." Wayne smiled at me as he leaned over his cluttered wooden desk—a big work surface for a big man. "We're happy that you'll begin working for us for the winter, Stacie, rather than volunteering part-time."

"I'm looking forward to it," I replied from the comfortable chair I sat in across from him in the also-cluttered office. I'd met with him this morning to discuss my becoming an employee again. Not that I would get a huge paycheck. The animal sanctuary ran mostly on donations, with some money coming in from visiting tourists. I'd spent time here volunteering on days off during the summer season when I worked at my dream job, leading nature tours on the local waters. And though I needed an income now, late in the year, to care for myself and my dog, I didn't want to take much money from this very special nature preserve.

But I intended to do a good job observing and helping the animals. I'd love it. Again. Even though my favorite job remained giving tours on boats in the summer. I reached down and patted my wonderful gray-and-white husky, Sasha, on the head. I'd brought her along, as always, and she sat on the shining wood veneer floor beside me. Most areas where wildlife roamed in this refuge were off-limits to her, although she could join me on many paths in areas where the animals tended not to come close to the fences. Hiking out there was good exercise for her—and me too. If I ever visited the locations where I might get up close and personal with some wildlife, which I hadn't yet, she could stay in an enclosed area in this main building. At least she wouldn't be home alone.

Wayne was a nice enough guy to permit her to be here even under limited circumstances, and I appreciated it. Most dogs weren't allowed in this sanctuary, but Wayne had met Sasha before and knew how well behaved she was. And even during visits when I brought her along while volunteering, there were times she sensed that one of the inhabitants needed help. She communicated this to me in her special way of staying in the area, looking into my eyes with her wonderful blue ones, and snorting without getting close to the animal. That had happened when a reindeer had injured its leg in one of the large areas of the preserve near a hiking trail, and another time when a young bear cub had gotten separated from its mother. Sasha's name means defender, after all.

I'd immediately notified the first staff member I found, and both times the animals had been rescued and received the care they needed.

So now most of those who worked and volunteered at this shelter were perfectly fine with Sasha coming along, just as she was welcome on the *ClemElk*. That's the tour boat where I work as the primary guide during the season when it isn't too cold or icy to be out on the Alaskan waters viewing the amazing wildlife in the water and along the shorelines.

That season was drawing to an end now, in chilly mid-October. I had a couple more tours to give this week, but then ClemTours would close for the winter. I'd had to determine what to do with my time till spring—mine and Sasha's. Not that it was hard to decide. I'm a naturalist by education and career—and love of animals. I volunteer at Juneau Wildlife World when I have time during the summer. And last winter I'd officially worked here, so it made sense for me to come back again.

Which was why I was here today—to confirm all was well and that I'd officially start in a few days.

"Sounds good," Wayne said. "We'll still have a few of our regular staff, but as usual, a lot have said they're heading back to the lower forty-eight for the winter. Not everyone can deal well with snow and harsh conditions."

"The animals have to." Not that I had to remind him. "All the more reason for their human protectors to do just that—protect them."

"I'm not one you need to convince," he said with a laugh. "But fortunately, you're not the only one who'll hang out to help. We have a few volunteers living in the Juneau area who said they'll continue to come."

"That's great," I said. "Anyway, I'll start first thing next week, after I give my last two tours of the season over the next few days."

"Fine. Hey, while you're here, you may want to check out who's in today who will also be working with us over the winter. We even have some newcomers."

"I like that idea. I assume things will work the same as last year? You're still providing instructions about who's to observe where and when, keeping an eye on our protected inhabitants, right?"

"That's right. As you know, the instructions are pretty general but mostly involve observation and reporting, and even tours if the weather is okay and any tourists arrive. You may also be asked to help prepare food for specified animal groups and distribute it at appropriate places for them. Other people will work on that too, as always. Of course, it's even more critical in winter, since the animals can do less foraging on their own."

Some, like the reindeer and elk, usually fed off the landscape. The carnivores pretty much had to be supplied with some of their food year-round, since the idea was to keep the inhabitants from eating each other. The preserve had been established years ago not just as a place where animals roamed in their natural habitats but also where they could be taken in because of injuries or because they needed a special place to go, which was why it included large but enclosed areas for their safety. The animals were all amazing to observe and care for, wildlife at its wildest and best here in Alaska. Naturalists like me, Stacie Calder, a woman long in love with wildlife, couldn't ask for anything better.

"Got it."

"I'm going downstairs for a few minutes," he continued. "You can join me, and maybe go outside to do your usual patrol of our grounds—with Sasha, if you'd like."

"I'm ready to go when you are, and so's Sasha."

We rose, my dog included, and headed for the office door. I paused to gaze through the wide windows that lined the far side of the hall in this delightful welcome building, which had apparently been constructed as a special part of the sanctuary. People on both levels could look out toward several parts of the grounds. Animals weren't always visible, but at the moment I saw a bald eagle soaring in the sky.

"Wow," I said as I watched. Sasha must have seen it too, since her head moved in the same direction.

"Yeah, wow," Wayne agreed.

The eagle soon soared out of sight, and I followed the director down the stairway.

In the lobby downstairs, one of the other employees was just walking in. I didn't know Marnie Korman well, but she was the main food preparation employee. She looked about my age: early thirties. My hair is of medium length and the shade I like to call dachshund brown, after the pup I had as a child. Hers? It was short and bright blond, probably with help. She was a pretty lady, and she was smiling now, as she usually was when I saw her.

"Hi, Stacie," she said right away. "And hi, Sasha." She joined us and bent to pat my loving husky on the head.

Like me, she wore a sweatshirt. Hers, a gray one, read *Juneau Wildlife World*. Mine was plain black. I was used to wearing shirts that said *ClemTours* on my water outings, but while I worked here, I'd probably wear a Juneau Wildlife World sweatshirt often too. And thick parkas outside as the weather got worse.

"Hi back," I said. "You're going to have to instruct me again in food prep soon so I can help you. I'll be working full-time in a couple of days."

"Ah, the Alaskan weather is driving you off the water again," she said, nodding knowingly. "Well, better here in the snow where you can watch and help our resident animals rather than dealing with snow and ice around tour boats—even though you won't get to see your seals and whales and other sea creatures."

"Exactly. But naturalist me is thrilled to get to visit with all kinds of native wildlife."

"I understand that." She looked toward Wayne, who now stood beside me. "And hi to you," she said. "I'm about to start getting more of our animals' food ready. Do we have anyone coming in to help—volunteers or employees?"

"As far as I know, we do," Wayne said.

"Great. Well, see you later, Stacie and Sasha." With that, Marnie pivoted on the tile floor and headed toward the rear of the tall, open lobby area, where a door led into a hallway and to the kitchen and some other important areas, like the on-site veterinary clinic.

"So, what are you up to now?" Wayne asked.

"Well, if Marnie had suggested it, I'd go help her with food prep. I may stop in later to check on whether she needs me to do anything. But for now, I think Sasha and I will take a quick hike."

"Sounds good."

Sasha and I were soon outside. I hunkered my sweatshirt around me because it was chilly, around forty degrees on this early-October afternoon. Colder at night. Would it get even colder? Absolutely, as autumn merged into winter and more precipitation, usually snow, fell. I could deal with this. I had for over a year now. But it was okay for me to admit to myself when I was a bit chilly.

There was a large open area at the front of the welcome building, mostly paved. Visitors, as well as employees and volunteers, could park their cars there, and today I'd also left my blue SUV there—at the end, so lots of people could park closer to the door. But there were only a few cars there at the moment.

As usual, Sasha was leashed beside me, wearing a harness so I wouldn't choke her if I had to slow her down or lead her in a different direction. Right now, we headed across the parking area to the nearest pathway, a wide one with a gravel surface that led between a couple of the reserve areas containing types of wildlife that shouldn't mix. They were all enclosed by tall chain-link fences, and some, farther away from here, also had very large, rounded, uneven caps that prevented the animals from scaling the tops. Both areas here were large, with rolling terrain covered with grass, where the resident reindeer, moose, and elk could graze. Hares and others hung out here too. They weren't all native to this area but had been brought in for different reasons, often because they or their mothers had been discovered injured somewhere else in Alaska and they needed a place to live.

As Sasha and I set off down the trail, we were alone. I'd given tours at this sanctuary as well as from my boat when I was volunteering here, but that wasn't why I'd come today—and there didn't appear to be any folks looking for tours today anyway.

I did see some reindeer in the distance, but none of the other animals. Still, it was always fun to see who was where.

We continued on for a while, and I saw some moose in the area on the other side of the trail, also far away. When I was on the job, I figured, I'd see a lot more, although when the weather got bad, maybe not. But I would file reports on who I saw when to help the sanctuary keep track of its residents. I'd also help get food out there, and when the ground was covered with snow, we'd augment what was left of the grass and other growth these animals would eat with other plants brought in to feed them.

In a while, I turned and gently pulled at Sasha's leash. "Come," I said. "Time to go back." We needed to say good-bye and remind Wayne when we'd return. As we continued along the path and neared the parking lot again, I saw a man approaching. A visitor, I assumed, who also intended to go out and see what animals he could. Was he carrying a shelter map? I didn't see him holding one, nor a phone where he could view maps on the app.

He was tall and thin, wearing a blue knit cap. He also wore a sweatshirt that said *Juneau Wildlife World*. Had he been here before? Just bought it?

"Hey," he shouted as he got closer.

I smiled as he hurried up to us. I hadn't seen him while volunteering, or at least I didn't think so. I started to welcome him to the sanctuary, but he stopped right in front of me and grabbed for Sasha's leash. I moved so he couldn't reach it.

"Why do you have a damned dog here?" he shouted. "This is an animal sanctuary. Pets don't belong. Didn't they tell you when you arrived and paid your admission?"

"Whoa," I responded through gritted teeth. "I didn't pay admission. I'm a longtime volunteer and am about to become a winter employee for the second time. The director, Wayne Deerfield, knows about Sasha and always lets me bring her."

My dog stood beside me, looking up at the scowling man, and I put my hand on her head, gently commanding her to stay still.

"I don't believe that," the man said. "Now, get the hell out of here."

"I don't care what you believe," I stormed back. "And who are you to tell me or my dog what to do?"

"I'm one of the managers, that's who I am. And your dog needs to leave. You too."

Really? A manager? "You must be new." I tried to keep my voice light, even friendly. "We haven't met before. As I said, I've been coming for a long while and am always allowed to bring Sasha. Like I also said, Wayne is fine with it." I paused as the guy continued to glare. "Tell you what. Let's go back to the welcome building and talk to him."

I didn't ask if he agreed, but leading Sasha with her leash, I walked around him and headed back along the path toward the main building.

I knew Wayne was fine with Sasha being here. But as an incoming employee, I'd undoubtedly run into this man again. If he really was a new manager—and why would he lie about that?—I'd have to figure out a way to get along with him and still have my wonderful dog with me.

Hopefully, Wayne, apparently his boss, would help.

I heard the fellow's footsteps on the gravel as he caught up and walked beside me, with Sasha on my other side. Okay, if he really was a manager, now was a good time to start attempting to get along with him. After all, he might wind up officially telling me what to do, Sasha or not.

I turned to look at him and made myself smile. "I'm Stacie Calder, by the way. I'm a naturalist by background and profession. I provide tours on one of the tour boats that goes out into the local waters during the spring and summer, and I've got a couple more to provide this year before the season ends. That's when I'll start working here—next week."

"Got it," he said, still somewhat curtly. But he followed my cue and said, "I'm Oliver Brownling. I've worked at various wildlife sanctuaries here in Alaska and started at this one about a week ago."

"I'll want to hear about the others," I told him. "I really appreciate all the places where local wildlife is protected and cared for. I've visited some when I can, but not as many as I'd like. Were any around the Juneau area?"

"A couple."

I got no further details after we crossed the parking lot and entered the building.

There were a few visitors in the lobby area, and one of the volunteers I'd known for a while, Larraine Placarde, was with them, showing them around. Larraine was in her forties and had lived in Alaska her whole life, although she'd been in Juneau for only five years or so. But like the others, including my new acquaintance Oliver, she was an animal aficionado. Her long brown hair was pulled back, held by a silver scrunchie at the back of her neck. She was pretty, with prominent eyelashes and a ready grin.

She showed that grin now to the people with her, who appeared to be a family with two young kids. They all wore fluffy parkas, even though the worst cold was yet to come. Then she spotted me with Oliver and Sasha and gave a brief wave. I waved back as I headed up the stairway to the second floor with my dog, Oliver behind us. Hopefully, Wayne was in his office.

Another volunteer came down the stairs just then, and I said hi to Bill Westerstein, who'd been here several times when I'd visited this season. Couldn't tell it on the stairway, but he was about my height. Though he wasn't much older than me, his hair was graying, but he still looked fairly handsome. He was a nice guy, originally from the San Francisco area, he'd told me, but he wanted to do something more frontierlike than he could there. He said he worked at one of the downtown Juneau restaurants now and was looking forward to spending his first real winter in Alaska. Well, he'd soon get that opportunity.

Following him was Shawna Streight, a native of Juneau. In fact, judging by her appearance, she might actually be a descendent of the original natives, with her dark skin and sharp features. I kind of envied her. She might be even closer to the animals than the rest of us, at least by her cultural heritage.

"Hi, you two," I said, then had to ask, "Are both of you going to continue to volunteer this winter?"

"Definitely," Bill called over his shoulder.

"Me too," Shawna said.

I wondered what the man following me was thinking. As a manager, he might be managing these volunteers too.

We soon reached the second floor, and Sasha and I led the way to Wayne's office. The door was closed, as I'd expected. I hoped the director was there and knocked.

"Come in," came the call from inside. I opened the door and entered, letting Sasha go in first. Oliver brought up the rear, and I wondered again what the new manager was thinking.

Wayne wasn't alone. Marnie, our food prep expert, sat on a chair across from his desk. But she got up at our entry and came over to pat Sasha, who lapped up the attention, as she usually did.

"Hi, Wayne," I began immediately, waving at Marnie and not letting Oliver start the conversation. "Sasha and I were out on the trail across the street, and Oliver joined us. He said he's a new manager, though we hadn't met before. And—well, he made it very clear he didn't think Sasha should be there, or anywhere else at this sanctuary. I can understand his concerns, but I'd really appreciate it if you'd enlighten him about my dog being permitted to be here, though there are rules Sasha and I need to follow, which we do."

Wayne rose and looked from me to Oliver and back again, his eyes not lighting on the dog in question. "Have a seat, you two." Wayne swept his hand in our direction.

As we settled in, Marnie also took over one of the chairs, keeping her hand on Sasha's head.

Oliver watched Sasha, and Marnie too. "I don't mean to be a pain in the butt, but I really give a damn about the wildlife, as you know, Wayne. Having a dog here disrupting things doesn't seem like a good idea to me." His tone was a lot gentler than it had been with me. Interesting.

"Oh, Sasha doesn't disrupt anything," Marnie said before Wayne could speak. "She even helps the wildlife. She's let some of us know when she's sensed they need attention or help."

"Oh, really? That's wonderful. I didn't know."

Boy, Oliver was really backing down. He even smiled a little.

"That's right," Wayne said. "And as Stacie said, we do have some rules that she follows with Sasha."

"That's fine, then. I won't say anything more, as long as they follow the rules. Maybe you can tell me what they are."

He was looking at Marnie now.

"Not up to me," she said. "And I need to get back downstairs for more food prep." She stood and again patted Sasha.

Oliver stood too. "You can show me a bit more about how that's done, then." He looked back at Wayne. "Sorry if I caused any trouble."

As Marnie left, Oliver followed, leaving Sasha and me with Wayne.

"It'll be a good thing if Oliver and you get along," Wayne said, after the others were gone. "He'll have responsibilities running and supervising things, and you'll report to him somewhat."

I felt a bit bewildered, but what the heck. "As long as he's okay now with Sasha being with me, that's fine. I'll do my best to get along with him." At least Sasha was a nice, quiet dog who seldom barked or whined, and that helped with her being around the wildlife. Maybe it would help with her being around Oliver too.

"Excellent. Now, why don't you go downstairs and watch more food preparation too? That will be some of what you'll be doing when you work here this winter."

"Fine. I'll find a place outside the kitchen for Sasha to hang out, at least this time. If she comes in with me, I think she'll want to sample everything."

Wayne laughed. "I wouldn't be surprised." He paused. "How much longer will you be around today?"

"Not much longer. But you'll see me again in a couple of days. Sasha too."

"I'll look forward to seeing you," Wayne said, "and putting you to work."

Chapter Two

I was in no hurry to leave, but I also didn't want to get involved with food prep today. What Wayne had said was a suggestion, not an order—this time. And I figured Oliver wasn't going to come after me again and argue about my having my dog along with me, so once again I led Sasha down the path that began across the parking lot. I was thrilled to see a moose—a male— much closer to us beyond the fence than I'd seen any earlier today.

But he was still far enough away that I wasn't worried about Sasha's presence. I just stood there with her so we wouldn't scare the moose away. I could see his antlers, but we weren't near enough for me to see the flap of skin beneath his chin, and I didn't pull out my small binoculars just to look for it. He appeared to be a loner, which was often true of moose, except in mating season.

I wondered how soon this guy would lose his antlers for the winter.

I didn't want to take the time now, but I looked forward to going farther into the sanctuary, hiking to areas beyond these where the landscape rose and other land animals that fascinated me dwelt, including wolves and bears. I sometimes saw both from my boat on water tours, but here I could get closer. And remain safe. And sometimes have Sasha with me.

I saw a few people head our direction from the parking lot, none of whom looked familiar. They appeared to be two couples, maybe in their twenties. This was still the time of year when at least some tourists visited Alaska. They could come to the sanctuary to view animals before it became more difficult thanks to consistently challenging weather: snow, ice, freezing temperatures—all the things that made Alaska such a wonderful and unique state.

"Hi," I said as they drew closer, and Sasha wagged her tail. "If you look over there, you'll see a moose not too far away."

"Oooh," said one of the women as she looked in the direction I pointed, and all of them seemed enthralled at the sight.

I hoped they'd see more wildlife, but it was getting late in the afternoon and they probably wouldn't stay much longer. Maybe they'd been here for a while viewing other areas. I hoped so, for their sakes.

But I didn't ask. I wasn't going to show them around.

And it was time for Sasha and me to leave.

I soon helped my pup into the back seat of my car, where I strapped her in for safety.

So, where to now? Home, most likely. I'd need to rest up a bit for the tour I'd be giving tomorrow.

Still, it was late enough that I'd soon need to decide what to do about dinner.

Before I got far in thinking about it, I noticed several people emerging from the welcome building a short distance from my car. Bill Westerstein came out first with Marnie. They both carried large boxes, and I assumed they would head for one or more of the distant areas to provide food for some of the animals inside the sanctuary. Oliver and Larraine followed, but their arms were empty. Oliver seemed to be hurrying forward to catch up with Marnie. I couldn't really tell what was going on but wondered if he had offered to help.

In any case, only Bill and Marnie continued with the food, heading for the big garage at the far end of the parking lot where the preserve's vehicles were kept. There were several large all-terrain vehicles with substantial tires that could be driven anywhere in the shelter in any weather, so employees and volunteers were able to check out all areas and all the kinds of animals. Also, there were snowmobiles for people to get around the shelter in bad weather, and some smaller ATVs.

Larraine continued standing by the welcome building door, and Oliver eventually returned that way. They both went back inside.

I considered joining them. I wouldn't go out to help deliver food, especially not with Sasha along, but since I'd be back soon to work with these people, it wouldn't hurt to socialize with them.

Still, I'd have time to do that when I returned here for my job. And I really didn't have anything to talk to them about right now. I turned on my car's engine and backed out of the space.

I had an idea what to do about dinner. I figured that once I got home, I would call my buddy—and more—Officer Liam Amaruq, a trooper with the new and special Initial Response Section of the Alaska State Troopers. I knew I was always welcome to call him, but he was generally quite busy, so I most often had to leave a message. I'd invite him to join me for dinner.

As it turned out, after I drove a good half hour from the sanctuary and onto the street in downtown Juneau where the dog-friendly apartment I rented was located, the phone in my car rang over Bluetooth. The screen indicated it was Liam.

I pushed the button to answer. "Hi," I said. "Just thinking about you. I was going to call and see if you were interested in grabbing dinner with me."

His deep voice sounded amused. "Same wavelength. I wanted to invite you to dinner, though it'll have to be brief. I've got another meeting later tonight."

Which also told me we wouldn't spend the night together. We had done so a few times, maybe not as often as I would have liked, and this apparently would not be one of them. But just having some time with him would be a good thing.

"I like the idea. When and where?"

We decided on a pub we'd eaten at before and agreed to meet there in about an hour. I'd brought Sasha before and knew she was welcome, so that was a good thing.

The Lucky Lady Pub was located off Franklin Street, a popular area in downtown Juneau. I found a parking space, and Sasha and I headed inside.

I wasn't surprised to see Liam already there, saving a table not far from the door. He rose when he saw us, and I soon joined him at the table, where we shared a hug and brief kiss. He patted Sasha on the head. He was good buddies with my dog.

He was good buddies with me too. I considered him one good-looking guy. His strong facial features were very handsome, with a wide brow between his smooth, dark hair and deep-brown eyes. And his physique? Hard to tell in the navy-blue sweatshirt over jeans that he wore right now, though I knew what he looked like—nice and muscular. He'd changed out of his trooper uniform for dinner, but I gathered he might have to put it back on later for the meeting he'd mentioned.

"Great to see you, as always, Stacie," he said warmly, motioning for me to sit down. "You too, Sasha." My dog reacted to her name by wagging her tail and drawing close again to Liam for a pat.

"And great to see you." I felt my smile grow broad. Oh, yes, it was great to see him. It felt like a long time since we'd been together, even though it had only been about a week.

We ordered our meals. I'd eaten their Irish pub salad a few times, which was fine, but I'd really fallen for the shepherd's pie that Liam always ordered, so we each got one of our own. Nothing there to give Sasha except a dab or two of mashed potatoes, but it was served with some really good soft rolls, and I also gave her small pieces of that.

The server was a young woman who wore a black shirt and trousers. She was friendly with Sasha but didn't pet her, and I assumed that might be partially because she didn't want her other customers to figure she had dog-dirty hands.

Since this was a pub, we both ordered a beer. We'd each drink only one glass. Neither of us was inclined to overdo it, especially Liam, who might be on duty later.

"So tell me how things are going in your life," Liam said.

I described my visit to Juneau Wildlife World that day and told him how much I looked forward to working there soon. "Not that I'm particularly looking forward to our Alaskan winter," I said, and he laughed.

I asked how things were with him, and he told me about how busy he was as a trooper, but he gave no details about any assignments, which wasn't a surprise. I was aware that at least some of it was confidential.

But as he talked about the little he was able to, I couldn't help thinking about how he had recently assisted me with his amazing skills as a trooper. Someone who'd been on one of my water tours had disappeared from the boat, then reappeared dead in the water the next day. It had appeared to be a murder, and our boat captain, whose family owned the ClemTours company, had been the major suspect. Liam had helped figure out who'd really done it.

And . . . well, so had I.

The beer arrived, and then our food. I enjoyed both, and the company even more.

I wished we'd be able to get together at my place after dinner. But not tonight.

When we were done, Liam paid the bill. I didn't always let him, but this time I did.

He walked Sasha and me to my car. It wasn't completely dark out—not at six thirty this time of year—but the sun had begun to set.

I opened the back door and fastened Sasha in. Before I got inside, Liam put his arms around me, and we kissed. And what a kiss, for being in public on a city street. Good thing he wasn't wearing his uniform, or it might have reflected badly on the troopers.

Or not.

"Let's do this again soon," I said. *And hopefully more,* I thought.

"Definitely."

I slid into the driver's seat. Liam returned to the sidewalk, and I saw him watching as I drove off.

* * *

That night, I read part of one of my favorite books on Alaskan wildlife to put myself to sleep. And the next morning I got up early, as usual on a tour day.

I walked and fed Sasha, grabbed a quick cereal breakfast, and then we headed to the tour boat port. I wondered how many tourists we'd have today as I walked up the plank.

I spent a little time talking with our captain, Palmer Clementos, and his assistant, Steph Porter, and then people started to arrive for the tour.

* * *

Oh, yeah! Another fun tour filled with seeing seals and bears and whales and birds. Even though we had fewer passengers than usual, they all seemed fascinated and watched and took pictures and asked questions. And my wonderful assistant, Lettie Amblex, young and slim and dressed in the standard ClemTours outfit, joined me on the top deck and even took over the tour for a while.

But all too soon, it was over.

Definitely fun. But somewhat sad.

This had been my next-to-last tour of the season.

I was hopeful that night of seeing Liam again, and perhaps not only for dinner. But it turned out that whatever he'd been working on last night was still taking up his time.

"I wish we could get together tonight," he said when we finally talked on the phone, and his wistful tone suggested he was telling the truth. "But tell you what. Plan on meeting up with me tomorrow night. And I'll stay with you, if that's okay. I know you start working at the wildlife park the next morning."

And I'd be getting up early. If Liam joined me, we'd be up a lot of the night.

Still, I wanted to take advantage of the opportunity. "Sounds good," I said.

* * *

The next morning, I engaged in the same routine I'd had now for months: shower, get dressed, walk Sasha, head to the pier, and lead another fun expedition with tourists who seemed to enjoy what I pointed out to them. I let Lettie lead some of the tour too, and hung out with Palmer and Steph maybe a little longer than usual.

This was, after all, probably the last time I'd see them till spring sprang again in Juneau.

Back at the port, we said good-bye to the passengers as usual, and then we said goodbye to each other, giving hugs we seldom engaged in otherwise.

Lettie sort of surprised me, though. "I got a job for the winter at a school cafeteria. It won't take all my time, so I'll be volunteering when I can at Juneau Wildlife World."

I felt like cheering. I considered Lettie a friend as well as my assistant. "It would be great to see you."

She left then, and so did I. The rest of our crowd dispersed too.

I sighed as I walked Sasha along the pier path. Few people were around at that hour. I doubted I'd see many others for the next few months. Oh, well. Spring would arrive eventually. And winter could still be enjoyable at the wildlife world, especially if I saw Lettie sometimes.

Once more Sasha and I settled into my car, and I called Liam, wondering if he really would be able to see me tonight.

He would, and did. We had a fun evening, eating out at another of our favorite restaurants, and then . . . well, yes, he did come home with Sasha and me.

And stayed the night. And yes, we engaged in stuff that was utterly enjoyable, as we had before.

If only it could be like this all the time. But we both led our own lives.

"So," he said in the darkness next to me early the next morning. "I'm on an early shift this morning. And it's your first day—"

"Working at Juneau Wildlife World." As we got out of bed and started getting ready for the day, I couldn't help saying, "Not sure what my schedule will be later, but I'll let you know. I might be free tonight."

"I'll keep my fingers crossed," he said.

I was later getting going than I wanted to be for my first day. We took Sasha for a quick walk. It was noticeably colder today, with a hint of precipitation in the air. Then I threw some breakfast together for Liam and me, exciting stuff like cereal and milk.

And soon, after we shared several heated kisses that made me long for when we'd see each other again, it was time for us to go our separate ways.

Chapter Three

Fortunately, the drive to the sanctuary wasn't too bad, though it took a little longer than the usual forty-some minutes, since I drove slower, as did other cars on the road. With the coldness and bit of rain coming down—not snow or sleet, fortunately—there was always the possibility of ice on the road.

I knew that today's weather was only a harbinger of what I could look forward to during the next few months as I worked at the sanctuary.

Still, I had a good objective: helping the animals who lived in the vast areas within the shelter deal with the winter, when fewer employees and volunteers would be at the preserve. But I'd be there.

Caring about wildlife was my life.

A good part of it, anyway.

"And you're a major part of it too," I called gently to Sasha in the back seat, as if she'd been able to hear my thoughts.

I heard her move in response. Sweet girl.

I wondered what I would be up to today as an introduction to the upcoming season. I would most likely get my first set of instructions from Wayne. Would I visit all the areas I could to check out how the residents were doing? That would be my preference. But I might wind up helping Marnie with food preparation. Or something else.

I parked near where I had the other day, almost at the end of the lot by the garage area, a short distance from the welcome building.

The building nearest to where I parked huddled in the chilly, gray air as I let Sasha out of the car. A section of it included small apartments that weren't rented out but were for workers and volunteers who needed to stay overnight should the weather become too treacherous to allow for driving home in a blizzard.

I wondered if Sasha and I would stay there sometime during this season. It was likely.

I was glad I was wearing a Juneau Wildlife World sweatshirt. It kept me warm enough. But I had tossed a jacket and a heavier parka on the floor of my SUV before leaving my apartment area just in case it got any colder. I assumed I would be out and about on the sanctuary's grounds, at least a bit.

As Sasha and I stepped inside the welcome building, I called Wayne to let him know we'd made it.

"Welcome," he said. "Oliver is on the main floor passing out our instructions for the day. I'll see you later, but you can talk to him about what's going on."

"Got it."

As we reached the door to enter, so did Bill Westerstein. He'd indicated he worked in a restaurant the last time we spoke, so maybe his busiest times there were weekends, freeing him up for weekdays. This was a Monday, first day of a new week and a new chapter in my life. Maybe his too.

"Hi," I greeted him.

"Hey," he said. "Are you starting today? You're a regular employee now, right?"

"That's right. And you're volunteering?"

"Yep. And I'll do all I can to make sure the animals do well."

Good guy, I thought.

As we reached the main door, Bill stooped to pet Sasha on the head, and my friendly husky wagged her tail in response.

I saw Oliver near the front desk. Yes, another sweatshirt similar to Bill's and mine. His was black with gold letters, more ornate than the rest. After all, he was a manager. He nodded. I figured, from what Wayne had said, that he was waiting to hand us information and tell us what to do.

"Hi, you two," Oliver said. "And dog." His tone became grim when he mentioned Sasha, and I wanted to kick him for it.

Okay, at least he wasn't trying to make us leave. Fortunately, thanks to Wayne, he knew better.

Marnie entered the waiting room from the door along the rear wall, where the food area and other areas important to the general running of the place were located. That included the large clinic, where veterinarians, including Dr. Skip Lawrence, visited often, especially if a new and ailing potential resident had been taken in. He often brought assistants along to help.

One of the rooms included a large video screen on the wall where guests could view a photographic array of the sanctuary's animals. Cameras and other high-tech sensors had been placed at multiple locations throughout the sanctuary, including inside the buildings for security. Though no one necessarily knew where any of the wildlife dwelling on the grounds happened to be at any moment, the motion detectors here and there sometimes caused outside cameras to go on. That meant whatever creature had caused the motion would most often be photographed and the images sent to the screen.

"Hi, all of you," Marnie said. She wore a long-sleeved T-shirt with an apron over it.

As before, she hurried over to greet Sasha, patting her on the head and stroking down to her shoulders. Marnie glanced at Oliver as if she knew she was goading him by doing it, but so what?

She then drew closer to Bill. "Good to see you. I gather you're ready to do some more food prep now?"

"Definitely," he said. "I plan to come a lot. I'll work it out with my job, maybe even take time off for a while."

"Even managers can help get nourishment prepared for our residents," Oliver said. Managers like him. Was he trying to be helpful? Maybe he was a better person than he'd seemed to be since I'd met him.

"Hey, I'm happy for all the help I can get," Marnie replied with a smile. "But do you have time to help me right now?" This comment appeared to be directed at Oliver, who was still holding paperwork in his hands.

"Well, I can later," he said. "But at the moment—"

"At the moment, I hope you have the instructions Wayne said you'd be giving to me," I said, getting involved in the conversation.

"I do," Oliver said. "And some for Bill too. I don't think they include working on food today."

"Let me see." Bill took his form from Oliver, who also handed one to me.

Did everyone have the same instructions? Probably not. Mine listed going out to some of the more distant sanctuary areas to observe for a few hours, then reporting back and filling in appropriate forms on the sanctuary computers. Food prep? Not today, which was fine with me. Nor were there currently any animals who'd been rescued and needed special care before being released back into the wild.

Today, I believed I'd be able to hike to those remote sanctuary areas and bring Sasha along, since all I had to do was observe and make notations about what I saw.

If I saw any injured animals or other problems with the inhabitants, I'd definitely need to do more. But there was no reason to believe anything would go wrong today, or so I hoped.

I couldn't help grinning. Wildlife. Observation. With Sasha. Sounded like the makings of a perfect day.

But that would, of course, depend on how things actually went.

As I pondered my instructions, Wayne walked down the stairway from his office with a few other people, including Larraine and Shawna and two folks I didn't know, a man and a woman. Or a girl, at least. She looked young. The guy did too. Were they visitors here to view the wildlife? Or new volunteers or employees who hadn't yet gotten their Juneau Wildlife World gear?

Turned out to be the latter.

"So, hi, everyone," Wayne said. He too wore a Wildlife World sweatshirt, but his was dark green and not at all as official and ornate looking as Oliver's. So who was really in charge?

"Most of you know each other, or have at least met," Wayne continued. "But I'd like you to meet a couple new volunteers, Jessie and Bobbie. They're here to do some work for us and help care for our wildlife, and get some credit for it at a class or two at University of Alaska Southeast, the Juneau campus."

Who was Jessie and who was Bobbie? Both names could be used by both sexes, and Wayne hadn't been specific.

No matter. I'd figure it out soon enough, since I'd at least be talking to them, maybe even working with one or both.

Everyone, including Larraine and Shawna, was holding printed instructions like me. Interesting that everything was printed out—not necessarily great for the environment. But it was easier than figuring out all our cell phone numbers and sending instructions that way. And there were recycle bins in various places around the building.

Soon we were all milling about the lobby, waiting to depart for our assignments.

"Who's supposed to help me with food prep this morning?" Marnie called.

"Me," Bill said.

"And me," said Oliver.

So were Shawna and one of the newcomers, though I still didn't know who was who.

"Then come on in." Marnie gestured for her crowd to follow.

Oliver and Bill started out at the same time, nearly running into each other. I caught a flicker of animosity between them as they glared at each other momentarily. Bill then moved his arm, gesturing grandly for Oliver to precede him. Which he did, quickly catching up to their food prep manager and striking up a conversation.

The male newbie student, also designated to help, caught up to them as they reached the door. "Hey," he said, "this is my first time doing this. I really want to learn it all. My name's Jesse."

At that point, I started spelling *Jesse* the masculine way in my head. I wasn't sure how Bobbie spelled her name, since there were several options, but I'd learn that too.

"Hi, Jesse," Marnie said. "Good to meet you. And I'll be teaching it all to you. We have to do a great job of getting things ready for our residents, and I make sure that happens."

That was the last I heard before the group slipped through the door.

"Okay, then, does everyone understand what you'll be doing today?" Wayne asked the rest of us.

Hungry animals needed lots of food prep. That would certainly be the case around here in the wintertime, when it would be harder for them to forage for themselves, I knew. But the sanctuary residents needed to be checked on to ensure they remained safe and secure, especially those who'd arrived because of health issues. And any possible changes in their environment had to be identified and described.

"Sure," Larraine said. "I get to visit areas of the sanctuary to observe our residents. You too, Stacie?"

"Yes, Sasha and me." I looked at Wayne. "And I'm sure you know I'll be careful about where Sasha goes so we don't spook any of the animals."

"I know you're careful," Wayne agreed. "And if either or both of you want to take one of the shelter ATVs, feel free."

I considered it. I knew there would be times I'd want to, but for today I just wanted to walk with my dog, despite the coolness and hint of dampness in the air. There'd be other times that riding would be a heck of a lot more comfortable.

"Not today, thanks," I told my current boss. "But soon, I figure."

"Same here," Larraine said. She looked at me. "We can start off in the same direction."

"Right," I agreed.

"Sounds good." Wayne nodded and smiled. "I'm sure you both will do fine, but be sure to file your report when you get back. You should return for lunch, then head out again. Or if there are any visitors wanting a short tour then, one of you can take care of that too."

Larraine and I both agreed. Then it was time for us to start our assignment of the day.

But when Larraine and I exited the restroom with Sasha before leaving the welcome building, Oliver was just coming out of the men's room.

"Hey. You're still here," he said. "You and that dog." He assessed Sasha. "And you're going to be visiting our wildlife with it along? You'd better be damned careful. That dog's big enough he could do some damage to our animals."

"Sasha's a sweetie," I countered angrily.

"Well, she'd better be." And with that, Oliver stomped back to the door into the back area.

"What was that about?" Larraine asked.

"I'll tell you about it as we walk. But the gist of it is that our manager Oliver isn't happy at all that I'm allowed to bring my wonderful dog along, even though Wayne's fine with it."

"Well, so am I," Larraine said, patting Sasha briefly. "Definitely." Then we headed outside.

We started out together on the same path Sasha and I had traveled a couple days ago, the logical way, although there were several other paths leading from the welcome building in different directions. But this way we could reach the largest number of areas most easily. And Sasha, as always, trotted happily at my side.

I didn't know Larraine well, so I began a conversation after we crossed the parking lot. "So why are you here? Are you a wildlife lover, or someone who wants to—"

"I want to do everything I can for animals," she said, aiming a smile at me as we continued onto the gravel pathway. "Including dogs." She patted Sasha again, and I smiled back.

We both wore boots in anticipation of worse weather. Our footsteps crunched as we made our way over pine needles and twigs as we walked. There was a slight wind now, so Larraine's hair, again held back in a scrunchie, began to blow. I wondered if she'd wear a hat, or a hoodie, on future shelter outings.

I might. I wasn't too uncomfortable now despite my hair whipping in different directions, but this was a good warning. I had my jacket on now and would keep my parka with its hood in my car for when I needed it while out on the Wildlife World grounds.

Yes, winter was on its way. The chill in the air reminded me along with the wind.

"I understand what you mean and identify with it," I told her, and described my college major in wildlife conservation and management at the University of Arizona, my work in the area at various places, and the tours I now gave for ClemTours. I kept my voice low, although I didn't see any animals on either side of the path at first.

Larraine also asked me about Oliver and Sasha, and I tried to make light of it, telling her that the manager clearly cared about the animals here and seemed concerned that my dog would scare or otherwise harm them.

"But she's been here enough in the past months while I've been volunteering, so Wayne is fine with her accompanying me, with some rules in place that we follow."

"Makes sense." And Larraine gave my pup yet another head pat, which again caused Sasha's tail to wag.

We went to an area farther into the preserve than any I'd visited yesterday. Soon a few Sitka black-tailed deer started approaching to our right, not close but definitely worth observing for a little while. Since it was past August, their coats, reddish in the summer, were turning darker. They appeared fine, not affected by the cooling weather, happily grazing on what was left of the brown grass along the ground. A distance beyond them, I also saw a small herd of reindeer.

I didn't need to point them out to Larraine. She was already staring and smiling and oohing and aahing softly. Her reaction made me grin.

We kept walking. Slowly, though, and I kept Sasha close at my side so she wouldn't spook anyone. We soon saw a moose, and then another to the left, far enough away that they weren't likely to pay attention to us. But we paid attention to them, and I made mental notes for my report later. I couldn't identify them individually, but I could tell all appeared healthy.

As we continued, Larraine told me a bit about her background—no formal education in wildlife but a longtime fascination that she'd fulfilled by moving from one area to another that had animals to be observed, including Colorado and a couple of places in Canada and now Alaska. She'd also provided tours of various facilities, and that was how she'd made a living for quite a few years.

"I move around too much to keep a dog, though. I envy you your Sasha. I also envy you your water tours."

I couldn't do anything about her lack of a dog but let her enjoy being with Sasha. But as to the water tours, I let her know she could contact ClemTours to maybe be hired to provide some of her own. My employer often hired other tour guides, or assistants like Lettie.

And I wondered when I would see my current assistant here at Juneau Wildlife World. Anytime soon?

We didn't walk much farther before Larraine said, "I think I'll head back to the welcome building and fill out the computer form about what we saw. I'll hang out there for lunch, then maybe go in a different direction to observe afterward. And you?"

"I want to continue here till we get near the mountain area. That'll take probably another half hour or so, I think. I hope to see bears or wolves or whoever happens to show up near the path there."

"I'll definitely want to do that one of these days," Larraine said, "maybe joining you again. But not today."

"Okay. Hopefully, I'll see you back at the welcome building."

"I hope so too." She bent down and patted Sasha's head a final time. "Bye, sweetheart." And then she turned, her boots crunching loudly against the gravel path.

Sasha and I continued forward in the same direction we'd been heading. Since the morning was growing later, the air warmed a bit, though it was still cool. No matter. Although the path meandered, I could see we'd eventually get to an area at the base of the shelter's nearby mountains. No plains there for anyone in the deer or related families to graze, but other kinds of animals I saw from a distance during my tour boats might be around.

I hoped I'd see some so I could report on them along with the other animals I'd already seen. Even more, I wanted to observe them, see them closer in their own habitat, and make sure they appeared to be healthy and safe.

I knew I was supposed to return to the welcome building for lunch, but figured I could be a little late, although maybe that wasn't such a good idea on my first day as an official employee. I decided I'd reach the base of the mountainous area, take a quick peek around, then hurry back with Sasha.

I heard a noise behind us and soon saw one of the small but large-wheeled covered ATVs from the garage drawing closer. I moved aside with Sasha so it could pass. As it did, I saw Bill at the wheel. Marnie was in the seat beside him, and I was surprised two people fit. They waved as they passed, and I waved back. I figured they were bringing food in this direction and was a little surprised they weren't using a larger vehicle.

Sasha and I soon stood at the part of the path where the chain-link fence we'd been walking alongside connected to other fencing, enclosing the animals we'd seen and more. It separated a couple of other wildlife areas that led deep into the hillsides. It also marked the end of the territory where Sasha was allowed. I saw a couple of gates where people could make their way inside those sections. Someday, whether or not I was delivering food, I hoped to go inside and hike and observe without Sasha. Maybe I'd even go as far as the areas where the bears were. But not today.

I realized this would be a good time for us to return for lunch. "Okay, girl?" I asked Sasha.

She looked up and wagged her tail, so we turned around.

I scanned the area one last time, hoping to see some of the resident animals.

And gasped aloud in happiness when I did.

There, not far in the distance, was a pack of four wolves. They didn't seem to have noticed us but were walking along the hillside, hunting, perhaps. Or hoping for humans to deliver some food, even though this time of year there were probably still rabbits around for them to prey on.

I couldn't help but watch for a few minutes, Sasha still at my side. I smiled, enjoying the view. And got excited when a couple started heading our direction, but they turned around before I could pull my binoculars from my pocket.

I heard a noise behind me. Apparently the wolves, with their excellent hearing, did too, since they headed off up the hillside, not appearing scared but also not hanging around.

I turned. Another ATV approached. Oliver was in it. He rolled to a stop when he saw me.

"I know your instructions told you to head this way, but same thing goes for some of the others. Are you alone here now?"

"That's right."

"I thought you were with Larraine. And didn't others drive out this way?"

"Yes to both, although Larraine headed back. I saw Marnie and Bill drive past before."

Oliver shook his head but didn't elaborate. "It's time for lunch. Hop in and I'll drive you back." He looked past me and frowned. "Your dog too."

I wanted to object. To say no, that we'd hurry back on our own.

But as a manager, he was one of my bosses. And I really did want to encourage a good relationship with him.

"Sure. Thanks," I said, then helped Sasha into the area behind the seats, fastening her securely, and got into the seat beside Oliver. "What's for lunch?"

Chapter Four

There was a separate, small concrete building on the other side of the welcome building from the apartments and garage that was a restaurant of sorts. At least, it contained vending machines from which people could purchase food and drinks. That included those of us who worked or volunteered at the sanctuary as well as visitors. I wasn't certain who was in charge of making sure those machines remained stocked, but I didn't think it was our animal food prep champion Marnie.

Manager Oliver, now? Maybe. I doubted that director Wayne took care of it.

But maybe volunteer Bill could take charge, since he also worked at a restaurant. Although doing that might be the last thing he'd want, since he now hung out at a wildlife sanctuary for fun.

The place had long tables and rows of folding chairs inside on the paved floor, so food purchasers could also eat there if they chose.

Oliver parked the ATV inside the garage, and we both got out. So did Sasha, and I kept my dog as far from Oliver as I could. Oliver still aimed a nasty glance in Sasha's direction as we entered the food building.

It was filled with people. Unsurprising, since it was lunchtime.

"Hey, Stacie," called a familiar, welcome voice, and I looked toward the seating area to see that Lettie had risen and was now dashing over toward us. I was delighted to see my tall, youthful tour guide assistant and was relieved that her schedule at the school allowed her to be around at lunchtime.

Oliver cast an unfriendly gaze in her direction. Didn't he like anyone? I recalled, though, that he'd seemed interested in food prep for the wildlife, so he hadn't scowled at Marnie.

And an interest in food was somewhat surprising, since he was so thin. But then, he wasn't eating the food prepped for the animal residents here.

"Great to see you, Lettie," I said as she reached us. "I'd like to introduce you to one of the managers here, Oliver Brownling. Oliver, this is Lettie Amblex. She's my assistant on my boat tours, and she's volunteering here part-time for the winter. She has great knowledge of wildlife."

"That's an asset here." Oliver didn't sound extremely impressed, though. Still, he held out his hand, and they shook.

"You'll join me here when you get your food, won't you? I've been chatting with the others sitting there, but there's still plenty of room for you both." Lettie's black hair, in its pixie cut, hung looser now than it did when we were out on the water, so it framed her pretty face. Her raised black eyebrows gave her an expression of perpetual surprise.

"Sasha and I certainly will," I told her. I didn't bother to ask Oliver. I glanced at the others who were there: Wayne, Shawna, Bill, the two newbies Jesse and Bobbie, and Marnie.

Another of the long, wood-topped tables nearby also had a few occupants, none of whom I recognized, so I assumed they were tourists taking advantage of the not-so-bad weather to visit the sanctuary. I'd have some time here after lunch, so I'd be able to show them around if Wayne asked me to.

That meant I might have to leave Sasha secured somewhere in the main building, and I wasn't thrilled about that unless I could be certain Oliver didn't hassle her.

I nibbled on the cold roast beef sandwich I'd bought from one of the machines, slipping small pieces of the meat to my canine companion, who snacked happily.

Otherwise, I mostly listened to the conversations. Oliver and Bill sat near Marnie, asking her questions about food preparation. Jesse, Bobbie, and Shawna joined in with inquiries of their own; Lettie too. She obviously had a lot to learn about Juneau Wildlife World. As far as I knew, this was her first time here as a volunteer.

The discussion veered to the animals in residence. That was when the veterinarian who visited periodically, Dr. Skip Lawrence, came in.

"Hey, Doc," Wayne called to him from the far end of the table where we sat. "Glad to see you. Would you like something to eat?"

Dr. Skip was in his midforties, with a stern, inquisitive-looking face that made him appear as if he were always assessing the health of those around him, even though his skills were in veterinary care. He was dressed in a loose green long-sleeved T-shirt, although I'd seen him mostly in blue scrubs when he was examining the few new residents who'd happened to arrive last winter and during the times I'd been volunteering—reindeer, moose, and even hares. Once, it had been a pregnant wolf.

"Absolutely," he said, and immediately went to the row of food-dispensing machines. Wayne joined him there and swept a card on the reader as Skip made his choices.

I was delighted that, after Skip gave Sasha a pat on the head—which earned a frown from Oliver—he sat only a few chairs away from me, just past Lettie and Wayne. I was hoping to hear whatever he had to say about the health and welfare of the animals here.

He began talking shortly after he bit into his sandwich and chewed a little. "So, who's seen some of our wildlife today? Everyone look okay?"

I was first to speak, letting him know I'd walked with volunteer Larraine at first. She wasn't at lunch with us, but I mentioned we'd seen, in various areas, some Sitka black-tailed deer, reindeer, moose, and farthest away, a pack of wolves.

"And did they cry wolf?" Skip asked, a big grin on his face.

"Not really. Crying wolf means they had to be asking for help without really needing it. And this pack didn't seem to be asking for help at all."

"Just as well," the veterinarian said with a shake of his head. "I wasn't there to help anyway."

"I saw them too," Oliver broke in, "when I drove out there to check on the wildlife."

"Glad you were out there checking on them, as usual," said Marnie, who was sitting beside him. "That's always so helpful, and reassuring, even though others do the same thing." She smiled at him, then took a drink of water from a bottle on the table.

Her comment made Oliver smile too. I wasn't used to his long, narrow face with pale-brown eyes looking particularly pleasant, so that was a good thing. He took a drink from his own bottle of water, as if to match Marnie's action.

It made me thirsty too, so I also took a sip. And figured I'd soon give Sasha a drink as well.

I couldn't hear most of the conversations, but it felt good to have so many people together here. Some discussions seemed intense, including an apparent argument between Bill and the newbies Jesse and Bobbie. At one point, Oliver jumped in to attempt to calm them.

I wondered what they'd all been talking about. And why it had gotten so heated. Did they feel as if they were competing with one another somehow?

A good thing for Oliver was that Wayne joined them and appeared to verbally pat his new manager on the back, nodding approval of how he was handling things.

I finished soon and stood, and so did Lettie, and eventually everyone else as well. Most milled around and talked before they dispersed. Marnie also seemed pleased with how Oliver had handled the argument. She asked when he'd join her for food prep.

"As soon as I can." He glanced toward Wayne, as if he didn't think his boss would be thrilled about the idea, but the director was occupied elsewhere. "Maybe tomorrow."

"Great," Marnie said.

"Are you ready to go?" Lettie asked me as I grabbed a paper cup from the counter and poured water into it for Sasha, earning me a glare from Oliver yet again. What was with that guy? I saw a few of the others, also about to leave, glancing at him before heading toward the door.

"Yes," I said, "as soon as Sasha's finished drinking. I'll be going back out to the open areas to see who's there and how they're doing. Are you coming with me?"

"I sure am. But I need to leave soon to get things ready for tomorrow's lunch at the school."

"Got it."

Lettie and I repeated my earlier journey across the paths near the welcome building. We took turns pointing out wildlife to each other.

We wandered for a while, Sasha included, all the way back toward the area where the wolves were. Turned out there were quite a few other workers in this area as well, including Larraine, who appeared to be showing tourists around.

Surprisingly—maybe—Oliver caught up with us there too, once more driving one of the ATVs.

Was he out here to view our wildlife inhabitants as well?

"So, who do you see there?" he asked us in a not particularly nice voice as he got out of the driver's seat.

"We've been observing quite a few of the residents as we walked here," I said calmly, as Larraine and the tourists joined us. "How about you?" I asked them. "Did you see many animals? Are you enjoying your walk?"

"Absolutely," said a young lady clutching the arm of a man who appeared about her age. Both wore parkas, and she was shivering. "But I'm glad it's not really winter yet. Don't think we'll come back here then, but maybe next summer. We live in San Diego. It's a lot colder here."

"I get it," I said with a laugh. "What about now? Do you see that pack of wolves beyond the fence?"

I'd noticed a small pack in the distance as we'd gotten near this area. Now I turned and saw they'd drawn closer since I'd looked a couple of minutes before.

And one of them—

"One of them is limping," Lettie said. That was what I'd noticed.

And when the poor thing stumbled to the ground, I handed her Sasha's leash. "Here. Watch her. I'm going to check on him."

I'd get as close as I could without getting attacked by the others. But the pack must have been spooked by their comrade's fall and by my opening the nearby gate to walk through it. I closed it tightly behind me. They ran off.

"What the hell are you doing?" Oliver yelled.

What he *wouldn't* do, I was sure. But I needed to check on the poor wolf's condition.

I yelled back, "Call Dr. Skip and see if he's still around. Tell him to come out here if he is."

"You stupid . . . Come back here! I'm the manager, and—"

"Please make the call," I interrupted as Sasha began to bark. Lettie calmed her, and I continued toward the injured wolf.

The animal growled as I approached but didn't attempt to get up. I could see he had a gash along his left rear leg near the paw. It was bloody, and I couldn't tell if the leg was broken.

I didn't want to touch the wolf, though I did wish I had soft towels or a way to wrap the wound. And my own arm, in case the scared, injured animal tried to bite this intrusive human, who he wouldn't know was just trying to help him.

How long could I stay here? How long *should* I stay here? Lettie had to leave, but I needed her to watch Sasha. I wanted to hang around till Dr. Skip arrived, but who knew how long that would be? And whether he was even still at the sanctuary?

And was I really helping by being here? At least the poor creature wasn't attempting to run off into the vast wilderness, which might hurt him even more. Nor did his pack members reappear, which might have caused additional stress, and maybe an urge to dash off with them.

One thing I did do was reach slowly toward his ear, where a tag had been inserted. Not all animals got that kind of identification, but some did, which helped keep track of who was where, since each tag contained a GPS tracker. These animals were also given names, as were others who hadn't been tagged but often showed up at the same locations and were therefore identifiable.

He moved a little, as if to bolt, so I stopped, hoping he wasn't any more scared than he'd been. I decided to think of him as Tikaani, which means *wolf* in the Inuit language. I doubted it was really his name, but at least I had a way to refer to him.

"Okay, Tikaani," I said softly. "I won't touch you. Let's just wait a while and see if help arrives."

And it did. It felt like forever, but I figured someone, Lettie or Oliver or someone else, must have called the welcome building, since another ATV arrived.

Two people got off, and I would have cheered if it wouldn't have scared Tikaani even more. They were Wayne and Dr. Skip. Both hustled through the gate, locking it once more, and hurried over to me. Skip carried a medical kit, and Wayne wore a concerned frown.

"What's going on?" our director demanded, his focus on the wolf. "What happened to him?"

The vet had his medical kit open on the ground near the still but growling wolf. I watched as he filled a syringe from a clear vial, then moved around to avoid any bite and injected the animal in the flank in one sure movement.

Okay, the wolf wasn't Tikaani to Wayne, and I didn't intend to refer to him that way in front of my boss. "I was outside the fence, observing the area and its inhabitants with Lettie and Sasha, and saw a pack of wolves. As we were watching, I saw this poor guy fall to the ground." I explained I'd entered the area to check him out, leaving my dog with my friend.

"I assume the rest of the pack ran off." Wayne's tone was a growl, as if he was angry with me. Well, that was okay. I knew we weren't supposed to get close, but I was a real wildlife aficionado, here to observe and help protect the animals, and would do nearly anything to do so. Fortunately, it had worked out okay for me.

But for Tikaani?

"Yes, fortunately, it did." I turned to look at Skip, who was wrapping a bandage around the injured leg.

"We need to take this guy back to the clinic," Skip said. "It'll be okay to move him. I've sedated him."

The wolf's eyes were closed, and he was still breathing as he now lay without moving, fortunately. Skip whipped a sheet out of his kit and wrapped it gently around the animal, lifting it into his arms.

"Grab my kit and open the gate," he ordered Wayne. "I'll hold him in the vehicle."

Wayne did as he was told, then followed Skip out the gate. After taking another look around to make sure the pack wasn't behind us, I slipped through it too. Wayne had locked the gate, but I couldn't help it. I had to check it too.

His smile at me felt sardonic, but he didn't say anything.

He took the covered wolf from Skip, then, when the vet had gotten into the passenger seat of the ATV, handed it back to him.

Tikaani's head lolled, his eyes closed and his long snout loose. Poor guy. I was glad when Wayne turned the vehicle and headed quickly down the path toward the sanctuary's welcome building.

Only then did I again notice the briskness in the air and the group of people—and the dog—staring toward the vehicle, then back at me. Lettie hurried toward me with Sasha at her side, and my dog stood and leaned on my chest, as if to comfort me.

"Are you okay, Stacie?" Lettie asked. "Will the wolf be okay?"

Before I could say I was fine and I certainly hoped so, Oliver stomped up.

"What were you thinking?" he demanded. "Running in there that way? Yeah, it's sometimes fine to enter the enclosures to check on the occupants, but we all saw the pack of wolves. They could have attacked you, and it would have been my responsibility. I'm a manager. I was right here. I might not give a damn about what happens to you, but it could have damaged the sanctuary if you were hurt."

He was more concerned about his reputation than anything else, or at least that's what I deduced, judging by his reaction. And danger or not, I'd done what I'd felt I needed to.

43

"Good thing you didn't have your damn dog with you in there," he continued. "It would have made the situation with the injured wolf even worse."

Back to his dislike of Sasha again.

I nearly bit my tongue to prevent myself from lashing back at him. What good would it do?

I noticed then that, in addition to those who'd already been there, a couple of newcomers had joined the crowd. Bill and Marnie were there.

Rather than saying anything to Oliver, I turned to them. "Are you here because you heard what happened?" I asked.

"Yes, and we saw Dr. Skip and Wayne heading back to the vet clinic with the injured wolf," Marnie said. "But we had to make sure everyone was all right. Are you?"

"Yes," I replied, "as far as I know—assuming I survive the tongue-lashing I just got from Oliver." Had they been here long enough to hear it? Maybe.

Bill shook his head, but before he added to the conversation, Oliver interrupted. "I just can't help getting angry when someone disobeys the sanctuary rules," he said, directing his comment to Marnie as if asking for her understanding.

And *I* couldn't help responding angrily, "I didn't disobey anything." And I hadn't. Not really. Well, not much. And I'd been careful, or I'd tried to be. And I did think I'd helped save Tikaani.

"Oh yes you—"

Before Oliver could finish, Marnie took a step forward. "It all looks okay to me," she said. "Everyone's okay, even hopefully the injured wolf, or at least he's getting some care."

Oliver didn't finish what he'd started but glared at me, then looked back toward Marnie. "All right. But I'm going to hang out here a bit longer to make sure it stays that way."

Which meant it was time for Sasha and me to go. Everyone else too, I figured.

Without another word to Oliver, I took Sasha's leash in my hand and started back toward the entry area.

Lettie caught up with us. "That was nasty. You were just trying to help that poor wolf."

"Yeah," I agreed, too irate to get into much of a discussion. I couldn't resist adding, "But then, Oliver is nasty, so I couldn't expect much else."

I wondered if he intended to hang around much longer. Out of curiosity, I turned back to look toward him. He was still talking with a small group, and as I watched, I saw a pack of wolves, maybe the injured one's pack, appear again on the brown rolling hillside in the distance. Were they checking on their comrade?

I wasn't the only one to notice. One of those still hanging with Oliver—Bobbie, I thought, though I couldn't tell from that far away—called out, "Look!" and pointed in the direction of the wolves. They most likely didn't notice, or if they did, they weren't upset about the human acknowledgment.

Everyone watched the animals. Oliver took a couple steps toward the gate. Really? Did he now want to meet those wolves? Commiserate with them about their injured packmate?

Apparently, the tourists started asking questions, though, and he stopped to respond. Good. That, at least, was what a manager here was supposed to do.

"I'm on my way now," I told Lettie, and started walking along the path with Sasha. She joined us.

We soon met up with Larraine, who greeted us, and we all continued up the path toward the others. I assumed she'd heard about the injured wolf and had perhaps come to see it. If so, she'd probably also seen the vehicle taking him to the clinic. But any other guess on my part about why she was here would be speculation.

When we reached the welcome building, no one else had caught up with us, nor had we seen any vehicles. Maybe the tour was continuing.

In any event, I decided it was time for Sasha and me to leave. The working day here was pretty much over for most of us. Lettie would undoubtedly leave too, since she'd said she wanted to head out even earlier. I hoped she'd still be able to accomplish what she needed to at her new job. I felt bad that I'd delayed her, even though it was for a good reason.

As if hearing my thoughts, she said, "Well, I'll get on my way now. I already told Wayne I wasn't hanging around long."

"We'll leave soon too," I told her. First, though, I wanted to peek in and see how the injured wolf was doing.

Dr. Skip was still in the clinic, and so was Wayne. I left Sasha in the waiting room, and they took me into a room where Tikaani was now sleeping on his side in a fully enclosed pen. His leg was fully bandaged.

"After doing an x-ray, I cleaned it up and stitched it. It's not broken, but there is significant infection that's going to require IV antibiotics and fluids over the next several days," the vet told me. "Hopefully, he'll be fine. I need to leave soon to return to my clinic downtown."

"I'll be in my apartment here and will check on him every couple of hours," Wayne said. His eyes held mine. "I agree it was somewhat foolish for you to go inside the fence and check on him, but I nevertheless appreciate it."

Despite the mild criticism, Wayne's comment made me glow inside. Somewhat. But he had mentioned the foolishness of what I'd done, and though I didn't want to, I recognized the truth in it . . . somewhat.

"See you tomorrow," he said. It was a statement, not a question, as it should be. I was an employee now, no longer a volunteer. And no matter what I thought about my least-favorite manager Oliver, I liked being at the sanctuary.

In fact, I felt a twinge once Sasha and I got into my car and headed toward town. I couldn't help glancing back toward the entry gate and the part of the vast sanctuary grounds that was visible through the fencing.

I saw animals far in the distance and figured they might be deer, but I couldn't tell, nor could I look for a long while on the road.

I talked to Sasha, my companion in the car, even though she was secured in the back seat. "Strange day, wasn't it? And I don't know what you think of the place, but I miss it already. Having more responsibilities than a volunteer feels good. But stressful."

She didn't respond, and I figured she was asleep.

So what would tonight be like? I had an idea, as I often did. I called Liam on my Bluetooth.

"Hi, Stacie," he said right away. "I want to hear about your first day of work." But before I could say anything, he added, "But I'm working tonight. Maybe tomorrow."

"Sure." I tried to make my tone light. "Sounds good."

Sasha and I just headed to our apartment, where I fed her and myself some dinner. Hers was regular healthy dog food. Mine was stuff from my fridge, mostly veggies, which were also healthful.

But when I'd eaten and settled down to watch TV, I felt antsy. Hey, I was now an employee at the Juneau Wildlife World. I didn't need to live there, at least not now, while the weather remained decent. But I could spend as much time there as possible.

Even at night.

And so, knowing it might not be the best choice, I loaded Sasha back into the car. The weather was nice enough for us to get back there in the usual forty-some minutes. I wouldn't stay long. I wouldn't bother Wayne, even though I knew he and a few others would still be around. If he was checking the security camera footage, he might see me, but he'd probably call me then, and I'd explain I just wanted to see the place, and whatever animals I could, at night.

Okay, maybe not the best idea, but I was already on my way.

The front gate was properly shut, so I got out of my car to open it. I'd already been given the security code, as all employees were. Then I stopped and closed it again.

I parked in my usual space and got Sasha out, keeping her on her leash. I saw few lights from the windows of the welcome building and figured it might even be locked. And only a couple of the apartments showed any lights.

There was some dim lighting along the hiking paths into the sanctuary. It didn't extend far out, so I wondered if I'd see any animals. And I didn't intend to go much of a distance.

After about twenty minutes of seeing no one, I figured I'd assuaged my curiosity enough. Daylight was best for wildlife viewing. And it did feel eerie out here with no one else around.

"Okay, Sasha," I said. "Let's go home."

We hiked back to the car. I drove to the gate and opened it again, then shut it behind us.

And then we went home for the night.

But I did get us back there early the next morning. The sky was light as I drove, the gray skies from the day before lifted. The gate was open when I got there.

And as I pulled in, I heard sirens behind us.

Larraine, Bill, and Marnie must have gotten to the sanctuary really early—although I believed Marnie mostly lived there. They were standing outside the entry to the welcome building, and they all appeared upset. One of the other managers was there, too—Neil Zesser, an older guy, whom I hadn't seen yesterday.

The police cars I must have heard approached the gate, and Bill stepped toward them. The cars pulled in behind us as Sasha and I approached the people standing there.

"What's going on?" I asked.

"Oh, Stacie, it's terrible," Larraine said. She was wringing her fingers, and her long hair was loose outside her hoodie. She was far from wearing her usual grin.

"What—" I began, but she continued.

"When Wayne took his early-morning walk this morning, he went back to the wolf area, and . . ." She paused, and tears began falling from her eyes. "He found Oliver. He . . . he's dead."

Chapter Five

"What happened?" I exclaimed, horrified. I hadn't particularly liked the guy, but I certainly hadn't wanted anything bad to happen to him.

Had he fallen somewhere in the sanctuary, off a hillside? Had he rolled his vehicle on the ride back? Or—

I imagined scenarios while awaiting the answer my mind was fishing for, but before Larraine could give me more information, one of the two cops hurried out of the vehicle and joined us. Their car displayed the seal of the Alaska State Troopers, the same law enforcement agency Liam belonged to. He was in a special unit, and though it might have been appropriate for the Initial Response Section to be here, he wasn't among these troopers. Maybe whatever had happened to Oliver didn't need much investigation.

But what was it?

"We don't know yet," Larraine said. "And—"

"I assume you all work here," the trooper said, interrupting her. He appeared to be in his thirties, scowling, and his name badge said he was Morlande.

His assumption wasn't unanticipated, since we all wore Juneau Wildlife World sweatshirts, mostly blue.

Sasha, leashed at my feet, whimpered, as if she sensed the emotional strain of the humans around her, and I bent to stroke her head.

"That's right," said Larraine, her voice rasping. "Though some of us are volunteers."

"We were called about someone who has been found deceased. Will one of you take us to wherever he is?"

Larraine had mentioned that Wayne had found Oliver in or near the wolf area. The area that had become even more important to me yesterday.

I'd been looking forward to learning how Tikaani was doing, but that would wait. Since no one else jumped in immediately, not even manager Neil, I said, "I'll do it." I glanced at Larraine. "Wayne was around the wolf area?"

She nodded. "That's what he said."

"Just a sec," I told the trooper, then started taking Sasha to my car. I intended to shut her inside after rolling down the windows a bit. It was even cooler today than it had been yesterday, so she definitely wouldn't fry in there. But before I'd taken even a few steps, Larraine came to me.

"I'll take care of her," she said, and put out her hand for Sasha's leash. I'd known Larraine for a while, and I'd no reason not to trust her with my beloved dog. She'd always seemed to like Sasha. And everyone here would see her take control.

Yes, I was being a bit paranoid, but I was more concerned than normal about Sasha after Oliver's nastiness about her.

But Oliver apparently couldn't be nasty anymore.

"Okay," I said to Larraine, handing her the end of the leash, which she took. Then she bent to pat Sasha and give my tail-wagging pup a hug.

Bill, who was standing near us, said, "I'd be glad to come along, although I can't stay too long. I also talked to Wayne before and have an idea where he is."

Since I'd heard where Oliver was secondhand, I figured it would be a good idea to have Bill along. And the police car was a four-seater, so that should work.

Manager Neil didn't offer to go, but with Wayne out in the field and manager Oliver . . . gone, it made sense for another manager to stay at the welcome building and be in charge. Maybe. Unless he had another reason for not wanting to see Oliver's body . . .

Presumably, the shelter would open for any tourists still in the area around nine o'clock, as it always did. Assuming the troopers allowed it, under the circumstances. It was only eight thirty.

But Bill was a volunteer. I appreciated his coming out to help find out where the . . . situation had apparently occurred. It was interesting that he was here this early. But why not? I didn't know what his hours were at the restaurant, but after yesterday, I figured he might be scheduled at his job more on weekends. Plus he'd said he was cutting his hours there. Out of curiosity, I'd have to ask him more about his schedule.

We were soon driving down the concrete path in the car. The trooper in the passenger seat—Officer Morlande, the same one who'd gotten out to talk to us before—turned to face Bill and me. "So tell me who each of you is and what you do at this wildlife place."

I winced at that rather disrespectful description of Juneau Wildlife World. But it *was* a wildlife place—and more—so I didn't say anything critical.

Instead, I began, "My name is Stacie Calder. I'm a credentialed naturalist and give tours on the ClemTours boats during the summer. I've volunteered here, and just started working as an employee at this sanctuary for the winter."

"And you know Oliver . . . what's his last name? The man we've been told about?"

"Not well," I said. "I just met him yesterday. He's a new manager here. His last name is Brownling, or at least that's the way he introduced himself."

"Got it," the trooper said, then aimed his gaze at Bill.

"My name is Bill Westerstein," my back seat mate said, leaning forward. His graying hair looked a bit mussed, and the expression on his face was full of concern. And why not? We were out here attempting to help the state troopers find where Oliver's dead body was located. I shuddered at the thought as Bill continued, "I don't have that kind of credentials. I just moved to Juneau recently, and my job's at Juneau Seahouse. I'm a server there, mostly on weekends."

Ah, that was the information I'd assumed, and now I had confirmation.

And at least we weren't attempting to protect any sea life out here in the wilderness area, so his serving it for meals sounded fine.

In fact, I enjoyed eating regular seafood, but I certainly wouldn't want to dine on any of the wildlife I pointed out on my tours.

"I like wildlife too," Bill continued. "That's why I started volunteering, and I intend to spend a lot more time here this winter. I've already told my employers."

"Got it," the trooper said. "I assume that's true of all of you, or why else would you be here?"

We reached the end of the initial pathway, and I pointed to one of the next trails, ahead of the car. "There, toward the right and beyond this part of the fencing, is the area where the wolves roam," I said. "I'm not sure where we're talking about from here. Do you know?" I asked Bill.

But he didn't need to answer. Not too far away, I saw a person stand from where he'd apparently been kneeling on the ground.

He was inside the fence around the area beyond the gate, and I gathered it was Wayne.

"Right there!" Bill shouted, seeing him too. Our pointing him out was probably unnecessary, since I noticed both troopers staring in that direction.

Well, at least we'd been helpful in getting them to the area. There were other ways they could have gone within the sanctuary, although this was the most direct.

I doubted they needed two civilians hanging around. I'd stay out of their way and assumed Bill would too.

They parked along the gravel road right beside the fence, though far enough away to allow those on the passenger side to get out, like me. All four doors were soon open, and the troopers stalked ahead to the gate, where Wayne stood, waving. It remained closed, which was a good thing, although I didn't see any wolves in the vicinity. But we didn't want any to get out.

At least Wayne could exit quickly if any showed up and appeared ready to attack.

Attack? Surely not.

And yet . . .

I approached slowly as Wayne opened the gate and let the troopers in. I'd already seen something on the ground and shuddered as I got nearer. I knew what it was.

Oliver lay there, unmoving. I still didn't know what had happened to him.

As I reached the opposite side of the fence from where his body lay, Bill right beside me, I could see blood around Oliver. Around his neck.

And what appeared to be gouges there, though I really couldn't tell much from this distance.

I'd seen animals that had been mauled by other animals, killed by them, and that could have been what happened to Oliver.

Not that I was an expert on such stuff.

"That's awful," Bill said, taking a step back. "I . . . Did one of the wolves kill Oliver?"

"It couldn't be," was the best I could reply. My words sounded garbled by my emotion.

But if that *had* been what happened to him, what would these troopers, or their superiors, even the government, want to do to our wolves?

I felt awful about what had happened to our manager, no matter how nasty he'd been. I couldn't think he'd been attacked by a wolf, though. But as much as I hated to think so, what else could it have been? *When* could it have been?

Had he stayed here later than anyone else last night?

We needed more information, but how could we find it? I didn't think any of the security cameras were around here, since they were mostly located farther out on the grounds, but I had to find out.

"I'm calling it in," the trooper who wasn't Morlande said. I hadn't noticed his name badge but saw now it said *Jonsk*. He looked at Wayne. "You're the director here, right?"

"Yes," Wayne said.

"Let your people know that a medical examiner and more will be coming," the trooper said. "They'll need to be brought out here too."

I was glad manager Neil was at the welcome building. He'd need to let the outsiders in.

Would tourists be allowed in today? Maybe that wouldn't be a good idea, but it wasn't my call.

I hoped Larraine was still taking good care of Sasha. I wasn't sure how long I'd have to stay here. The troopers could find their way back on their own, and maybe Bill would stay with them.

I'd stay for a while, maybe till the medical people showed up. Or not. My stomach twisted. I didn't know how long I'd be out here or what had befallen poor Oliver.

I could walk back, and maybe see some wildlife on the way.

That might cheer me up under these circumstances. And I certainly could use some cheering. Oliver and I might not have been best buddies, but I felt really, really sorry that he had died.

I didn't know how long it would take for the medical examiner and the others to arrive, and even when Neil let them in the gates, they wouldn't know where to go any more than these troopers had. Even if I hurried, it would take me at least fifteen minutes to get back to the entry area, but maybe I'd be of more help showing the new outsiders where to go.

Which was what I did.

Sure enough, just as I reached the main area once more, an array of vehicles was pulling up to the gate. I hurried into the main building, looking for Larraine and Sasha. Fortunately, they were waiting in the lobby, so I got to say hi.

"What's going on?" Larraine asked.

I told her briefly, without going into any detail about what I'd seen of Oliver's body, but even that little bit made me grimace and shudder.

"I won't ask questions now," she said softly, "but I gather it's pretty bad."

I nodded, then turned to go back out. I pivoted again, though. "Are you okay watching Sasha a little longer? Someone needs to show these newcomers where to go to . . . get Oliver."

"I can take them to the wolf area," she said, and I felt a bit relieved. I didn't really want to go back to that place and watch . . . whatever they'd be doing.

"Sounds good, if you're okay with it." I told her where to take them. And hoped she wouldn't see too much.

I suggested to Larraine that they take only one vehicle, if possible, since the pathway wasn't very wide and turning around wouldn't be easy. Plus there was already another vehicle there.

Soon the medical examiner and the others were on their way with Larraine guiding them. I'd followed her outside. I had Sasha's leash now and bent to hug my pup, more for my support than hers.

"So tell me what's going on." Neil had come up to us in the parking area.

I briefly explained what I'd seen, and he shook his head the entire time. He wore a knit cap, even though the weather was far from the worst it would get here. I knew his silver hair was short and sparse, so his head probably got cold. His thin lips were pursed, and his concerned expression accentuated the wrinkles on his face.

A chilly wind began to blow, possibly a brief harbinger of the winter to come, and I shivered and said, "Why don't we go inside?" I wanted to get into the main building and the clinic to check on Tikaani's condition.

"Soon," Neil said. "Don't know if we'll get any tourists today, but I probably should stay out here and turn any away, at least until the authorities leave. Maybe you could help with that."

I nodded and agreed to remain with him. He was, after all, a manager. Tikaani wasn't exactly waiting to see me. I could visit him in a while.

In fact, a couple of carloads of visitors soon arrived. Neil didn't let them through the closed gate but had them idle in the entry area, where he explained that there was something going on here today and we couldn't let anyone visit. "Please give us a call in the next day or so, and hopefully we'll be open again then."

No one seemed happy about leaving, and I could understand why.

After they left, another car pulled up, and the driver, a pretty lady in a thick jacket, held out a card to Neil. There was a man in the seat beside her, holding a camera. Sightseers hoping to see wildlife?

That speculation was dashed immediately. "Hi," the driver said. "I'm Dannie Briggs with the *North Juneau News*." Wasn't that a small weekly newspaper?

The media had already heard.

The media were everywhere, and it was no surprise, really, that word had gotten out about a death, presumably by way of the troopers or the medical examiners or whoever.

But that made the situation even more horrible. What would any negative publicity do to Juneau Wildlife World—especially since it looked as if one of the wolves might have been the culprit?

I wasn't about to buy that, but the public might. And what would that do to this wonderful sanctuary and its inhabitants?

And what if it did turn out to be true? No!

The reporter stayed in the car, stubbornly refusing to leave, claiming the right to enter, as her companion began taking pictures out the window, despite the fact that there wasn't much to see that way. He couldn't get a good angle, even through the windshield, to see much of the wildlife preserve, let alone anything going on inside.

I was nevertheless relieved when they finally gave up, and the reporter, yelling she'd be back, finally drove away.

I hoped that she wouldn't return and that no other media people would show up, but I realized it was just an idle wish on my part. More information would get out, especially when they took Oliver to . . . wherever they took him for a final examination and autopsy. Ugh.

Neil finally went back inside through a side opening in the gate. Fortunately, no other cars were in sight.

Soon a procession of the two official vehicles carrying the troopers, the medical examiner, and, apparently, Oliver finally reappeared at the main area. They were followed by Wayne, Bill, and Larraine, who walked behind.

Wayne made his way around the others and said something to each of the drivers, then let them out the front gate along with the couple of cars they had parked near the welcome building.

"I think we need a short meeting," he said to all of us. He checked to make sure the gate was locked again, then motioned for us to follow him inside the welcome building.

He walked up a couple of steps toward his office and turned to face all of us.

"I figure you want to know what's going on," he said. He appeared dejected, and no wonder. One of his managers was dead, found that way on land comprising part of the fantastic sanctuary of which he was director. The large guy's shoulders sagged beneath his Juneau Wildlife World sweatshirt, and though he was only in his fifties, he suddenly appeared much older.

"Yes, please," Marnie called out. I hadn't seen her since I'd arrived; she had apparently stayed in the building while some of us went outside. We all wanted to know what had happened, I felt certain, but she might know less than any of us.

Wayne kept it brief. "When I came out of my apartment early this morning, Oliver's car was still in the same spot as I'd seen it yesterday and I didn't see him around, which worried me. I started looking for him in the area I last saw him." Wayne had seen him near the wolves too, when he'd come with Dr. Skip to help save Tikaani. Of course, Oliver could have left that area afterward, but it made sense to look for him there first.

Wayne then indicated where he'd found Oliver's body and said the poor man's throat had been lacerated. "He was, unfortunately, deceased, which the medical examiner confirmed when he got here, although it was pretty obvious, and I'd checked for a pulse and all that." As bad as that was, I dreaded whatever Wayne would say next about Oliver's condition and what the medical examiner believed was the cause. *Who* the ME believed was the cause.

Presumably, it was one of the wolves, considering where Oliver had been found and the types of wounds. I dreaded hearing that, even though it was probably true.

Would anyone speculate as to why Oliver had been out there? Or why a wolf had been able to sneak up on him? Around what time it had been?

And why was I thinking about all of that?

Because I was worried about the wolves, of course.

"Could the medical examiner tell what had happened to Oliver?" Marnie asked. She sounded choked up, and I knew Oliver had been her friend. Or so it had seemed.

"He said he had to do further examination," Wayne replied. "But he did point out some things to me, which I hated seeing but wanted to know."

The bloody area . . . I shuddered but admired Wayne.

And then the director continued: "Although it looked like an animal could have bitten Oliver's throat, the way the examiner was talking and pointing, and the way it appeared to me . . ." He paused, his head shaking slowly. "Of course, I don't know anything about it. The examiner will have to figure it out. But he seemed to think, and it looked to me, as if a *person* might have used some kind of pointed weapon to dig into Oliver's throat and kill him and make it look like an animal's teeth could have been the cause."

Chapter Six

Oh, wow. I forced myself not to exclaim aloud as I stood in the warmth of the large lobby with everyone else at the base of the steps, listening to our distressed director, who'd just shared the current status of the investigation into Oliver's death.

Oliver had been murdered—by a person?

I found myself really hoping that it had been a human who'd killed him. As horrible as that would be, it certainly would be better than if he'd been mauled by a wolf under protection here. But who would have done such a thing?

Beside me, Sasha moved, snuggling up to me as if she knew I needed comfort as we both heard the shocked exclamations and questions the other employees and volunteers around us had started to vocalize.

I was filled with questions too. If it had been a person, who had done it? Oliver wasn't exactly the most popular guy around here, but who'd hated him that much?

And then I nearly fell over, steadying myself quickly. Sasha drew even closer against me and snuggled her nose to my sagging hand. I patted her gently, needing the reassurance she was conveying.

For I realized that, of everyone, I probably looked the most likely to have killed Oliver, since I'd been arguing with him about Sasha from the moment we'd met.

The fact that I'd come back to the sanctuary last night, after leaving, wouldn't look good either, if anyone found out.

The security system, the cameras around this building and heading out on the trail, would rat me out.

They would proclaim my presence.

The fact that there weren't any cameras directly where the activity had been in the wolf area yesterday, and where Oliver had ultimately been found, wouldn't exonerate me.

I'd been involved in a murder situation before, just a few months ago, though I hadn't been a major suspect. But I had been under suspicion, since I'd argued with the victim.

Instead, I'd helped figure out who'd really done it.

Would I have to do that again now?

To save myself?

Okay. Once again, as I often did, I was overthinking. Worrying too much.

I hoped.

"Are you okay, Stacie?" asked Bill, who stood next to me.

My thoughts and emotions must have been screaming out at the world, which wasn't good.

"How could any of us be okay?" I asked. "It's bad enough Oliver's dead, but now the authorities have to figure out if a person did it or a wolf, and it evidently appears to be the former. And if so, they have to solve the crime and arrest the killer. Someone who's been around here, or at least was yesterday. It's all so . . . it's all so horrible, in so many ways." I felt my eyes tear up. The whole situation was so awful, so sad, no matter how I'd felt about Oliver.

Cry Wolf

"It really is," said Marnie, who'd edged over toward us. Tears pooled in her eyes too. "There are no good possibilities. Any one of us could be guilty, or at least the cops might think so."

I didn't mention my arguments with Oliver, including his words with me yesterday. They all knew. Trying to reassure everyone that I was innocent would just call attention to my earlier attitude.

Instead, I looked up the staircase toward Wayne. He was observing all of us.

Was he listening, assessing who said what, attempting to determine who among us was guilty?

Or could he be the guilty one? He'd known where Oliver was yesterday. He'd come out to the wolf area to help Dr. Skip with the injured wolf. He'd seen his manager along with some others, including me.

Did he have an axe to grind, so to speak, with that manager? Or a smaller, toothlike weapon . . . ?

"Wayne," I called up to him. "Thanks for keeping us informed, and I hope you'll continue to do so with whatever you find out."

"I . . . I can't believe it would have been anyone here who did that," Marnie said. She was standing just below Wayne. I noticed then that Shawna Streight was beside her. I hadn't seen her earlier, so she must have just arrived.

Even if tourists couldn't come in under these circumstances, I gathered that employees and volunteers were still welcome.

Shawna might be luckier than the rest of us. Since she hadn't been here yesterday, she wouldn't be a suspect.

Although . . . anyone who knew the place could have sneaked in. But hidden from the rest of us?

Sneaked off to kill Oliver?

63

No, I didn't believe that could have happened, with Shawna or anyone else. Still, it might take suspicion off me.

Assuming it was on me. I could hope, at least, that people at the sanctuary knew me well enough to know better. But past experience had taught me to expect the worst.

And in reality, people around here didn't know me well at all.

Okay. Enough of this. No sense worrying this much, at least not now.

Wayne started talking again, probably in response to what both Marnie and I had said.

"I do wish I could give you more information. I promise I'll let you all know anything I hear that could help. I'll also be talking to the authorities, but if they tell me to keep anything quiet, I'll have to listen to them. Right now, though, I'd like you all to get to work. At least in pairs, though, to protect each other—and let me know who each of you is working with. We need to make sure this sanctuary and its inhabitants are doing as well as always, despite the horrible thing that happened here to a human."

That was enough to get us all going in our usual directions. But before I went out along one of the trails to do some observation, I decided I could take time to go check on Tikaani.

Sasha and I went through the door to the inner hallway and began walking toward the end.

"Are you interested in doing some food prep today?" Marnie was right behind me. "Is that why you came in here? I don't think Wayne scheduled you, but—"

"I'd love to one of these days, Marnie. Feel free to mention it to Wayne. I will. But no; right now I wanted to take a peek in on that injured wolf in the clinic."

"Oh. Got it. I should have guessed that first." Marnie grinned, then looked down at my dog and back up at my face. "I know how much of an animal lover you are."

I smiled back. "What a surprise." It felt reassuring to have what seemed like a somewhat normal conversation with another employee, and so as Marnie slipped though the doorway into the food preparation kitchen, I felt a tiny bit better.

At least for the moment.

"Sit," I told Sasha as we reached the clinic door. It wouldn't be a good idea to bring my dog in. The wolf might be awake and could be stressed by seeing another animal there, even if it was sedated.

Of course Sasha obeyed, and I then told her, "Stay," putting my hand gently in front of her face to emphasize the command. I also looped her leash around the door handle.

I slipped inside. I wondered when Dr. Skip would be in. With an injured patient, I figured he would at least visit, although he might have given Wayne sufficient instructions for caring for the animal a day or so before he returned.

Assuming the wolf was doing well enough after that terrible wound.

Dr. Skip visited often anyway, or that was what I understood, and now he had reason to come back soon.

For now, I walked through the entry area to the clinic and into the large room at the rear where animals under treatment were kept.

Considering the types of animals who might be cared for, that room had to be large. It also had several enclosures separated from each other by walls so the wild patients would be less agitated if others were nearby. A reindeer might not be thrilled if there was a wolf around, for example, although the place was pretty empty now.

Only Tikaani was here, as it turned out.

Just one of the areas had its door closed, so I opened it slowly and carefully and peered in.

He was sleeping on the floor of his enclosure. Perhaps the sedation was still in effect. But as I watched, I saw him breathe. His injured limb remained bandaged. A half-full bag of IV fluids hung from a rack in the enclosure, its tube leading into an unbandaged upper portion of the wolf's right leg. I really didn't know enough to determine how well he was doing.

I'd have to ask Wayne, or better yet, Dr. Skip if I saw him.

As I turned to close the door behind me, I was startled to see the main door open. It wasn't Dr. Skip but Neil.

Was the manager also checking on the wolf?

"What are you doing here?" His tone was sharp and definitely not welcoming.

I told him I was checking on the patient, partly because I'd been there to help him when he'd been found injured.

"Yeah, yeah, I know. Well, Dr. Skip is coming to check on him this afternoon, and I'm supposed to keep an eye on him in the meantime. Did he look okay to you?"

"Yes," I said, "though I'm far from an expert, and I didn't get close."

"I figured. Well, you can leave now while I take a look. Oh, and Wayne knows I'm here now."

I wondered at the aging guy's nasty attitude. And then I wondered, since he'd made it a point to tell me our director was aware of his location, whether he thought he was telling someone he assumed to be a murderer she'd be caught if she dared to harm him too.

Okay. That was a bit much.

But I realized I'd wonder a lot about people's attitudes toward me till this mystery was solved.

And I couldn't be certain that wasn't what he was thinking.

"Sure," I said. "Sasha and I will go check out some of our residents now." I almost told him he didn't have to worry about me, but I caught myself.

I didn't really know what was on his mind.

I did lead my dog out of the main building after that. No way was I going to follow the main trail just then, since it led to the wolf area.

Instead, I went to another, smaller trail that led from the back of the welcome building and toward another couple of large, fenced areas where more wildlife resided. One of them, in the distance, contained quite a few brown bears. Another, closer to the welcome building, held additional moose and reindeer, and since it led to vast hillsides, there were also mountain goats. I still didn't know why these particular animals were here, but I assumed they had been enclosed in these locations for their safety, possibly because of injuries or because they hadn't been able to remain in their original locations for some other reason.

This pathway didn't segue off the parking lot, and it still had some gravel but was mostly dirt. I was already wearing sturdy boots for walking, and I'd put on my parka with a hood, since rain was predicted for the afternoon. The temperature was in the low forties, so I didn't anticipate sleet or snow, but I also knew that could change.

Fortunately, Sasha, as a husky, had a nice, warm coat and didn't seem to mind it even when the weather turned cold. I didn't want to take her on muddy trails, though, if it rained, and would put dog boots on her if I thought her paws would get uncomfortable, depending on the amount of muck, ice, or snow on the ground.

I hadn't seen anyone else when we headed out, which was probably a good thing. I wanted to be alone.

Well, alone with my wonderful dog.

It was late morning, but I didn't figure I'd return to the vending machines for lunch. I didn't have an appetite. And I didn't particularly want to talk to anyone again, at least for a while.

Although I wouldn't be surprised if troopers wanted to talk to me.

No. I wouldn't think about that. I'd just perform my job, which would be a welcome distraction, considering how much I enjoyed seeing animals.

Our hike took a nice long time, and I wound up getting glimpses of several of the creatures I'd hoped to. I took pictures on my phone. I also made notes on note cards I'd brought, which I hadn't done yesterday and regretted. I hadn't yet added my report to the sanctuary's system, and I figured I'd remember everything I'd seen, but with my mind the way it was now, I wanted to do more to reassure myself that I wouldn't forget any animal.

I certainly wouldn't forget yesterday's wolves.

I jotted down when and where I saw the six different bears on the hillsides as I viewed them from a distance. All were roaming individually, which wasn't surprising this time of year, considering it was far from mating season.

Beyond one of the many long fences, I glimpsed a porcupine, which was fun, though I was glad it wasn't at all close to Sasha and me.

And then, when we turned onto the farthest path on this route, I saw mountain goats on the hillsides, several together. From this distance, they appeared to be of similar size, so I assumed they were all female, and they were shaggy enough to have begun growing their winter coats.

Oh yes, I was enjoying this. Sasha, at my side, seemed happy too.

But finally, it was time to head back.

I entered the welcome building on our return and went directly to the small office reserved for us to do our reports. I hurried with Sasha to avoid seeing anyone, and fortunately, no one else was around.

I didn't spend long at the computer but drafted my reports for yesterday and today, making sure that when I wrote yesterday's, I was totally professional. I was specific in my description of the area where the wolves were, where I'd helped Tikaani. I didn't mention how many other people had been around or what had happened to Oliver.

And while I was online, I checked. Various media sources had already reported Oliver's death, including Dannie Briggs of the *North Juneau News*. They'd apparently spoken to the authorities but not interviewed anyone at the sanctuary. Good.

It was finally time to leave. But first, I texted Wayne, holding my breath in case he wanted to talk to me.

He acknowledged my text but said nothing else.

I wondered what, if anything, had happened in the investigation into Oliver's death while I was out.

Maybe they already knew who'd killed Oliver and had arrested their suspect.

I doubted that. But I could hope.

Before leaving, I stopped once more to check on Tikaani, leaving Sasha outside. This time, Dr. Skip was there.

"He's doing fairly well," he said, when I asked how the wolf was healing. And then he aimed a speculative smile at me. "How about you?"

Drat. I gathered he'd heard not only about Oliver's death but also maybe from those who were trying to guess whodunit. I might be somewhere on that list for a few people who had seen us arguing, though I hoped not.

"I'm concerned," I admitted. "Too many bad things happened around here yesterday." I left it at that and hurried out of the clinic, offering Larraine a quick wave in the lobby on the way out. I noticed Lettie talking to others in the corner, but I didn't stop.

At least I might be able to get some insight about what was happening with the investigation from Liam, even though I knew he'd have a professional responsibility to keep the case details confidential.

I called him on Bluetooth as soon as I'd driven through the gate and shut it behind me. Was he going to be available to talk?

Even more important, could I see him that evening?

He answered immediately. "How are you, Stacie?"

Which made me gulp. That was a bit weird, as if he knew I had reason not to be doing well.

Okay, he *did* know that. He knew where I worked and that someone had been murdered there. Of course he knew.

Or was it more than that?

"I'm fine," I said firmly. I could pretend that I was, at least.

"I was going to call you later," he said. "Can we get together for dinner?"

Really? Were we going to have another highly pleasant evening, and perhaps night, together?

Or . . . My mind continued to leap in terrible directions. Maybe he was under orders to interrogate me but make it look as if it were just a date.

Was that even legal?

I'd just have to be careful. And ignore the fact that, at least for the moment, I didn't completely trust this man I'd come to like a lot.

Any more than I trusted anything else about the situation.

"I was hoping you'd say that." Which would have been the truth if things right now hadn't been so difficult.

"Great."

We made plans to meet at one of our favorite restaurants, DelishAFish, one where I could bring Sasha with no problem.

Good. We'd be out in public. Surely, even if he was assigned to investigate me, he wouldn't do it where other people could possibly eavesdrop.

I drove home first, walked Sasha briefly, then fed her the special dog food I always gave her. I changed into a nice outfit—a frilly, long-sleeved shirt and slacks. I wanted to look dressy, but I also wanted to wear something appropriate for the chillier weather now.

I looked at myself in the mirror before I left, and not just to refresh my minimal makeup. I wished there were something I could do to brighten my eyes and emphasize my currently non-existent smile.

Oh well. Maybe just seeing Liam would help with both.

Or make them even worse.

"Let's go, Sasha," I said, after putting on my jacket. I approached my dog in the kitchen, where she was still licking her bowl. She didn't object.

The restaurant in downtown Juneau wasn't too far from my home and there wasn't any traffic, so we arrived quickly. I called Liam once I found a parking spot.

Sometimes he picked me up, but he hadn't suggested it this time and neither had I. I kind of assumed he was leaving at the last minute from his office. But once again, my mind tried to add an ulterior motive, like he didn't want this to feel much like a date, especially in case anyone he worked with noticed us. He could always say we'd agreed to meet so we could talk.

Enough.

Sasha and I walked inside the moderate-sized restaurant, which smelled like seafood, but in a pleasant way. It was perhaps a bit more crowded than I'd seen it before, which might be a good thing. Too many people around to do much talking about anything that needed to remain private.

Liam was already there. He'd gotten us a two-person table not far from the entrance, and he'd already ordered us the kinds of beer we each liked.

He stood as we approached—and gave me a quick kiss. That would be obvious to anyone observing us, but I liked it. A lot. I even felt a little relieved by the way he approached me. Of course, I responded in kind.

"Hi, Stacie," he said with a grin on his handsome, craggy face as we pulled away and I put my jacket on the back of my seat, revealing my dressy blouse, and sat down. "And hi to you too, my husky friend." He scratched Sasha behind the ears, then took his own seat, also removing his thick jacket, as my dog settled beside me.

I glanced at the menu briefly, though I didn't need to. We soon clinked beer glasses in a silly toast and each took a sip. I appreciated the cold, tangy taste of the dark ale.

"So, how have you been doing?" I asked to start the conversation, since we hadn't seen each other for a few days.

"Relatively well," was all he said in his warm, deep voice, before our server, a woman in a pink shirt and slacks, came to take our order. As usual, I ordered salmon and Liam ordered halibut.

When the server left, I pondered what to say next, but Liam beat me to it. There was something about his almost blank expression that I didn't understand. I guess I was used to him showing some emotion toward me, which had become increasingly warm as we'd come to know each other better.

Not now.

"I'm sure you realize," he said, "that I have heard about what happened at Juneau Wildlife World last night. But in case you wanted to discuss it—well, I can't. I'm not working on the case, but I'm still not permitted to talk to anyone about it at all, even my fellow troopers, or access any files or further information, since my superior officers are well aware that I'm involved with a person of interest."

Chapter Seven

My heart sank. I felt tears rush to my eyes.

I'd wondered if I was a suspect, figured I might be. Now I knew I was a person of interest.

And even the man I cared for most thought so. Even if he supposedly couldn't talk about it, he'd just done so by saying he couldn't. He hadn't really offered an opinion, but neither had he denied that I should be considered at least a person of interest.

He hadn't asked my opinion about what had happened—not that I knew anything. But I certainly could reassure him I'd had nothing to do with Oliver's murder.

Although he'd said he couldn't discuss it. Even so . . .

"I see," I said, and took another sip of my beer. Then another.

I wasn't going to chug it, though, or order any more. Getting drunk wouldn't help the situation.

Even if it did help to mush up my mind.

Our meals were finally set on the table before us. Could I convince myself to eat now? I supposed I could always take leftovers home, even if it turned out to be my entire salmon serving.

But would I even be home to eat it?

"Okay," I said brightly as I made myself take a bite. "What can we talk about?"

Cry Wolf

Liam never talked much about the cases he was working on anyway, so that was seldom a topic of our conversations, although he occasionally gave hints about the kinds of matters he was pursuing. He actually did that now as we both ate—yes, I managed to—mentioning he'd received an interesting assignment regarding a tourist who'd gone missing. He couldn't say much regarding anyone suspicious who might have accompanied the tourist or other circumstances related to the case. But he'd told me before that he'd worked many cases where people who'd come to Alaska had disappeared for a while, sometimes permanently. All he could say about this one was that it was different because that person's spouses had filed reports, so they'd apparently known he'd come here.

"Spouses, plural?" I asked.

"Yes, and they evidently didn't know about each other—before. But that certainly gives us a clue about why he's missing. Though whether he's remained in this area is one of the things we're looking into."

Okay, that *was* interesting. "Hope you'll keep me informed, to the extent you can." I added the latter because confidentiality was always important in situations that the Initial Response Section got involved with.

"Sure, to the extent I can," he emphasized.

The rest of the meal went fine. I tried to keep my worries at the back of my mind, and though I didn't fully succeed, I allowed the things we talked about to take more of my focus.

He didn't say much more about his missing two-timer. But then I started talking about my winter job at Juneau Wildlife World and the hikes I'd been taking to observe the animals. I mentioned the various types of wildlife, the way the vast areas had looked, and the feel of the wild Alaska air around Sasha and me. I talked about the reindeer and moose, the bears and mountain goats and more, noting how far away they'd all been from us and the fencing. I even mentioned the wolves, including the injured one. I explained why I called him Tikaani and how he'd been taken into the sanctuary clinic to be treated for his wounds.

I didn't mention any people who'd been around.

And I most certainly didn't mention Oliver.

Eventually, dinner was over. I'd enjoyed the company. For the last time?

Under other circumstances, I'd invite Liam to come home with me and spend the night. But I figured that at a minimum, he'd have to say no because of his job and the direction he'd been given about me as a . . . person of interest.

And so I just said, in as light a tone as I could, "Guess it'll be a lonesome night tonight." I made myself grin at him. "Just think of all the fun we could have had."

He grinned back in a suggestive leer that made me laugh. "Oh, we can still have some fun."

That startled me. "But—"

"As long as you don't mind some company who may not talk much, I'd be delighted to get an invitation to your home tonight."

I felt myself blink. I forced myself not to overthink this. I had no idea what the atmosphere might be like, but I nevertheless said, "Then consider yourself delighted. You're invited."

And so, after insisting on paying our bill again, which he did more than half the time, Liam followed Sasha and me home. He accompanied us on our final walk of the night. And then he came inside.

It was an enjoyable night. We watched a couple of comedy TV shows, which didn't exactly lighten my mood, but at least they didn't make it any worse.

And I did appreciate the company.

At bedtime, we both showered. But—well, I wasn't really interested in anything particularly intimate.

"I gather you're not in the mood," Liam said as I kissed him, but not as heatedly as when we were about to really dive into a night of fun.

"No, sorry, I'm really not." I felt myself tear up again. Was I going to turn him off altogether, so we'd never have another sexual night?

His job, his attitude before, what he'd said . . . I just couldn't get excited.

And so, we put on our pj's—he'd started keeping a pair here, and I kept a set at his place—and simply got into bed together, with Sasha lying on the floor on my side.

Liam and I held each other. Tightly. It felt comforting.

"Hey, you know what?" he asked softly as we lay there, the night-light at the foot of my bed illuminating his handsome face slightly.

I was exhausted and wired and wondered if I'd sleep at all tonight. "What?" I asked.

"Has Sasha ever attacked anything? A person?"

"What!" I pulled away and sat up. "Are you implying that my dog could have . . . done what you're not supposed to talk about? If so, no way!"

The smile he aimed in my direction looked grim in the faint light. "I didn't think so, but—well, forget I've mentioned it at all. But I know those in charge of the unnamed investigation are also looking into whether a canine could have done it, presumably a wolf, considering the nature of the injuries. And I figure a different kind of canine could also be a suspect. Along with . . . people who were present."

"No way!" I exclaimed again. "Not Sasha. And not me. You can be sure of both."

"That's what I figured," he said. "Not that I can pass that along to my colleagues. But you're likely to meet some of them tomorrow. I gather they'll be conducting more of their investigation at Juneau Wildlife World."

I swallowed. "I . . . I kind of wondered. And you're telling me now—"

"Maybe I should have waited until breakfast, or not mentioned it at all. Do you think you'll be able to sleep tonight?"

"I wasn't sure before," I admitted. "And now—"

"And now, come back into my arms and let me hug you again. I wasn't sure I could sleep either with all this on my mind. But now, if we stay close, maybe we both can relax at least a little."

"Maybe." I knew I sounded doubtful.

But even though my mind swam around the situation and what Liam had said—*Sasha guilty of harming a person? No way!*— I did manage to snuggle against the man whose warm body pressed against mine. I thought I heard his breathing deepen.

And sometime later, I fell asleep too.

* * *

I woke early the next morning, thanks partly to feeling Liam moving beside me. He'd awakened first.

"Good morning," he said as I pulled slightly away. We'd remained in each other's arms.

For the last time?

He'd said I might meet with investigators today. Would they arrest me?

Okay, for the moment I would act as if all were fine, that this was just another morning we'd woken up together.

"Good morning," I responded. "What time is it?"

It was six thirty. I knew he sometimes had to get to work early, especially on those days he wasn't scheduled for an assignment at night. I didn't need to get up this early, since my work at the sanctuary didn't officially start until nine or so in the morning. Or at least it hadn't so far. I supposed if I ever got into food prep and not just observation of our residents, I might have to get there earlier to get food ready to take out to some of the animals.

I threw on casual clothes first thing and took Sasha out for a quick walk, and Liam joined us. He had breakfast with me, as he often did; I kept a kind of cereal he preferred in my pantry along with my favorite. Neither one of us cooked anything, thanks to our usual need to keep on the move.

Soon, after discussing nothing much other than what Juneau's weather would be like that day—it had started out even colder than yesterday when we'd been out with Sasha—and whether there'd be any visitors to the sanctuary, we bundled up a bit and walked out of my apartment. Then we each headed toward our cars, Sasha at my side as usual.

Yes, it was chilly. And despite my jacket, I felt cold and concerned, and not merely because of the weather.

It was misting, but the roads were slick, so I drove slowly. It was a good excuse not to hurry.

When we arrived, the main gate was closed, as usual. I got out and opened it, wondering if tourists would be permitted to come today.

I wondered also if any tourists would *want* to come today, considering that the weather was growing worse.

Soon, it really would be winter, and then probably no one but those of us who belonged at the sanctuary would come.

I certainly hoped I'd be able to.

I had to stop worrying and get on with living my life. As long as I was able to.

I parked in my usual area and let Sasha out, then took her for a brief walk in the chilly air, trying to ignore the black, formal-looking SUV parked near the front of the welcome building.

It wasn't an official Alaska State Troopers vehicle, or at least it didn't bear the decals. But who knew who'd driven here in it?

Liam had said I'd be interviewed eventually, and unfortunately, today made sense, since I hadn't been yesterday. I would anticipate the worst and hope for the best.

Soon, Sasha and I headed inside, and I removed my jacket, hanging it on the rack for employees near the entrance. I did my routine of texting Wayne that I was here. Were any other employees or volunteers here? When would we receive our instructions for the day?

We'd get them from manager Neil, I assumed. I decided to go to his office, which was upstairs, not far from Wayne's.

Before I got there, Wayne appeared in the hallway. The large man's Juneau Wildlife World black sweatshirt seemed even thicker than those he usually wore, which wasn't surprising, even though we were inside. It wasn't that cold yet, though.

"Oh, good," he said. "You made it in. There are a couple of detectives here today who are questioning everyone about . . . about what they were doing when Oliver was killed. Not too many of our staff are here yet. They're questioning Neil right now, and they asked me to schedule our other people as they arrived. I'll put you down next."

Oh, you can put me at the end of the list, I wanted to tell him, but I said, "Okay. Where are they conducting their questioning?"

He nodded toward the door at the beginning of the hall, an office I understood was currently empty.

"I guess I'd better not go out to observe any of our wildlife, then," I said. "Has anyone else been on the trails this morning?"

"Not yet," Wayne said. "Hopefully, you'll get to head out there soon. Choose which trails this time."

Hopefully. That implied I might not get to go for a while.

Or maybe at all.

Once more I was worrying too much without needing to.

"Should I maybe go see if Marnie needs a little bit of help first thing?"

"Good idea."

But before I could start down the steps with Sasha, the door Wayne had indicated opened. Neil came out, along with a man in a black suit, white shirt, and pale-blue tie. He didn't exactly look like a tourist come to check out our animals. He was followed by a woman who wore similarly formal clothing.

I'd assumed most Alaska State Troopers wore uniforms, but maybe that wasn't true of detectives.

"Oh, good, Stacie," Neil said. The manager appeared haggard, and I wondered how stressful his interrogation had been. "You're here. The detectives were hoping to talk to you soon."

I guessed I was about to find out about that stressfulness myself.

Before I could respond, the woman approached me. "Hello, Ms. Calder," she said. She was about my height, maybe around my age, and she had black hair clipped short. Her expression remained neutral, although her hazel eyes appeared to assess my face. "I'm Detective Lillian Christopher, and that's Detective John Daniels. We're assisting the Alaska State Troopers in their investigation of Oliver Brownling's death."

I found it interesting that they apparently weren't with the Alaska State Troopers, at least not directly. They had to be homicide detectives, didn't they?

But not part of the troopers? I wondered if it might be because of Liam and our sort-of relationship.

No matter. I'd tell them the truth, same as I'd do if they were clearly troopers like Liam was.

"Hi," I said, attempting to sound friendly. I even smiled. "What happened to Oliver was really a shame. It's so shocking." I was being honest. I didn't have to like the guy to feel terrible about what had happened to him.

"Very true," Detective Christopher said. "We'd like to talk to you about it."

I don't know anything, I wanted to shout. Instead, I said, "Sure." Then I found myself adding, "And I'd imagine you have some form of ID to show that you're authorized to do this."

I knew I'd be earning at least one strike against me by saying that. But what if they were media or something else, rather than truly assisting the troopers?

"Certainly." Her tone was calm. "We already showed it to Mr. Deerfield when we arrived, and to Mr. Zesser when we started talking to him. We'll show you too, once we get started."

Maybe they were legit and understood that civilians needed some degree of proof that they were who they said they were. I glanced at Wayne, who stood nearby watching us, and he just nodded.

"Let's go inside this room and talk, Ms. Calder," Detective Daniels said.

"It's fine, Stacie," said Neil, who also hadn't walked away.

He and Wayne were both my superiors here, although I didn't need to obey them in this situation.

But I knew I would be questioned. Liam had told me so—and I'd figured as much anyway.

"All right," I said. Pulling gently on Sasha's leash, I followed Detective Daniels inside while his colleague came behind me, making me feel trapped.

Well, as detectives who might not be part of the troopers, they probably couldn't arrest me, right?

I'd just have to see how things went.

* * *

Things went about as well as I anticipated, which is to say, not well at all.

They had me sit behind the desk in this small, unoccupied office while they sat on chairs facing it. That seemed odd. It felt like I should be in charge, but it was just the opposite.

First, they asked about my background and credentials and what I was doing for the sanctuary. That part was easy, and I let them know I was a naturalist with a degree in wildlife conservation and management from the University of Arizona. I said I'd come to Alaska to use my background and love of wildlife in an enjoyable way. I also told them about my regular job narrating tours out on the water during the summer for ClemTours, but I didn't go into detail about it. I said I was working here at Juneau Wildlife World for the winter because ClemTours didn't provide tours during the inclement Alaskan winter weather.

That was the easy part.

Then came what they really wanted to talk about. They provided me with official-appearing credentials from the Alaska State Troopers, indicating that the troopers had hired a detective agency called Christopher Detectives to assist in a current investigation. So Lillian was in charge, evidently.

Was this normal? I didn't think so. Again, I wondered why they weren't using their own people. I'd ask Liam but figured he couldn't talk about this either. I wondered if they were a third party hired to investigate me while avoiding any conflict of interest with Liam and the troopers.

I answered their questions as well as I could. Yes, Oliver and I hadn't gotten along well, thanks to his bad attitude toward my dog. I bent down and patted that sweet dog on her head, and

Sasha looked up at me. Even that slight move on her part, and the way her eyes locked on mine, reminded me what a protector and defender she was.

We continued on. Yes, Oliver and I had been arguing on the afternoon of the night he was killed. No, I hadn't threatened him in any way. I would rather have left my job here than continue being harassed that way.

And, I added, if they suspected me of killing him? Well, that hadn't happened, I stated bluntly. I'd never kill a person. I'd never even kill an animal, unless it was euthanasia because the creature was suffering.

Their questions, and my answers, meandered. No, I wasn't a vegetarian, but then, neither were the carnivores I loved to observe. I bought meat when I needed to. I didn't kill to get it.

"When was the last time you saw Mr. Brownling alive?" asked Detective Daniels. They both took notes on tablets of paper, although they'd made it clear they were filming the interview and recording everything I said. Daniels loosened his necktie and was leaning forward on the skimpy-looking wooden chair. The expression on his midforties face appeared bland, most likely by design. His brown hair was pushed back on his head, and his brows were straight, as though they were part of his dull-appearing professional demeanor.

"It was outside the fence surrounding the large area that is the wolf habitat." I described how I'd gone through the gate to help a clearly distressed wolf, leaving my dog with one of the others, who remained outside. I'd helped make sure that the wolf was as okay as possible until the sanctuary's veterinarian arrived with director Wayne, then watched as they took care of the injured wolf and headed back to the shelter clinic with him.

"Oliver was outside that fence with a few other people," I said. "He—well, he clearly wasn't happy that one of the employees he supervised had dared to go inside and risk herself that way. Though I assured him I was fine, he still gave me a hard time about it, so I took Sasha's leash back and walked to the welcome building. I saw the vehicle bringing the poor wolf this direction. And I didn't see Oliver again."

"Not even when you returned to this sanctuary later that evening?" Detective Christopher demanded. Her tone was sharper than it had been. Why? Was she officially accusing me? "We've been given evidence about who left that day and when, thanks to some of the security footage from around the entry gate. You left. And later, you came back."

She glared, as if she expected me to deny it.

But I didn't. "That's right," I said, as calmly as I could. "I spent time later that day in a different area of the sanctuary, observing some wildlife that I hadn't seen previously since I officially started working here, like some mountain goats. And then Sasha and I headed home. But now that I'm an employee, I thought it would be a good thing to return and do some additional observation that day. Which I did, but not for very long. And although I did initially head down our original pathway with my dog, I didn't see many animals and figured they weren't getting near enough to the fencing to view at that hour, and so I headed back home again."

I didn't mention that part of my reason for returning was a touch of sadness that I wouldn't get to see Liam that evening; I'd needed something more interesting to do with my time than hang out at home and watch TV.

"And before you ask," I added, "I didn't see Oliver on that return trip. Or any sanctuary vehicle he might have driven along the trail, if he'd stayed there or returned to the wolf area."

"Did you notice whether his own car remained in the parking lot near this building?"

"No," I said. "I didn't really pay attention to who else might still be around."

They didn't ask much more after that. But I did say honestly, "I can understand why I could be considered a person of interest, since I'm sure people around here heard me arguing with Oliver. But none of it was all that harsh, and I certainly wouldn't threaten him. And I definitely didn't kill him."

I wished they'd reply with something like "Of course not," or anything that suggested they believed one word of what I'd said.

Neither said anything, though, until Detective Christopher stood and turned off the recording equipment. "Thank you for your input," she said.

Which was too neutral and noncommittal to make me feel any better.

Questions I wanted to ask them bombarded my mind, things like who else they considered to be suspects; who they thought had been the last people to see Oliver alive; what they really thought had been used to slash his neck, assuming it wasn't the canine teeth it had apparently been designed to look like. I was really curious about that. What had the weapon been?

"You can go now," the lady detective added. "You have work to do today, right?"

I nodded. "I haven't received my official assignment of the day, so I'll check with Wayne, but hopefully I'll be sent off into the sanctuary areas to do more observation."

"Fine. Before you go, though, we'll want you to fill out this form."

I was a bit surprised they hadn't asked for more contact information from me earlier. Maybe they'd thought I'd be more open with what I said if I didn't think they'd be able to find me easily when I wasn't here at Juneau Wildlife World.

But the form they had me complete required my name, address, phone number, even my driver's license information. I had an official Alaska driver's license, since I'd been living in the state for over a year.

Then, at last, I was free to go.

But my mind was far from free after what I'd just been through. Or what I was worried might come in the future while I remained a person of interest in Oliver's murder.

Chapter Eight

It was still early. As I stepped out of the small office into the hallway, I sighed in relief. At least that interrogation was over.

Would there be more?

I wouldn't be surprised. I wondered what my blood pressure was like right now as I headed quickly down the steps, Sasha at my side. The welcome building felt warm, maybe too warm, so I knew the heating system had kicked on. It smelled rather musty to me, and I wondered how bad it smelled to my poor dog at my side, who had a much better sense of scent than I did.

"Are you okay, girl?" I asked. She glanced up at me as she too walked quickly down the stairs. She seemed concerned, as always. "Yes, I'm okay," I reassured her.

Sort of okay. I had a sudden pang of fear.

I almost wanted to head home right away. Or at least get into my car so I could scream about what I'd just gone through, what I might face in the future.

But I didn't. If Oliver had been here, if he'd been alive, I wouldn't have given him the satisfaction. And now that he wasn't, I still couldn't let what had happened to him control my life—not unless I was ultimately wrongly arrested.

Cry Wolf

I was at the Juneau Wildlife World for a reason: to do all I could to help the wildlife sheltered here. I knew that observing them, making sure they ranged around and were okay as well as finding any who were hurt, like Tikaani, helped a lot. What I'd done so far since starting as an employee had been somewhat productive, at least.

I wanted to continue. To do more.

To forget I had become a person of interest in a murder.

And going out in the shelter areas and observing the best way I could seemed aspirational for today. I might even help more animals, although I certainly hoped I wouldn't find any more in Tikaani's condition.

Trekking out to observe would surely be good for Sasha and me too. As long as we didn't run into anyone else who had any kind of grudge against me.

Time to make good on that.

Tikaani, though. How was he?

I decided to check on the poor wolf later rather than now. After all, others were looking after him.

I saw a few people in the large lobby: Marnie, Neil, and—thank heavens—Lettie. At least I'd have one friend present, someone who wouldn't just assume I was a murderer.

She'd even been around, assisting here and there, as I'd helped solve the murder a few months ago that involved the ClemElk tour boat where we both worked.

She was talking with the other two people with her, and I wondered what they were saying. They all turned to look toward us as Sasha and I approached, and I made myself smile. "Good morning, Lettie and Marnie," I said. "And hi again, Neil."

The manager's expression appeared quizzical, as if he was trying to read on my face how badly things had gone for me during my interview. I held my smile as I looked at him.

"Hi again to you," he said. "I have your instructions for the day that Wayne put together."

So that probably was what he'd been discussing with the others—what they would be assigned for today.

"Great," I said. "Thanks." I approached and took the paper he held out. I waited for him to say something else, like inquire what I'd been asked, whether I'd survived okay . . . maybe whether I'd admitted to killing Oliver.

But he fortunately didn't ask anything. Just looked at me.

Was it some kind of ploy to make me think I was his number one suspect too? Or possibly to hide that he, in fact, had been the one to do away with his co-manager?

Not that I was going to ask him.

I instead looked at the paper, hoping my assignment that day would tell me to hike out again to the far pathways surrounding some of the sanctuary wildlife areas and report later on who I'd seen there and how they were doing.

Naturalist me loved that part of working here.

Though not when I wasn't the only one out there and one of the other observers was giving me a hard time about my dog.

Okay, I couldn't exactly stop thinking about Oliver. I knew that. And now, once my mind was on him—well, I really felt bad about what had happened to him, even if he hadn't been my favorite person. In any case, I didn't have to keep focusing on him. I had to point my mind in other directions.

I focused on my assignment sheet.

I couldn't help grinning.

"Must be good stuff," Lettie said as she looked at me. She was standing beside me now, holding a similar piece of paper.

"Definitely. I'll be hiking again today, spying on some of the sanctuary's residents. How about you?"

"Ditto, and I'm really glad."

"Great. Let's do it together."

A couple of people in the same location at the same time was fine with Wayne. I'd learned that before. And if one was an employee and another a volunteer, so much the better. He mostly didn't want the entire group collected at the same spots. Better that more locations be visited and more animals observed.

Although when tourists were around, a bunch of people at the same sites was just fine.

And when Oliver had been out there giving me a hard time with others around, he'd been a manager, so he could get away with a lot more than we peons could.

I talked to Lettie about the possible places we could go. She hadn't visited many yet, so we decided to go back to the far-out areas I'd been to yesterday, where I'd gotten to see not only bears but mountain goats and a porcupine.

"Oh, I hope we see all of them again, and more," Lettie exclaimed. Her background in naturalism wasn't at the same professional level as mine—she had no degree in it, at least—but I knew from the way she pointed out wildlife on our boat tours how much she too loved animals.

She was bundled up today in a currently unzipped parka and boots, as I was. We should do fine hiking on the open trails. And Sasha, with her heavy coat and husky heritage and the boots I'd put on her, might even enjoy it more than our earlier excursions this year, even on the boats.

I had the option of driving one of the ATVs like the one Oliver had taken out to the remote areas, but we chose to hike.

Outside, we fastened our jackets against the increasing cold, and the three of us embarked on the trail behind the welcome building that I had most recently ventured along. This was a narrower trail than the ones at the front of the building. It led to a group of vast enclosures with distant hillsides that appeared to have begun icing over.

It was chilly, and mist hung in the air. Still not the real Alaskan winter, but a harbinger that it was coming.

We walked briskly, but also carefully. It was a good thing that we'd worn appropriate boots; neither of us humans wanted to slide or fall if we didn't have to.

Fortunately, husky Sasha remained at my side, walking as she usually did, not appearing to have a problem in her doggy boots.

"Do you see anything?" Lettie asked. She'd pulled her parka hood over her head, though I hadn't.

Hoping I'd get this kind of opportunity today, I'd stuck small but powerful binoculars in my jacket pocket before leaving home, and I pulled them out. I thought I saw animals in the distance but couldn't tell what they were yet.

Yes! They were mountain goats—light in color, so they were hard to observe on the icy hillsides, and their dark horns weren't particularly visible this far away. But their movement helped me spot them. I'd figured we'd view some today as I had yesterday, and I pointed them out to Lettie, letting her look through my binoculars. It was hard to tell from here, but they could again be females with the beginnings of their winter coats.

"Wow," Lettie sighed. "They're wonderful." Still wearing her gloves, she pulled a small notebook and pen from her pants pocket and began writing notes, even as I snapped photos on my phone, which I realized wouldn't be very helpful from this distance. "For our report later, right?" she asked.

"Right." As on our tour boat, Lettie was again a wonderful assistant.

The mountain goats didn't get any closer, but as we continued walking to the next enclosed area, we saw reindeer much nearer to the fencing.

Both of us oohed and aahed as the herd ventured a little closer. We both took photos, and Lettie made more notes.

The reindeer were cousins to caribou but acted a little differently, especially when they were in danger. Reindeer stuck together, while caribou tended to run away. Or that's what naturalist me understood, and I mentioned it to Lettie as we watched.

Both males and females grew antlers, but the females were smaller creatures. I wished we could easily go into the vast enclosure and see them more closely, but that wasn't a good idea, either for them or for us, so we continued to watch from where we were for a while.

If they were aware of the gawking humans, they didn't show it. That was probably a good thing. We weren't scaring them.

But soon the herd did turn and start off toward the nearby hillside. We watched a little longer, then started to move on.

It was past lunchtime now, and I figured we'd better go back to the welcome building. But my assistant came through again. She'd brought along snacks, so we ate pretzels and cheese crackers as we continued. And I fed Sasha dog treats I always kept in my pants pocket for her.

I was just as glad not to head back. The detectives might still be at the welcome building, questioning other people. If I saw them, I'd have no appetite anyway.

"I haven't been this far back in this area," I told Lettie a while later. "Not even while I was volunteering." We saw more reindeer as we reached the farthest part of the enclosure and watched them for a while too. And yes, took more pictures.

Eventually we headed back along the trail to the welcome building.

I didn't see the vehicle I believed the detectives had arrived in, which was a relief.

Not that I'd expected them to interrogate me any more today, but who knew?

I did see other official-looking vehicles as well as uniformed troopers and others who were likely conducting their on-site investigation. That made sense. I just hoped whatever they found helped zero in on whoever had killed Oliver.

Not me.

We went inside, and I let Wayne know we were back. He came into the room where we were entering our report into the computer a short while later.

"So how was it out there today?" he asked, and we both gave our testimonials about how wonderful it had been.

I met the large guy's brown eyes more than once, trying to use them to see inside his head. Did he know who else the detectives had questioned?

Did he know if any of those out investigating today had found anything to point to whoever had done it?

Did he know what they thought, whom they suspected?

Anyone other than me?

His expression remained bland—except I had the sense he was trying to see inside me too.

Well, I wasn't going to tell him any more than he told me.

After we finished our report, it was time to leave. "See you tomorrow," I told both Wayne and Lettie.

"Hope we have as wonderful a time as we did today," Lettie said, a big smile lighting up her young, pretty face. Her short black hair was a little mussed, probably because she hadn't combed it after removing her hood when we returned.

"I hope so too," I said, not mentioning that not everything I'd done today had been wonderful.

I certainly didn't want a repeat of the first part of it tomorrow.

Cry Wolf

But going out on the trails again and viewing the wildlife? Oh yeah.

After we said good-bye to Wayne. I popped into the kitchen to see if Marnie was there preparing food. Since she wasn't there, I figured she might be out on the grounds leaving food for the animals.

"I'd love to try food prep soon," Lettie said. She'd followed me.

We left for the parking lot then, Sasha at my side as always. I felt relieved—sort of. I was leaving on my own.

How would I feel at home alone tonight, with only Sasha for company?

Did I dare call Liam?

Did he know what I'd gone through today?

If so, how could we talk without discussing it?

If not—well, I'd have to at least mention it to him, right?

Better that it just be Sasha and me for tonight.

Still, I did what I probably shouldn't as I drove Sasha and me home. I called Liam.

I was almost surprised when he answered right away. "Hi, Stacie. How are you?"

He asked me that often, but this time felt different. I had to wonder, as I had before: Did he know much about what I'd gone through?

Would we discuss it?

"I've been better," I said as noncommittally as I could.

"I figured. Hey, how about if I bring dinner to your place tonight?"

Really? How would things go if he did? How would I feel if he'd known more about what I was in for and didn't tell me? He'd hinted at it, but—

I needed to answer. "Sure," I told him. We discussed what to eat, then hung up.

And I wondered how our evening would be.

95

Meantime, I drove home, going slowly and carefully, not seeing many other cars on the winding roads, though there were more as I got into town. As I tended to do, I found a parking space just outside the door to our unit in the development I liked so much. I took Sasha for a brief walk and noticed that the temperature here didn't seem quite as chilly as out at the wildlife center—but neither was it especially warm. Our place was nice and convenient, on the ground floor, easy for taking Sasha in and out.

Easy for kicking Liam out if we got into an argument?

I hoped I wouldn't have to find out. Better yet, I hoped we wouldn't discuss my situation today at all, let alone argue about it.

Inside, I removed my jacket and boots and left them in the area in the kitchen near the door. I changed into a casual, though nice, pants outfit to wait. Although it was approaching six o'clock, I wasn't particularly hungry. A good thing, since I wasn't sure when Liam was arriving, though I assumed it would be fairly soon.

And no matter what my appetite was, I knew my wonderful husky, whom I didn't overload with treats during the day—though I always gave her some—was undoubtedly hungry. I fed her a usual meal of healthy kibble combined with probably tastier, also healthy, wet food.

I stood in the kitchen, watching her, and realized I'd be fine with eating soon. Liam and I had decided on something easy, pizza, and one of the restaurants not too far away had takeout pizzas with various healthy toppings available. I'd asked for a few veggies, such as green peppers and tomatoes and spinach, as well as a little pepperoni.

And extra cheese. Not quite so healthy.

Liam was picking it up. I already had beer in my fridge, so I figured we'd wind up with a nice, largely unhealthy meal. But I doubted even that would smooth over the discussion we were likely to have.

I even considered starting a bottle of beer before Liam arrived, to try to soften my insides a bit so I wouldn't get too emotional about what was said, or wasn't said.

He'd already indicated I would be interrogated. Did he know what had been said today? He apparently didn't work directly with—

My doorbell rang just as I'd taken a couple of steps behind Sasha, almost inadvertently heading toward my refrigerator.

Good. Fuzzing up my mind for this conversation really wouldn't help.

Sasha stopped eating and barked, heading toward the door. She knew what a doorbell meant, smart dog. But she was smart about everything.

Would she protect Liam if she perceived that I was angry with him?

I took a deep breath and followed my dog to the door.

Liam was there, dressed as a civilian in a plain, thick jacket, blue sweatshirt, and jeans, as well as boots. Had he simply changed clothes, or had he not been on duty today?

Was he on leave because of his kind-of relationship with this person of interest? He'd indicated that he was in a bit of trouble about it.

And was he blaming me as I was blaming him for his silence and attitude?

"Hi, come on in," I said, trying to smile as I stepped back and let him in.

"Hi, Stacie," he said. "Okay if I just take this to the kitchen?" He nodded toward the large pizza box he held—the one Sasha kept her nose near as she sniffed at it.

Never mind that I was leery about what he was thinking, how our discussion would go—I couldn't help smiling at my dog. And I passed the glance toward Liam too. "Of course," I said in as bright a tone as I'd used when we were just buddies. Or more.

I followed him into my kitchen, where he'd been before, often, and watched him set down the box, covering most of the top of my small table.

"I've got beer in my car," he said as he turned to look at me.

"I have plenty in my fridge," I responded, and found myself surprisingly happy to bask in the glow of his smile.

Were we going to be as friendly as we'd been as recently as a few days ago, before all this had happened?

Before someone I'd been arguing with had been murdered?

He didn't say anything else as he removed his boots and left them near the door by mine, then also hung his jacket on a hook beside mine.

Sasha remained near the table, her nose not far from the box, but she knew better than to grab anything. "Good dog," I said, then turned to get two bottles of beer from my shining steel refrigerator. I felt somehow more comfortable with my back toward Liam.

Yes, I was dreading the conversation to come. If only I could rely on this trooper to at least assume my innocence. Maybe even help me.

But—

Okay. I couldn't delay for long. I carried the two bottles to the sink and opened a drawer to take out the cap remover, then opened them.

I turned and handed one to Liam. I took a healthy swig from the bottle I still held.

"Hey, I'm ready for some pizza," I said. "Are you?"

Before he could answer, I moved to put my bottle on the counter and carefully wash my hands. Those hands needed to be clean, after all. They'd be my eating utensils.

Liam had opened the box, and a couple of paper plates sat on top of the pizza. As I approached, he handed one of the plates to me, then went to wash his own hands.

Cry Wolf

Soon we both were sitting at the table. Sweet Sasha had lain down and had her head on the floor, though she rolled her eyes up at me as I looked at her. I'd give her a little pizza crust and some cheese. I knew not much of what was there would be healthy for her, but that little bit should be okay.

I placed my beer bottle and paper plate on as much of the small table as I could, then took a slice of pizza. I took a bite. I saw that Liam was doing pretty much the same.

Who was going to talk first?

Me. I could at least control that.

"So," I said. "Tell me whatever you can."

Chapter Nine

L iam only looked at me at first, over the slice of pizza he'd taken a couple of bites from. Those brown eyes of his were unreadable at the moment. Bland, maybe. Unemotional. Was he simply assessing me the way I was him?

"So, are you willing to talk about it?" he finally said.

"About what?" I asked, playing dumb.

His expression changed to one of irritation. "How about what it felt like to use . . . whatever it was you used to slice that guy's throat?"

I couldn't help gasping. "Liam—I know you're not serious, but—"

"No," he said, his face hardening into a scowl. "I'm not serious. But whatever happened, whatever your involvement, it's affecting not only you but me as well, and even my Initial Response Section."

I took a deep breath, unsure of how to respond. I wasn't sure what he meant, though I had some idea, partly based on what he had said previously about his employer's command that he stay away from the situation.

Still, even with Liam not involved, why had detectives from outside the Alaska State Troopers come into the investigation?

I made myself take another bite of pizza while I considered what to say next. I'd liked the flavor before, guessed I still did. But the taste was somehow flowing away, replaced by a really bad essence not only in my mouth but everywhere within me.

Liam must have figured that I was thinking about my next reaction. Or maybe he was also pondering where we should go from here.

Would it be better for him to leave?

I swallowed hard at that idea, not downing any more pizza. If he left, he might still consider me a suspect.

If he stayed . . .

I'd told him before I was innocent, but at least some of his fellow troopers must believe otherwise.

And maybe, by now, he did too.

"Okay," I finally said. I put the small remainder of my current piece of pizza on the plate in front of me and picked up my bottle of beer. "I know you said you're under orders not to talk about the situation, but since you're here, I assume you're willing to do so, at least a little. I may not have convinced you before that I had nothing to do with what happened to Oliver Brownling, and can't be sure I'll be able to now. But . . . if nothing else, I can let you know how today went, from the time I reached Juneau Wildlife World and was almost immediately confronted by unofficial but possibly officially hired outside detectives. I assume you're aware of them, right?"

"Yeah," he said. "But I don't know much else. Please describe what happened."

Trying to keep my breathing under control, I told him everything I could recall from the time Sasha and I had reached the sanctuary that morning till I was directed to go inside the office, and the questions I was asked by the two detectives.

"I tried to be entirely honest, since I had no reason not to be. I admitted that Oliver and I were arguing and why, that he didn't like Sasha out on the grounds, apparently for fear of scaring the wildlife. But I explained how I handled that. Grumping back at him, yes. Doing anything violent against him? Of course not. And even if I did want to do him in, I definitely wouldn't have used a weapon that could make anyone think he'd been attacked by a wolf or any other animal. You know how I love wildlife."

I looked him straight in the face, and his gaze appeared to soften, at least a little. "Yes, I definitely know that." He took another bite of pizza, as if he was relaxing, and I did the same.

Since he was using this get-together to discuss what had happened, I figured I could too. "The thing is," I said, "I haven't been informed what the murder weapon really was. I gather it hasn't been found, or if it has, there aren't fingerprints on it that would clear me. Do you have any idea what it was? And yes, I realize your fellow troopers are probably not telling you a lot, if anything."

He shook his head. "No, best I can do is speculate. I'm not aware of any existing utensils that might have pierced Oliver's throat like fangs, though maybe there are some. But I'm figuring that whoever did it planned it for a while, maybe created some kind of strong implement with a handle and curved, sharp wires sticking out one end that could be shoved deep into skin and yanked hard to sever arteries."

I couldn't help shuddering, but that made sense. "Maybe so. That's not something I'd ever have thought of, let alone make. I'd love to know if those detectives are attempting to learn if any of their suspects bought any kind of equipment like that."

A horrible thought crossed my mind. I didn't think anyone doing food preparation would have something like that, but maybe they'd know where to get it.

I didn't really suspect Marnie—did I?

And others besides those who prepared food for the animals might research how animals killed, what the injuries might look like, or how humans could imitate a predator's attack . . .

Others who worked at a wildlife sanctuary like Juneau Wildlife World might have that kind of interest and resources.

"Hey, I can guess where your mind is going about this," Liam said. "Let's cool it for now. Talk about something else, like more about the animals you've seen in the last few days and what the plans are for observation and caring for them during the winter. You've been working there long enough now to have some idea, right?"

"Sure. Some idea, at least." I felt a bit relieved at the change, or at least moderation, of subject, though my mind didn't really leave what I'd been thinking about, just focused on our conversation instead.

After we finished dinner, we took Sasha for another, longer walk.

Our moods had eased. Liam and I both talked about the way the weather was changing, how it would continue to grow colder and snow would blanket the area even more. This was Alaska, after all.

So we both could be warm at least for the night, we agreed that Liam should stay. I knew, though, that I wouldn't be satisfied only to be held by him.

It was a wonderful night. We watched a couple of sitcoms again, no news, then headed to my bedroom.

I managed to focus more on my company than anything else going on in my life. I enjoyed that company. A lot.

After we engaged in some fun, I even slept well, certainly a whole lot better than I had for the last couple of nights.

But morning arrived. I wanted to head to Juneau Wildlife World early, and Liam said he had an assignment to work on that day. He didn't tell me what it was, but I knew it wasn't anything to do with me or what had happened to Oliver.

We showered, got dressed, bundled up a bit, and took Sasha for another walk, and then I fed her. Liam and I next ate a breakfast of scrambled eggs and toast, which I put together. Rather a normal morning, similar to those after other nights we'd spent together.

I started feeling bereft as we ate, though. Liam had gotten my mind off my woes temporarily. But today was another day.

Before he departed, he looked at me with his caring brown eyes. He was definitely a handsome guy. I liked him—a lot.

But how long was he likely to stay in my life, especially now?

I was quite surprised at his next words.

"Okay," he said. "Never thought I'd be telling you this, but maybe you really do need to do some snooping this time—as long as you're really careful about it. Consider everyone you see at your wildlife world to be a suspect, except, maybe, the animals. And don't talk to me from there unless you're sure you're alone, unless you need immediate backup. Okay?"

Was he really telling me this? Oh, yes. And I appreciated it.

"In fact," he continued, "I know I should stop seeing you at all, since I'm under orders not to talk to you about the situation and it's hard to avoid thinking about it, let alone discussing it, when we're together. But my superiors know me well enough to know I'll be in touch with you and, if so, it'd be hard not to approach the subject at all. But I will at least stay far from the investigation and follow orders—sort of. I have a couple guys I'm close enough to that I can admit we're still talking. I may even tell them I'm using my relationship with you to investigate you." As I opened my mouth to protest, he said, "Not that it's true."

Not entirely, I figured. But if I admitted anything to him—not that there was anything to admit—I knew he'd be a good trooper and report it.

Still, even if we couldn't talk about the elephant in the room—and yes, elephants were a form of wildlife I appreciated, even though they weren't wild in Alaska—having Liam remain in my life in any way, and be there at least as emotional backup, would be a really good thing.

I hoped.

For now, I said, "Okay. Do what you need to, and so will I. And I'll appreciate any suggestions or help you can give."

"Sure."

"And if we can keep warm again sometimes like we did for the last couple of nights, I'd really enjoy it."

"Me too," he said.

When we walked out to our cars a short time later, Sasha with me, I thought again about how much I appreciated Liam. My mood last night had gotten off to a rocky start, but it was certainly improved this morning.

As I aimed my car carefully over the somewhat icy road toward Juneau Wildlife World, I considered how I would approach things today.

"So, Sasha," I asked my back seat companion, "what's your opinion?"

She didn't respond, but I wished I could give her a hug as thanks for the emotional support.

I let my mind go over my conversation with Liam.

What stuck out was that, even though he had ostensibly not wanted me to get involved with the murder investigation connected with my tour boat, this time he'd suggested that I dive into some snooping.

I felt proud that he felt I was skilled enough to do that.

And scared that he must think I was enough of a suspect that I needed to get involved to help save myself.

The roads from my apartment toward Juneau Wildlife World weren't too slick today. I wasn't sure how I'd have handled a sliding car as well as my scary sliding thoughts.

There wasn't much traffic either, especially when we left town and headed toward the boonies where the sanctuary was located.

Hills rose on both sides of the road. No animals appeared there, but I glanced at the landscape as my thoughts reeled.

If I was going to investigate Oliver's death, being an amateur with only a hint of experience, I knew I'd have to be careful and astute.

And I doubted I'd dare ask my best resource much, if anything, as I dug in. After all, Liam might have suggested I start snooping for a reason, but he wasn't supposed to talk to me about the situation. Maybe not talk to me at all, though I was glad he was at least partially ignoring his orders.

Mostly, I'd be on my own . . . although I might attempt to learn Liam's opinion if I found anything that appeared useful.

As I conducted a murder investigation.

Maybe to save myself.

Probably only a few people at the sanctuary had any idea I'd been involved in a murder investigation before, and one was my wonderful assistant Lettie, but I didn't want to let even her know it if I did dig in to solve this killing too.

As if I'd be able to keep it from her. Not if I really did a good job and nosed my way into what had happened and the attitude of everyone at the sanctuary toward Oliver.

Maybe I could even ask for her help. She certainly wasn't the killer. And she'd been good backup for me on the tour boat last time.

We reached the outer gate to Juneau Wildlife World. And I really hadn't come up with a plan for my investigation.

But I hadn't exactly had one last time, either.

"Sasha, we're here." I heard her move in the back seat. Once again, I got out of the car to open the gate. I wasn't one of the esteemed few who had a remote control to the gate. Not a problem, since I knew the code to get in. But I hoped I could avoid getting out of the car during the worst weather. One of these days I'd have to ask again about getting a remote.

Assuming I would still be coming to work and not be incarcerated for Oliver's murder.

I had to be smart about this. And organized. Maybe as organized as I had to be to keep track of the wildlife I observed and filed reports about.

Which I'd done just fine, even when I hadn't taken notes, but I would be even better about that in the future, I told myself as I drove inside the sanctuary. I got out of the car and closed the gate again behind me.

Me. Organized. I could do it.

I'd have to determine who seemed most likely to have wanted to harm Oliver. Someone other than me who'd argued with him, maybe.

I'd reached the area where I usually parked. A few other cars were there too. I didn't know whose was whose, but learning who came here when might be helpful.

Did any belong to the authorities? Most likely, although I didn't see any investigators at the moment.

It would be particularly helpful to know who might have stayed late the night Oliver was killed. Or even lived here . . .

Could Wayne be guilty?

At the moment, I couldn't take anyone off my currently completely mental list. No matter that I didn't yet know any motive. I had to be open to learning.

"Okay, girl," I said to Sasha after I opened the back door to let her out. "Too bad we can't communicate better," I added with my voice low, not that any person was likely to hear me at the moment. "Maybe you and your great sense of smell could help me figure it out. Your other senses too. If only you could tell me who you think hurt Oliver. Or even help to find the weapon used, assuming it wasn't a wolf's teeth. And I definitely assume that's true."

Sasha just looked at me, ears up, her tail wagging as I held her leash.

I saw Neil entering the main door as we approached. Not that he could hear me, even if he wanted to.

But since he, like everyone else at the moment, had to be on my suspect list, I'd have to be careful what I said around him. So I didn't say anything else to Sasha about helping me find the killer. Not then, at least.

I still wasn't sure how I was going to conduct my investigation, but one thing I was certain of: I couldn't allow anyone to know that's what I was doing.

Oh, we could all discuss what had happened to Oliver, how terrible it was, and maybe even any suspicions we had.

I'd love to hear what everyone else's suspicions were, after all. They'd all, including the one who'd really done it, be pointing fingers toward others.

As I would be.

They'd expect it of me too, as I expected it of them.

But how was I going to ferret out the truth?

Ferret it out. Yes, naturalist me loves animals, but there were no ferrets around here, in Alaska, that I could ask to help, although there were ermines, which came from the same natural family.

There was only my wonderful dog, but I doubted Sasha would be much help in determining who'd murdered that human and had made it appear as if she, or another canine, could have done it.

Or me.

My mind had been focusing on what I was really up to as I approached the same door Neil had entered, but I had to cast those thoughts aside. Or at least keep them at bay while I did what I was supposed to around here, as long as I was able. While I also attempted to figure out what had actually happened.

We'd reached the door, and I held it open for my pup.

Neil was still in the lobby. So were Larraine, Marnie, Bill, and Carlo Randallo, another Wildlife World employee I'd met before but hadn't seen since I'd begun working over the past couple days.

I hadn't seen him the day Oliver was killed. And yet, had I actually seen everyone who was here? This place was large. And I hadn't been at the welcome building a lot.

As an employee, Carlo most likely had at least met new manager Oliver. What had he thought about him?

I hadn't officially started making a list of suspects, but I figured I could add that somewhat heavy midthirties guy to it. He looked strong enough to wield a nasty fake-fang knife.

But under the right circumstances, like if Oliver wasn't expecting it, nearly anyone could have slashed him that way.

Even a true canine. But Oliver might have been watchful for an attack if a wolf was actually around him.

Another reason to figure out who had done this. Fortunately, it wasn't likely to be a true canine.

Certainly not my canine best friend.

As I was overthinking this, as I did so many other things, I'd approached the others in the lobby. They were standing near the stairway to the second floor, holding a conversation, and didn't seem to pay much attention to me, even though I was a current newcomer in the area.

"Good morning," I said brightly as I reached the group, and Sasha started sniffing Marnie's hand.

Did it smell like food preparation, or was my pup just being friendly? Maybe both.

Marnie just laughed and began petting Sasha's head.

"Hey, you're here," Neil said. "I assumed after the grillings most of us got yesterday, including you, that you'd have been arrested by now."

Chapter Ten

"What!" I glared at Neil, wanting to shove him or elbow his ribs or do something physical to get back at him for his absurd comment.

But doing something physical might make what he'd said appear reasonable, and that was the last thing I wanted to do.

I'd never attacked anyone and wasn't about to start now, no matter how I felt. Especially not a senior guy like Neil, whose Juneau Wildlife World sweatshirt seemed to hang on him today as if it was a few sizes too large.

Instead, I stepped back and made myself smile at his wrinkly face. "But here I figured, after all that, you'd be the one who would be arrested. They spent a long time questioning you, didn't they? And surely they'd have gotten the truth from you. Weren't you mad at your new co-manager?"

It was a shot in the dark. I had no idea whether that could be the truth. And even if they hadn't gotten along great, I didn't know of any motive Neil might have had to kill Oliver.

The detectives had questioned everyone because they wanted more information about the people at the sanctuary, or they wanted others' perspectives about what had been going on.

Still, they'd been a bit nasty in the way they'd questioned me, so I had to believe they hadn't zeroed in on anyone else, including Neil. Since I knew Neil had been present the day Oliver was killed, he would have to be on the list I intended to develop, no matter where the detectives were in their investigation. And since Neil had had the temerity to accuse me, I assumed there might be a reason.

Like, to draw suspicion away from himself.

Maybe because—

"Like I told those detectives who questioned us," Neil said, stepping closer to me again, which made me the one who stepped back this time, "I didn't know Oliver well. Can't say his first impressions were that good, and I didn't always agree with what he said. Like the way he treated your dog." He glanced down toward Sasha and smiled, as if patting her on the head from a distance, contrary to Oliver's attitude. That, at least, was a plus on his side. "But over many years and other jobs, I learned to work with fellow employees who weren't my favorite—not kill them."

"Got it," I said. And to hopefully get him, and the others, to stop thinking it was me, I said, "Same goes for me. Yeah, I had a bone to pick with Oliver, so to speak, since he kept insulting me and my poor Sasha, but I'd never physically hurt him, let alone kill him. And a wildlife lover like me doing something like that to appear to frame a wolf, or even my dog? You don't have to know me well to realize that just wouldn't happen."

"Of course not," Marnie said, smiling at me. She'd drawn close and again patted Sasha.

But she had also been here the day Oliver was killed. She knew how to use sharp instruments.

If she had a motive, though, I didn't know it.

Yet.

Two people on my mental list so far, even though I liked Marnie. But likable people could still do bad things.

Undoubtedly, there were more suspects to come. And I'd start writing up my thoughts and ideas about each of them when I could.

How would I narrow them down? That I didn't know yet.

But I knew I had to at least attempt to figure this out.

To save myself.

And maybe even Sasha or the wolves.

"Hi, all of you," came a voice from the stairway. Wayne was heading down, presumably from his office. "What's going on here?"

Like, *Why are you all here instead of doing your jobs?* That's what I figured was really on his mind.

"We're just trying to determine who killed Oliver," Carlo said. He was also wearing a Juneau Wildlife World sweatshirt like the rest of us—a black one. He grinned as Wayne reached us.

"Easy for you to say," said Bill, who was now standing just behind Marnie. "You weren't even here that day."

I had to ask—as I probably would with everyone. "Did the detectives question you too, Bill?" I didn't have to remind him he'd been here that day too.

He nodded, his expression wry. "Of course. I wished I'd changed my schedule to work at the restaurant yesterday and not been here when all that was going on, but I was. From what I gather, I was the fourth person in that office yesterday—after Neil and Larraine and you."

I glanced at Larraine, who also looked unhappy but resigned. "Yeah, me too," she said, as if I'd asked.

I'd been glad to flee from the welcome building as soon as I could yesterday, but I now wished I'd been around to see who else had been questioned. Everyone here who'd been interrogated seemed to be admitting it, at least, and I'd hopefully learn if there were others.

Still, I asked Marnie, "And you?"

She nodded. "Oh, yes. And before you ask, I didn't admit anything—although I did let them know how sad I was about what happened. Oliver seemed like a nice guy to me, though I didn't know him well."

I recalled that she and Oliver had seemed to be friendly, or at least that was the impression I'd gotten.

"I'm sure he was," I admitted, "even though Oliver and I weren't really getting along."

"Are we through with this conversation yet?" Wayne asked. "I'd like you all to get busy with what you're here for. Okay? I've got your instructions." He began passing out the papers he held in his hand.

Fortunately, I was again scheduled to go out and observe our wild residents, which was always what I liked, as Wayne knew. Today he wanted me to visit some of the closer sites. But I'd go farther out later in the day if I could.

One of these days I hoped he'd have me venture way out toward the farthest ends of the grounds, which he also knew I enjoyed. I'd most likely need to drive one of the ATVs if I did.

Though the types of animals might not be different, I wanted to view their habitats everywhere.

And stay away from the welcome building as much as possible.

As long as I remained free.

I assumed Marnie would start preparing food. One of these days, I kept telling myself, I'd work with her again, as I had last year when I worked here for a while. Maybe get to know her even better. She seemed like one of the nicest people at the sanctuary.

Assuming she wasn't the murderer.

That would keep me closer to the welcome building, except when we were out distributing food, but at least I'd be in good company, including Marnie, Sasha, and the animals we visited.

"I'm assisting you today," Bill told her. His smile was broad. The restaurant worker must enjoy the idea of feeding the wildlife.

"Sounds good to me," Neil said. He must have known what he was to be doing without instructions. Nodding to his boss, Neil moved to go upstairs, presumably to his office.

"Okay," Larraine said. "Stacie, if you're going into the preserve, maybe we can start out together again." Good. Perhaps we could discuss her interview with the detectives.

Not that I really thought she'd done it. But until I knew who did, everyone would be subject to my hopefully pleasant conversation—and questions.

"Sounds good to me." I pulled my jacket off the long row of hooks in the closet near the doorway, and others assigned to go outside did the same, including Larraine.

"I'm going that way too," Carlo said. He had also grabbed his jacket. Now he followed Larraine and me as we approached the building's front door. "I'll join you, if that's okay."

"Fine with me," Larraine said. "We can all walk together for a while, then take our different paths."

I nodded. "Always fun to start off that way and check out at least some animals together."

Sasha at my side, we all took the common path at the far end of the parking lot, between the fencing of the nearby large enclosures. We zipped our jackets, and our boots crunched on the gravel.

"Do you see anyone yet?" Larraine asked after several minutes, squinting into the area at the right as she pulled slightly ahead. But no moose or elk or anything else were visible there.

"Hey, though you didn't ask me while we were inside talking," Carlo said, drawing a little closer to me as we walked, "I was questioned too."

I glanced at him as we continued. Now he was also bundled into a thick beige jacket.

"I thought you weren't here that day," I said. "Or yesterday, when we were questioned."

"I wasn't either time. Even so, they came to my apartment yesterday afternoon. Since I work here, I guess those detectives figured I might know something. Or maybe that I knew how to sneak in and kill Oliver without being seen."

Interesting that he'd phrase things that way. "And did you?" I asked with a smile, as if I were only joking. And I was—unless I wound up with reason to believe it was true.

"Do you think I'd admit it if I did?"

"Of course, to protect the rest of us," I said, turning to continue along the path.

He kept up. "Definitely. I'm such a good guy." He snorted. "Not. But I'm also not a killer. Oliver and I got along okay."

Maybe so, though I hadn't seen any interaction between them even when I was volunteering.

"Good to know," I said. We continued walking silently for a while as I pondered what else to ask him. Larraine ventured back and forth ahead of us, still trying hard to be the first to see one of the animals, I supposed. Carlo had already proclaimed his innocence, which wasn't surprising. "So, what's your background with wildlife?" I finally inquired. That was nice and neutral, and maybe I could learn more about why he was here—and how well he had known Oliver.

Denying guilt didn't necessarily make it so.

"Loved it since I was a kid," he said, staring out at the expanse beyond the closest chain-link fence as if searching for whatever animals were out there, as all three of us were. "But not these guys here. I grew up in the Baja area and loved to go out on boats whale watching. But my family moved to the U.S., to Chicago, and I wound up studying math in school while visiting zoos and wildlife parks whenever I could—but not much whale watching anymore. Still, I always appreciated all kinds of animals, including those in the water. I visited Alaska on a cruise while I was in college and got hooked, though I worked for computer companies for a while before I actually moved here. But here I am—and working for Juneau Wildlife World seems perfect to me."

Nice guy. Good background.

But I still needed to learn what he'd thought of Oliver.

Not right now, though. "There!" I called out quietly as a moose appeared not too far away, approaching from over a hill.

We all just stood there for a while observing him draw even closer. I made sure Sasha stayed nice and quiet at my side. I didn't think the moose was coming this way to observe us. No, he appeared to be grazing, even though the growth along the ground was sparse and brown.

But there was still some vegetation, and he appeared to be enjoying what was left of it. Or at least he kept on foraging. And another couple of moose, one appearing to be female, seemed to follow him, though at a distance.

More, more, more, I thought. The awed and pleased expressions on the others' faces suggested that they too were delighted to get our first glimpse of wildlife of the day. And we hadn't gone too far down the trail yet.

We watched for a while, none of us talking, all of us observing. Probably taking mental notes. Enjoying the view.

But after a short while, the bull nearest us turned and started heading toward the others, who were grazing. Soon all of them walked back in the direction of the hillsides. We could stay there watching them till they disappeared over one of the ridges, but instead we all started walking again.

If we kept going this way, we'd eventually reach the fencing behind which the wolves were enclosed. Would we go that far?

Did I want to see that area again right now?

Maybe so. I always enjoyed seeing wolves. And I didn't believe what had happened to Oliver was their fault, even if someone had attempted to frame them. Though the person apparently hadn't done a very good job of it.

In any case, with the weather chilly but mostly dry, this was a wonderful day so far at the sanctuary.

Especially since no one was questioning me.

But I still had to do something to save myself. And definitely help to find Oliver's killer. Interrogating these two might be useful.

"Hey," Larraine said, "I think I'm going to go onto the other pathway."

To the right, I assumed. The way I'd intended to go.

"Sounds good." I didn't have the feeling she wanted company. Even so, I figured I could tell her I'd join her and watch her reaction. "I was thinking about turning off on the next one to the left, but—"

"Me too," Carlo said, surprising me. Then he added, "I've had some really good luck seeing reindeer out there, which seems appropriate, considering we're getting later into the year. Eventually, it'll be December. Christmastime."

I laughed. He didn't indicate he wanted to take the path alone, so I said, "I'd love to see them with you, if they're there."

"Why don't you and Sasha join me?"

Perfect. He wasn't number one on my suspect list, but he'd known Oliver for a while, so it wouldn't hurt to learn more.

Larraine took off immediately down the same pathway we were on for now, but to see the reindeer, Carlo and I would soon turn left on a different trail.

I considered how to initiate the next part of our conversation, then asked, "How long have you been working for Juneau Wildlife World?" I knew he hadn't been an employee when I worked at the sanctuary last winter, but my volunteering over the summer months had been sporadic, so I might not have met him if he'd been around then.

Sure enough, he had. "About six months," he said as we hiked side by side.

Sasha, good girl that she was, remained mostly at my side, but she did pull a little ahead, her nose in the air as if something smelled interesting. Not a surprise.

"I don't think I saw you when I volunteered now and then over the summer." I mentioned my real job on the tour boats, then asked, "How did you come to work here?"

"I came to visit, and I couldn't help asking to speak to the person in charge—Wayne. I had no idea if he was looking for help, but I mentioned I'd be interested in a job. Nice guy that he is, he humored me and invited me to his office. I told him my background, my love of animals, how impressed I was with this place, and all but got down on my knees and begged him to hire me. Which only caused him to laugh. And make me an offer."

I was the one who laughed then. "Sounds like you handled it just right."

He chuckled too. "Guess so."

We continued on for a while as I considered how to approach my next questions.

Before I did, I saw them—a few reindeer, not close, and walking in the same direction we were. "Look!" I exclaimed.

"Oh, yeah." Carlo sounded in awe, even though as an employee he must see a lot of the sanctuary's wildlife at various times.

His attitude was another reason for me to like him.

Even so, I had a mission in mind. The best thing would be for him to say whatever was necessary for me to remove him from my suspect list.

Would he?

We discussed the reindeer softly, the small herd consisting of what looked like two males and four females, a couple of which were small enough that they might be fairly young. No way of knowing right now how any of them had arrived at this shelter, although I figured the young ones had probably been born here. But the parents might have been native to this area—or rescued and brought in.

It was fun talking about them. We even stood still for a short while as we observed them, and I pulled note cards from my pants pocket and jotted notes to include in my report later, plus I took a not-so-great picture on my phone.

Sasha just sat down, also looking in that direction. My dog knew better than to do anything to frighten them.

They soon started moving, and so did we.

"Wow," I said. "It's always such a wonderful experience to see the wildlife."

"I agree with that," Carlo said. As we walked, he glanced at me. "I know I shouldn't push this, but I've heard that you're a suspect in what happened to Oliver. I doubt you'd admit it to me if you'd been the one to kill him, but I need to ask anyway."

My laugh was bitter. "You're not the only one. But as I've said to everyone who's asked, the answer is no. You don't really know me, but even if I would do such a thing—which I wouldn't—the last thing I'd do is attempt to make it look like a canine, my dog or one of the wolves, was the guilty party. I like animals better than people, and I particularly love canines."

"I thought that might be the case, even though I don't know you very well. And you don't know me very well either."

There was something about his tone in that last sentence that made me stop observing the reindeer and turn toward him. I was the one he was watching. Studying. His expression was somehow both wry and challenging. What was he thinking?

And I wondered just then if I'd made a major mistake heading out this way with this employee who might be an animal lover too. But was he a murderer?

Surely not. He was just someone I'd intended to question to stick at the bottom of my suspect list. Right?

"Well, tell me more about yourself," I said, trying to keep my tone light, even though inside I was kicking myself for deciding that I could go out in the fields of the sanctuary alone with just anyone to hurl questions at them and not put myself in danger.

"Oh, you've heard pretty much about why I'm here," Carlo said, "but I guess I could talk a lot more about myself. Doesn't everyone? But if you're hoping I'll start rambling till I confess I'm the one who killed Oliver . . . well, gee, maybe I will."

Chapter Eleven

"What!" I exclaimed, then made myself laugh. Or hoped I sounded as if I found his statement funny.

Instead, I was terrified inside.

Sasha sensed my fear. She stood and started pacing at my side on the narrow trail, still on her leash.

Sweet pup. My defender. But I hoped she wouldn't have to try to defend me from this human way out here in the middle of nowhere—or at least in the middle of the vast shelter grounds, with no other people around. There weren't even any wildlife close on the nearest areas behind the chain-link fence—not that any of them would even think about coming to the assistance of a human under attack, no matter how highly I esteemed the animals around me.

"So, you don't really suspect me? Or you don't want me to think you do?" Carlo took a step closer to me despite Sasha stepping between us. He looked me deep in the eyes with his dark brown ones.

I knew I was breathing hard despite attempting to appear amused. The chilly air suddenly felt hot. I wasn't sure how I'd protect myself out here if I needed to, but I would. Undoubtedly with Sasha's help.

But for now, at least, I'd act as if he was joking.

And maybe he was.

I hoped.

"Okay, then. Here goes. Should I suspect you? Are you the one who killed Oliver?" I continued to smile, as difficult as that was.

He took another step toward me, his brown eyes blazing, his expression as furious as if he intended to attack me.

As he had Oliver?

And then, as Sasha, at my feet, began to growl, Carlo started laughing and stepped back. "Gotcha. In case you haven't figured it out yet, I'm joshing you. I didn't kill Oliver. Don't even want you to think I did. But since I figured you're playing your own detective game—right?—I decided to play along."

"Then, even though you just looked like you wanted to attack me, you're saying you didn't, and you're innocent?" Once again, I tried to pretend to be amused, but I was anything but. At least I was starting to relax a bit. But I had to remain on guard.

"Exactly." He reached down and petted Sasha, who'd stopped growling but remained close beside me—my wonderful defender. When he looked back up at me, his expression appeared rueful. Or at least that was how I interpreted it. Wrongly?

"Okay," he said. "Here's the deal. I know I wasn't really being funny. But I also figured you'd be nosing around to try to figure out who killed Oliver—mostly because I heard from some of the others here that you might be at the top of the cops' list. And even though we hadn't met before, I'd heard of you, since you worked here last winter and volunteered over the summer. I also heard that you're such a fan of wildlife that you give tours on tour boats. And—"

"And I assume there've been rumors around here about how I helped solve what happened to one of our tourists who disappeared off our boat last summer because he'd been murdered."

"Exactly. So yes, it's in my best interests to have whoever killed Oliver outed soon, since I guess I may be a suspect like everyone else around here, even though I wasn't around when Oliver was killed. It wasn't me."

Maybe. But I would still have to be careful. He might be doing this just to throw me off the reality of his guilt.

"And I assume now that it wasn't you," he added.

"That's right." No matter that I was a person of interest.

"Right. So let's keep going. I want to see more of our wild residents. We can talk as we go. And I promise I won't attack your throat—or anywhere else. Okay?"

I found myself laughing. A little. "Okay. Same goes for me."

We started walking again. Sasha seemed calm by my side. The drama appeared over, at least for now.

But I would remain on guard. And keep Carlo somewhere on my suspect list. Closer to the top, since he'd behaved so strangely.

And I wasn't going to just let things go. I wanted to know more about Carlo.

But before I asked another question, I gasped quietly. "Oh, look!" We were nearing the end of the large enclosure, but I had just glimpsed several elk near the rise of the closest mountain. "It's a gang!"

Did he know that was a common name for a group of elk?

"Hey, yeah! I always enjoy seeing our gangs around here, as well as all of the herds and packs and all."

So he did. We watched for a while using our binoculars and both made some notes, mine on a note card from my pants pocket and his on a small spiral notebook he drew from inside his jacket. Plus another couple of pictures.

The elk soon began walking away from us after scrounging along the ground for something to eat. At least with the weather the way it had been, I could tell there was a remnant of plants for them to consume.

"Okay, let's keep going," Carlo said. "I'd like to visit the wolf area—notwithstanding what happened there. Or maybe because of it."

Really? Well, that still didn't mean he'd had anything to do with it. He could just be curious, as I figured a lot of people probably were.

"All right."

I doubted we'd see anything that would help me in my search for what had happened, but I could hope we'd see some wolves, even if nothing else exciting appeared.

Part of me wondered again if this was a good idea, coming out here alone with a man I didn't know well.

But if Carlo had been telling the truth about his involvement, maybe we could protect each other if anything went awry.

It was growing later in the morning, warming just a little. Eventually, we'd need to go back to the welcome building, maybe grab some lunch. But I wasn't in any hurry.

And right now I was eager to see who else was on the grounds. Wolves? I certainly hoped so.

Meanwhile, we could still talk as we continued. And maybe I could get more of my curiosity satisfied.

We plodded forward between the two chain-link fences, Sasha sniffing along the trail. I wondered what she smelled. She seemed highly interested.

But that was nothing new.

Our conversation fell into a lull with no new wildlife to observe and talk about.

I eventually said, "You indicated you've worked here for about six months, but since we didn't meet before, I guess our schedules have been different. I volunteer during the summer when I can, but it's most often on weekends or occasionally after one of my boat tours, if it's over early."

"Yeah. My schedule has mostly been early mornings during weekdays, almost never on weekends."

"Well, I'm glad we finally met." Was I really? I wasn't sure, but I figured it sounded good. "I assume you plan to work at the sanctuary for a nice long while, right? It's certainly an amazing place. I'm glad for the opportunity, even though I know the weather will soon turn terrible."

"Right. I haven't been in Alaska when it's been really bad yet, but I figure I can handle it. I know it'll be a lot worse than Chicago, but it does get cold and snowy there in winter."

Oh, that's right. He'd mentioned he had grown up in Chicago. "Well, at least that would be an introduction to the kind of weather you'll face. I had quite an experience last year. Oh, I knew what winter was like, but I grew up in Los Angeles. I attended the University of Arizona before I came to Alaska—and LA and Tucson are quite different from Alaska that time of year."

Carlo laughed. "I figured. What did you study at U of A?"

"You can probably guess: wildlife conservation and management."

"Well, my background in math and computers didn't prepare me as much for this job, but I really enjoy it. I've been trying to learn all I can and do everything possible to help the wildlife here."

"That's great," I said, and meant it. I continued to watch our surroundings, but all the animals in the area were keeping to themselves at the moment. We'd soon reach the change in fencing, so maybe we'd get to see the wolves. Or so I hoped.

"Yeah, it is. I think I've learned a lot, and Wayne seems to like me and how I'm progressing. And—"

There was something in his tone that made me look at him. He was watching the ground in front of him, and his expression seemed . . . angry.

What was that about?

Of course I had to ask. "And what? Everything okay?"

He laughed and looked at me, although he didn't really look amused. "Well, sure. It's just that I guess I did theoretically have a motive to do away with Oliver. He was even more of a newcomer than I was."

"Right," I said, puzzled.

"But Wayne brought him in as a newcomer, a stranger, and made him a manager. I'm one damned good employee, and though I hadn't been here long, I'd been here longer than Oliver."

Oh. Interesting. I thought I understood what he might be referring to. "And you hoped to become a manager."

"Yeah, especially when Wayne mentioned he was about to start bringing in more managers. I mentioned I'd be really pleased to be considered."

"I get it. Sorry that didn't work out." Would he be considered for promotion to manager now? That might give him a motive to have done something to Oliver. "What did you think of Oliver as a manager?"

"Oh, he was okay, I guess. But he knew I resented that he'd been brought in. And I know what you're probably thinking. But that still didn't motivate me to do away with him. I pointed out his flaws now and then to Wayne, but that was all."

Was that true? Well, I'd already determined to keep Carlo a suspect in my mind. Maybe I'd move him up a few notches to the top of the list again.

But with the way we were talking, I figured he was most likely being honest.

Most likely.

Rather than accusing him again, I asked, "Do you know of anyone else who resented Oliver, or who let Wayne know about his imperfections?"

Imperfections like hating my wonderful Sasha, who was still absorbed in the scents along our hike.

"I've been pondering that," he admitted. But before he could tell me if he'd any thoughts in that direction, he pointed to our right.

We'd nearly reached the divide in the chain-link fence with the gate just beyond it.

The area where Oliver had been killed.

But before we actually reached it, I heard howls in the distance, and three wolves loped over the nearest hillside in our direction, still far away but in our sight.

Which made me smile and pull out my binoculars again. Carlo did the same.

I wished I'd checked on Tikaani this morning, although I intended to when I returned around lunchtime. This was near the area where I'd gone inside the fence to try to help save his life.

I mentioned that to Carlo.

"Yep, I'm aware of what went on that day, before Oliver was found in this area. I've kept an eye on our injured wolf's progress, even assisted Dr. Skip now and then to change bandages and give meds."

The wolves stopped in the distance, and I had a sense they were eating. Probably prey who'd shown up in their enclosure. That definitely happened in the sanctuary, even though food was provided to inhabitants to keep their nibbling on each other at a minimum.

But wildlife acted wild, as they should.

We watched for a while longer, Sasha seated at my feet with her attention also focused on those distant creatures. But here she didn't disturb them, which was a good thing.

And as we eventually started our hike back to the welcome building, an unkindness of ravens cawed around us and flew by. They were far from the first I'd seen and heard on this expedition, but we weren't necessarily supposed to concentrate on them. Even though it was getting later in the year, there were always a lot around.

And though tradition indicated ravens could be difficult and unkind, at least it wasn't a murder of crows.

Carlo and I had fulfilled our observation obligations for the morning, and we'd file our reports when we returned to the welcome building. But not quite yet.

Wanting to keep our conversation going, but in a good, neutral way, I asked, "So what are your expectations, working here during the winter?"

Working here, not *as a manager*. That unspoken stipulation circulated through my mind, and I wondered if the same thought was going through his. He'd be doing pretty much the same thing I anticipated doing: observing, reporting, maybe preparing food, and trying to make sure that all went well at this wonderful sanctuary and that the animals remained safe and as healthy as possible.

But neither of us would be telling others, like employees or volunteers, how to make that happen, though being in that role might be his goal.

"Well, doing pretty much what we did this morning, as long as weather permits. And even when it doesn't. I don't mind hiking in the rain, or even the snow. The animals don't have a choice about it, after all, so I'll do all I can to make sure they're okay. How about you?"

"About the same," I said. "Do you live in one of the apartments now? I figure Sasha and I will move into one when the roads become impassable. Maybe even before that."

"You and I seem to be on the same wavelength."

And so Carlo and I and Sasha hiked back to the entry area together with what seemed to be a burgeoning friendship.

But he might still consider me a murder suspect, as I did him, though possibly less so than when we started.

As we reached the welcome building, we slipped into the office and entered our reports into the computers. We weren't alone. Larraine had already returned too, and she was still there when we arrived. I thought over my morning hike with Carlo. It had worked out okay. Maybe better than okay, since I wouldn't have been able to question the two of them together that way.

And I kind of liked how the discussion with Carlo had gone. Even though it had been uncomfortable at first, he'd been teasing. And then I'd been able to really press him for answers about whether he'd been the one to kill Oliver, as he'd also seemed to do with me.

I couldn't fully believe him, but what he'd been willing to tell me was interesting.

And I felt like my amateur sleuthing about Oliver's murder had started out okay.

But there was more to come. Like with Larraine.

"So did you see a lot of wildlife?"

"Yes," she said. "I went fairly far out and saw a herd of mountain goats. Loved it!"

"I identify with that," I told her.

We completed our reports and decided to go to the vending machine building for lunch. The room wasn't too crowded, even though it was lunchtime. I was delighted to see Lettie punching buttons on one of the machines.

When she spotted me, she dashed over, her blue parka over her arm, her short black hair neatly framing her face. "I just got here," she said. "Will we be able to go hiking together this afternoon?"

"Hope so," I said. And I did, sort of. But as much as I liked my tour boat assistant, she wasn't one I felt I needed to interrogate about Oliver's death.

She'd definitely not been around when it happened and had nothing to do with it.

Although she'd been helpful when I'd quizzed people on the boat about what had happened there. Maybe she could help . . . somehow. I'd need to ponder that.

For now, I bought an egg salad sandwich and a bottle of water, which I'd share with Sasha along with the dog biscuits that were still in my pocket. I sat down with Lettie, and Larraine joined us.

We had a nice conversation about what wildlife Larraine and I had each seen earlier, and Lettie said, "Even though I'm just volunteering and was told I didn't need to get here till early afternoon, I think I'm going to work things out so I can start coming in the morning and hopefully joining one or the other of you. Or maybe both, if that's okay."

"Oh, I think it might be okay sometimes," Larraine said, "although the usual plans are for only one or two of us to go out on our own. But we'll see."

Before we were done eating, Wayne, who had been standing by another table, came over to us. "Hey, did you all have a good morning of wildlife viewing? I'll want to check your reports this afternoon." He then aimed his glance at Lettie. "I know you just got here a little while ago, so I'll wait till later to hear about the animals you see today."

"That's right," Lettie said with a sigh. "I'm thinking about trying to change my schedule so I can come earlier, although I may have to look for something else to do besides work in a school cafeteria this time of year."

"Well, I may be able to hire you here to help out eventually," Wayne said. "For general observation, plus our food preparation will get busier soon, since the animals won't find their own as easily."

"Really? Oh, I'd love that." Lettie moved her gaze from Wayne to me, and I nodded my happiness with the idea too.

She wouldn't be my assistant here, but she was always my friend.

"And by the way," Wayne continued, "the reason I came over to talk to you is because I've been checking the weather report, as usual. It looks like things are forecast to get a lot more Alaskan soon."

"Here comes the snow," Larraine said with a smile that didn't exactly look thrilled.

"Oh, yes," Wayne said. "And I'll want to meet with each of you individually, both employees and volunteers, to work out who'll get which apartment assigned for days that commuting into town isn't a possibility."

Interesting. I'd planned on it, though I hadn't known when this might happen. I knew that was part of working here over the winter, and Sasha and I had in fact been assigned a unit last winter, though we'd only stayed sporadically, since the local crews had mostly kept the roads navigable.

Would that be the case this year? Judging by Wayne's comments, he didn't think so.

"Sounds good," I said, and the wheels in my head immediately started to turn.

I really doubted that Wayne had been the one to kill Oliver, but now that I'd started my own amateur investigation, it wouldn't hurt to test my sleuthing questions on him, as I had with Carlo.

Would questioning Wayne actually make me suspect him? I hoped not. But I'd have to see.

More likely, his responses would be useful in determining what to ask the others as I got the opportunity.

Assuming Wayne didn't get angry and fire me.

Chapter Twelve

G ood or bad, I wasn't the first one Wayne chose to take to
   view an apartment.

Manager Neil already knew which unit was his Juneau Wildlife World home away from home, but he requested that Wayne go with him to take a look at it. He said he'd popped in now and then recently but had a few questions.

On my request, Wayne said he would take me into my apartment after he took Neil. Which meant I got to go before the volunteers, since Marnie already stayed here often to aid in her food preparation. She already knew where her apartment was.

Wayne indicated he'd be ready in about half an hour, which suggested he figured he'd have to spend a little time with Neil. Oh well. I'd use that time wisely. It didn't give me much opportunity to go out and view our wildlife, but I figured I'd try.

Hopefully, I'd see some, and if not, I'd know to take another trail later.

And so Sasha and I headed toward one of the rear pathways. Lettie asked if she could join us.

"Sure," I told her.

We started out on the one we'd ventured on before together but veered off on a dirt side path that was different, although unsurprisingly also lined with a chain-link fence. The closest landscape here was flat, although like most areas within the sanctuary, it soon rose into vast, rolling hillsides.

This time, instead of mountain goats, we saw reindeer in the distance. "Oh, look!" Lettie breathed. I'd seen them at the same time and gestured for Sasha to sit as we observed. The small herd didn't get close anyway, which wasn't a surprise. Their antlers were magnificent. They seemed to be scavenging for something to eat, and despite the chill in the air, I figured they'd be successful.

And soon, when the bad weather Wayne was forecasting occurred, I could only hope all the animals found what they needed, especially when food prepared for them here wasn't available when they wanted it.

As always, I had an urge to stay and watch them. But I had to go back to view my apartment.

And talk to Wayne.

Both were definitely important to me. And so I said to Lettie, "Time for Sasha and me to get back and see where we'll be staying when the weather gets bad."

"Doesn't seem so bad now," Lettie said, putting her face in the sky and smiling.

I allowed myself to feel the coolness on my cheeks, inhale the fresh, chilly but not icy air, and agreed with her.

"But this is Alaska," I said, as if I had to remind her.

"Oh, yeah," she said. "It'll get worse. Probably a lot worse, and probably really soon. See you later. I'm hanging out here for now. But I hope to get assigned an apartment too." So she must intend to spend a lot of time here later, despite her temporary job.

She pulled a small notebook from inside her jacket and started making notes.

After Sasha and I walked back to the welcome building, we went straight into the separate apartment building. I assumed Wayne would be waiting for us there.

Which he was. In the lobby. Still talking with Neil.

And I wondered what the subject of their current conversation was.

The issues with Neil's apartment that I suspected he'd wanted to discuss with Wayne? Something else to do with this wildlife park?

Something to do with Oliver . . . ?

The last idea wasn't very likely. But who knew?

If so, would Wayne mention it as we talked?

Yeah, right.

Wayne noticed Sasha and me as we entered the small lobby and nodded in our direction, then apparently said something to let Neil know we were here. We drew close to them, and Sasha sat at my feet when we stopped.

Neil, whose back was toward us, turned and smiled briefly. "Hope you like your apartment," he said. "They're all small but nice."

Even a manager's was small? Maybe so, although I'd not seen a manager's unit before.

What about the director's? I thought, though, that Wayne's was on the ground floor of the building and was fair sized.

Maybe I'd find out, although I doubted Wayne would invite me there. I could always invite him to hang out in the unit he assigned to me, if we needed to talk somewhere other than his office or out in the fields.

Assuming he'd want to talk to me at all, except about our resident wildlife.

Sasha and I crossed the gray textured tile floor that wouldn't be very slippery when wet, a good thing around here. Wayne wore a long-sleeved plaid shirt, not a sweatshirt or parka, even though he'd had to go outside the welcome building to get here. It wasn't far away, and I figured someone like him who'd been in Alaska maybe his whole life was warm-blooded and didn't always need to be bundled up.

He reached down and petted Sasha.

Our director was definitely not Oliver. But then, Wayne had okayed Sasha's being here and had even told that to the manager who'd reported to him.

Not that it had mattered to Oliver.

But Oliver's rudeness certainly wouldn't have made me kill him, despite the suspicions I knew remained on me.

Where were those detectives now? What were they doing?

I couldn't help worrying, all the time, that they were still gathering false evidence and preparing to have me arrested.

Not a good time to think about that—or was it? I did hope to quiz Wayne in a few minutes. Despite not really suspecting him. But maybe he had thoughts about who could be guilty.

"So," Wayne said, his hand still on Sasha's head. My pup was panting just a little, not because she was warm but because she appreciated the attention. "I've picked out a unit that I think will work for you two. It's on the second floor but near the stairs, so it shouldn't be hard for you to go outside. Or not harder than any other place. Since you'll be here when the weather isn't exactly inviting you to leave the building, no place is likely to thrill you. But I'm sure you'll want to take Sasha out a lot while you're staying there."

We'd had a place on the third floor last year during the few times we'd had to hang out at the sanctuary, which Wayne knew. It had worked out okay, but getting Sasha in and out had sometimes had its challenges.

It was nice of him to consider that this year.

"Sounds good to me," I said. "And Sasha, I'm sure. Thanks. Can we go see it?"

"Of course."

He led us up the stairway, then stopped at the first door on the right. "This one," he said, taking a card key from his pocket and swiping it along the reader. Then, handing me the card, he reached past Sasha and me and shoved the door open, motioning us inside first.

I kind of knew what to expect after last year. I'd found the welcome building and all of its rooms I'd visited so far, including the lobby and some of the offices, to be nice and efficient and appropriate for a wildlife sanctuary where more of the finances had to go to keeping the animals safe. The apartment building also seemed suitable for its use.

This unit was actually cute—nicer than my last one, which had been starkly plain. Beige and boring but functional.

Oh, I didn't imagine a whole lot of money had been invested to create this one. But there was a lot of charm in the pale-blue walls of the living room that we first entered, with a matching blue tile floor and comfy-appearing furnishings—a sofa and armchair, with a small coffee table and another table across the room supporting a television. The kitchen was off to the right, not in a separate room, but also decorated in blue, with a raised counter and stools plus a small stove and fridge. I guessed that the open door at the far side of this room led to a bedroom and bathroom.

Nothing large, but all quite nice and efficient. And welcoming. I'd definitely been raised a notch or two when it came to our facilities this year.

Not a bad place to hang out during winter days when we couldn't go to our real home.

"As before, you can fill your refrigerator with things from the vending machines," Wayne said, standing in the kitchen doorway and waving around. "Although that won't include dog food." He smiled again at Sasha, which made me like the guy all the more.

Which only made it more difficult to consider the inquisition I intended to confront him with.

Still. "Any coffeepot here, and coffee?" There had been a coffeemaker in my last place. "If so, how about if I brew some for us, and we can take a quick break and—"

"And you can ask me what I know about what happened to Oliver and how it's being investigated." The large, bearlike guy in charge of this animal sanctuary was still smiling. Although, if I interpreted correctly, his smile was hiding anger.

Because I considered him a murder suspect?

Because he was a murderer?

"Well, yes," I said, attempting to look rueful. "You've got me pegged. I know you're aware that I helped solve the murder of the man who was killed on my tour boat a few months ago. And you're also aware that this time I'm apparently considered suspect number one."

"Yes, those detectives asked a lot of questions, apparently of everyone, as if any of us could have been the one to harm Oliver. But some of what they said indicated that at least one of us was highest on their suspect list."

"And I'm that suspect," I said with a sigh.

"Yes. Anyway, let's sit down at the table if you want. No need to brew coffee, though. There should be bottled water in the fridge, and that works for me. I can't stay long, but I can tell you what they said—as long as you promise not to murder me because of it."

I couldn't help staring into Wayne's brown eyes as they looked back at me. I figured he was kidding . . . about me. But would he poison the water? Do something else to get rid of me?

I didn't really think he was the one who'd killed Oliver, and I'd no real reason to believe he'd do away with me now.

Still, I knew better than to fully trust anyone right now, even this apparently nice guy who was my boss.

And had been Oliver's boss too.

Which meant he could have gotten rid of that manager, if he'd wanted to, without killing him.

I knew my mind would go back and forth over this a lot. It was the way I was.

And I knew I had to question everyone about what they believed had happened to Oliver.

Who they believed had happened to him.

And without necessarily eliminating whoever I was talking to from my suspect list—but determining where they belonged on that list.

I'd done that with Carlo.

Now it was Wayne's turn. Which he appeared to know.

But he still seemed willing to talk to me. Right?

Before I asked him anything, Wayne got a couple of water bottles from the refrigerator and put them on the table while I poured water in a bowl from one of the cabinets and put it on the floor for Sasha. We both sat down, and Wayne took a drink from one of the bottles, then said, "Okay, before you start, let me tell you what I know."

Really? Maybe he thought that would limit my inquisition.

I'd just have to hear what he said.

"Fine." I looked at him and took a sip from my bottle.

"Number one: I didn't kill Oliver, but I figure you know that." His brown eyes narrowed, as if he was trying to see inside my head to make sure that was true.

"Of course." I pretty much believed it was true. I hoped it was true. Others around here remained higher on my suspect list than the director, who could simply have fired Oliver if he'd really disliked him.

Unless there was some reason he couldn't get him to leave that I didn't know about . . . ?

"Number two," he continued. "I don't know who did it. Like you're undoubtedly doing, I've been churning the possibilities in my mind. I think Oliver was the nastiest to you—" He lifted his hand off the table, as if to keep me from butting in with a protest or a reminder that I didn't do anything to Oliver. "But the guy wasn't the friendliest in general. I sometimes regretted hiring him, especially as a manager. But when he came in for his interview and interacted with the employees and volunteers those couple days, he seemed nice. And when he and I went out on the grounds, he appeared charmed by the wildlife, as we all are. Plus his background working at other Alaskan sanctuaries was damn good, and the references I contacted had only good things to say about him. I didn't have the sense that they were complimentary just to get him to leave their facilities and get hired elsewhere."

"I get it," I said. And I did. I figured Wayne had been pondering whether hiring Oliver had been a mistake, if he should have somehow known the guy would rub someone the wrong way so much that whoever it was would kill him.

But how could he have known that?

"Anyway, I wouldn't necessarily admit this to anyone but you and maybe a few other people around here, but I'm glad the cops have concluded a person killed Oliver and not one of our wolves. Or even your sweet Sasha." He put his hand down, and Sasha, who'd been lying beside me, went over to Wayne for a pat.

"Same here," I said vehemently. "But I just wish they weren't zeroing in on me just because Oliver was so nasty about my pup. I suppose he figured having a dog here could scare the wildlife, and he was right, to some extent. But I do all I can to keep Sasha out of situations where she'd frighten anyone."

"I know, and I agree with all you do."

We sat silent for a minute. Then, before I could lead back into my questions, Wayne said, "And in case you're wondering, I won't tell you the people around here I suspect the most. But there's no one I could point my finger at, to the authorities or anyone else, and say they had to be the killer. I didn't see any real motives. And I guess that might be what's going on with the cops too, since they haven't arrested anyone. No matter what they told you, they may figure that your minor spat with the victim wasn't bad enough for you to have killed him over it. Or even if they think you really did it, they must not have found enough evidence that they think they can convict you. At least not yet."

"They never will, unless it's manufactured. And I certainly hope they recognize my innocence, even if they haven't told me so." I grinned grimly at my boss and nodded.

"I suppose it doesn't hurt that you've been seeing one of those troopers socially, right?"

"Right, as far as the fact that Liam and I have become friends." No need to mention that we were sometimes more than friends. "But he's let me know he's better off not seeing me at all right now, till this is resolved. And in any case, he's not supposed to discuss it with me."

"Makes sense. Anyway, I need to get back to introducing our people here to their apartments. I assume this unit's okay with Sasha and you?"

"Definitely," I said. I hesitated briefly before adding, "And I appreciate this discussion. I didn't really consider you a suspect, but I'm glad we talked about it. I wish you knew who it was and told me, of course. Or better yet, told those detectives. But I guess we'll all just have to keep on considering the possibilities."

"Till someone's arrested and, hopefully, convicted. The sooner the better. And in case you're wondering, I'm still trying to figure out who my next manager will be, someone already here or someone else." Wayne had stood and grabbed his water bottle. "Oliver may not have been my favorite person or yours, but he was an okay manager. He did his job. Someone else has to do that now." Before I could respond, he turned and headed toward the door, Sasha at his feet. "Talk to you later." He patted my dog once more, then left.

Whatever his good points and his bad points, Oliver had apparently been an adequate manager, at least in terms of the way he had cared for the wildlife.

But I had even less reason than before to believe Wayne had killed that manager, and I hadn't really suspected him earlier.

He apparently didn't suspect me either.

But what if someone was arrested soon? Would I have to continue trying to figure out who did it?

Definitely, if that someone happened to be me.

This part of my day, and my inquiry, was over. "Let's take one more walk through our new place," I said to Sasha. She wasn't wearing her leash inside, but good dog that she was, she stayed close to me while I walked around the small unit again, checking out all the accoutrements more closely.

Everything looked fine. I hoped we wouldn't be staying here a lot this winter, but assuming this Alaskan winter would be like most others, I figured we'd hang out quite a bit.

Which we'd deal with.

And I'd remain careful, of course. Until someone other than me was arrested for the crime, I would continue to attempt to figure out who had killed Oliver, and just the fact that I kept snooping might put me even more on that murderer's list to do away with too.

What I was doing here wasn't exactly new, unfortunately. I'd done something very similar on my tour boat after that passenger had been found murdered. There were a lot more possibilities for killers then, including other passengers, but I had questioned the people I knew on the boat and those I'd recognized as taking our tours before.

Surely, it should be easier for me to figure out who was the killer this time—especially since I needed to protect myself.

We soon left the unit. I checked to make sure I had the key card, then confirmed that the door was locked, and we headed back to the first floor.

Now it was time to go observe more of the wildlife. Alone, for the rest of the afternoon, with no other people with us? No other employees or volunteers for me to continue conducting my inquiries with?

Maybe so. Whoever was doing that kind of observation was most likely already out on the trails, not around here. And I couldn't be sure I'd see any of them while I was out and about.

That should be okay. After all, I'd been able to question two possibilities already today.

And if the weather turned bad soon, I'd be here with a bunch of them in situations where I might be able to get them alone to talk to them.

Carefully.

For now, I decided not to go way out on the sanctuary trails, since it was already midafternoon. Instead, I chose a path Sasha and I could take from the parking lot that veered off in one direction, then another. The nearest mountainsides had patches of trees, which would be a good winter environment for the Sitka deer I soon saw on the nearer rough landscape.

Sasha at my side, I watched for a while and made my notes and reveled in the experience, as I always did. I kind of wished I was giving a tour, pointing out the wonderful Alaskan wildlife to tourists who might never have seen any of these animals before.

I enjoyed not only having the experience of finding them, but also pointing them out to others and sharing the awesomeness with them.

But even if I didn't get the opportunity to share what I saw, I loved seeing it. Seeing *them*. The fantastic animals who lived out in the wilds and added to the wonder of the world, and especially the world of Alaska.

And so Sasha and I walked for quite a while. I bundled up as much as I could in my parka, thanks to the chilly, though not horrendous, weather. Sasha seemed fine with it, as my sweet pup always did. In colder, wetter weather, I'd at least put boots on her again, and maybe a doggy jacket too.

I saw a few hares jumping around on the landscape now and then. Small ones, probably snowshoe hares.

Eventually, I pulled note cards and a pen from one of the many and deep pockets of the warm but casual pants I wore and made notes about the deer and hares.

Did I regret that, except for Sasha, I was alone out here and not able to quiz anyone to determine who'd killed Oliver?

Not at the moment. If I was arrested later, I'd beat myself over the head—proverbially, of course—for not being more diligent. But for now, I was enjoying myself.

After a while, I knew it was time to go back to the welcome building. Since it was late afternoon, the temperature had warmed up slightly. I hoped that was an indication of good weather tomorrow too.

Would I be able to grab coffee—and a conversation—with any of my suspects when I returned to the welcome building?

The answer turned out to be no. Far as I could tell, Wayne was the only one there by himself. From what he indicated when

I popped in to let him know we were back, most of the others, including Lettie and Larraine, were out on the trails doing observation. Even Marnie was out, distributing the food she'd been working on. I didn't learn who was helping her, but I figured someone was.

And so, after drafting my report for the day, I decided it was okay to leave. Sasha and I went upstairs to report to Wayne first, though.

"Sure, it's fine if you leave now—while you can. The weather report for tomorrow doesn't sound great, although I'm not sure how the roads will be. You might even get to spend the night in your apartment here then."

"Well, I definitely like the apartment." I sent him a smile that I hoped appeared grateful.

"But you're not looking forward to being forced to stay in it. I understand. But hey, I'm one of the very few people at the moment who's staying here overnight. It'll be fun to have extra company when the weather finally forces more of you to remain around me."

I laughed. "We'll see how fun it is—maybe sooner than I'd like to think. Anyway, see you tomorrow."

And I'd most likely see the others, those whom I considered closer to the top of my suspect list.

What would it be like when they, as well as Sasha and I and Wayne, stayed here at Juneau Wildlife World for long periods of time without being able to go anywhere else easily?

I'd find out. And maybe I'd finally whittle down my suspects and determine who was most likely to have killed Oliver.

Who'd actually done it.

It started raining just as soon as I'd settled Sasha in the back of my car. A cold, sleety rain.

Which didn't bode well for the roads.

I just hoped I'd be able to return here tomorrow. Not only because I liked it here and was happy having a job involving wildlife when I couldn't give tours.

No, I was determined to snoop, the way I'd been doing.

Even if it proved difficult, I was determined to return here tomorrow. Maybe even start staying before I had to. I'd pack some of my clothes and necessities for Sasha and keep them in the back of my SUV.

Staying here, out of necessity or some degree of choice, meant I wouldn't see anyone else in town.

I wouldn't see Liam.

As I drove slowly along the winding roads toward town, I considered calling Liam. This might be the last time I'd get a chance to see him for a while, assuming he was available this evening.

But I considered it. Thought about it a lot more than I tended to do when I had a possible opportunity to get together with my friend the trooper.

The trooper who'd been ordered not to talk to me, and who'd ignored that.

To some extent.

The guy I was attracted to—but whom I found particularly difficult in this situation, when I was a murder suspect and he knew it. Our relationship, or nonrelationship, was particularly muddled.

"You know what?" I called back to Sasha, behind me. "I think you and I will go for a nice long walk when we get home. And then we'll stay home alone together tonight."

Would I regret it—especially if the weather did in fact turn bad enough that I wound up staying at the sanctuary?

Maybe. But I decided that, in any case, that was the way it would be.

No Liam tonight. And maybe for a long time.

Chapter Thirteen

As it turned out, Liam was the one to call me. Which wasn't particularly surprising, at least considering how much we had kept in touch . . . before.

He wasn't supposed to talk to me now, or so he'd said, even while making it clear that at least some of the people he worked with knew he'd talk with me anyway.

The call came in on the Bluetooth in my car as we neared town, and since his number was known, his name showed up. "Hi, Liam," I said, attempting to sound delighted to hear from him. And in a way I was, even though I'd decided that seeing him tonight, even though it could be the last time for a while, wasn't a great idea.

"Stacie, how are you?"

"Fine." But I wondered why that was his greeting. Was he expecting me to say I was horrible?

Under arrest?

Well, he'd surely know if that was the case.

"Glad to hear that. I keep thinking about you out there so far from anything but your wildlife—especially considering what happened at your sanctuary."

"What you're not supposed to discuss with me." I didn't make it a question.

"Right."

I nevertheless half expected him to start asking me questions about whether I'd learned anything, even though that would go against the orders he'd received.

Or maybe he wanted to get together this evening. Despite the fact that I'd already decided against it, I found myself hoping that was what was on his mind.

"Anyway," he continued, "I'm working on a case that will keep me occupied tonight, maybe over the next few days. But I'm concerned about you and your safety, especially if you're actually doing what I stupidly suggested and engaging in your snoopiness."

"Not so stupid," I said, slowing as I approached one of the turns that would get me off the highway and onto a street.

"Then, like I figured, you are doing it." Before I could answer, he said, "Look, Stacie. I don't know how things are progressing in the investigation, because I can't ask. But I'm worried about you, and not happy I can't be with you and—"

"But you can't. I understand. And though I'm doing what I need to, I'm being careful, so you don't need to worry." Well, kind of careful. "Anyway, sorry we can't get together for a while." I wasn't sure if that was true, but at least it sounded good.

Okay, I really would miss him on some level, but so what?

"Me too. But let's be sure to stay in touch."

"Of course."

Maybe.

We said our good-byes, and I felt more than a little sad. And somewhat relieved. We had seemed to be starting a relationship—before. Now I'd just have to see what happened between us in the future.

I decided to stop at a supermarket before going home to pick up some supplies that I could leave in the back of my SUV and take to my new apartment at Juneau Wildlife World tomorrow.

Despite the fact that I bought a lot, it was a quick visit, and no one ever complained if I brought Sasha inside with me. I'd picked up some extra good-quality food for her, as well as some ingredients for easily mixable meals for me—and a frozen dinner for tonight.

I also stopped at a drugstore to pick up pepper spray. Not that I expected to have to use it, but anticipating being out in the wilds more with people I'd be interrogating as possible killers made me want to be prepared, just in case.

We returned to our first-floor apartment, and I looked it over again after bringing in the few things I wouldn't be taking with me and walking Sasha. The evening went quickly, but when I took Sasha out for her final walk of the night, it was really cold, and it had started to snow.

I wondered what the roads would be like the next day.

I learned after we woke early, took another quick walk on sidewalks that had about an inch of snow on them, ate our usual doggy and people breakfasts, and got into my car to head to the sanctuary once more.

It was still snowing. Not heavily, but I had to drive carefully and somewhat slowly on the winding, slick roads. Would we be able to return home tonight?

Would I want to, considering that the weather might continue to grow worse?

I stopped outside the gate to the sanctuary and got out to unlock and open it, glad I'd dressed well for the weather that morning, including putting on boots and a nice warm parka.

Still, I'd have to remind Wayne I needed a remote control to open it. I was an official employee for the season, after all.

The short road leading to the welcome building had already been plowed, and so had the parking lot. I assumed that was Wayne's doing, or maybe manager Neil's.

I noticed there were more cars in the lot this morning than I'd seen this early since I'd started working here. Not many, but maybe a few other people had decided to move into their apartment yesterday, after Wayne had introduced them.

Or maybe there was an official car or two. Maybe the investigation continued.

One of the cars, surprisingly, was Lettie's. I recognized the white SUV partly because we parked in the same lot near the docks during the months we sailed on the ClemTours boats. She was here already? I'd have to find her. And learn which apartment was hers, whether or not Wayne hired her. We'd need to stay in touch better during this season of hanging out here.

For now, I decided to unload my groceries and other stuff before going into the main building. I got Sasha out of the back seat and walked her for just a few minutes, then removed a couple of the paper grocery bags from the back of my car and entered the apartment building, taking the bags and my pup upstairs to our unit. I used paper since I didn't know if I'd get to reuse them, and paper disintegrated in the garbage.

I opened the door with the card and left Sasha inside when I deposited the bags, so I could go back for the rest of the stuff I'd bought without having to worry about where my pup was.

When I returned to the stairs, Lettie was just coming down. My summer assistant was dressed as warmly as me, in the parka and boots I'd seen her in before, so I figured she was going outside, although her parka remained unzipped and she wasn't wearing the hood over her short black hair.

She was coming from her apartment, I thought. "Good morning," I called to her as she joined me. "Where did you stay last night?"

"Good morning. Great to see you." She grinned. "Looks like I moved in here sooner than you did."

"Looks that way, although I'm in the process of moving some stuff into my unit. Where's yours?"

"Next floor up, the second door on the right. I'll show it to you later, and I hope you'll show me yours."

"I'd be glad to show it to you now, especially if you'll help me bring my groceries in." It was my turn to grin at her.

She did help, going down to my car with me and taking a couple of bags as I did, making it my last trip.

Yes, I'd probably bought too much stuff, but I figured that when I actually moved in here, it would be too difficult to grab more things. And I told Lettie I'd be glad to share with her.

She seemed as delighted to see Sasha as my dog was to see her, and then all three of us headed to the welcome building.

"Do you know what you'll be doing today?" I asked Lettie.

"Not yet, although I'm hoping to get the same assignment as I've been, going out on the grounds and observing, although in different areas."

My favorite assignment too.

The only one I'd had so far.

But as much as I liked Lettie, I hoped I'd have an opportunity to talk to one of the other people today.

Although, if I actually was moving here for the winter and others were too, I was sure I'd be able to talk to each of them eventually.

But I really hoped I'd determine who the killer was soon. Really soon. So the rest of us could be safer, once the authorities arrested the actual culprit.

Assuming they did. And assuming they could, if the weather turned really bad.

Better yet, maybe the authorities could figure it out themselves and end all the suspense. Figure out how to resolve what had happened to Oliver, and get it right so they'd leave me alone.

But I didn't dare rely on that.

When we entered the welcome building lobby, it was empty despite it being about the time Wayne usually handed out our assignments for the day. But I noticed him appear on the stairs along with Neil. Marnie and Bill entered from the hallway to the kitchen.

Had they all stayed overnight? Some, definitely, like Wayne and Marnie. Maybe the others too.

"Morning, all," Wayne called out. He was wearing a black Juneau Wildlife World sweatshirt, so I figured he'd either been outside or was going out, though maybe not too far in this weather.

We all met on the bottom floor and greeted one another.

Carlo was also there, and as Wayne passed out instructions, Bobbie and Jesse came in. So did Shawna. I figured these volunteers hadn't stayed overnight. Had they been assigned apartments? Would they stay here other nights? I supposed that even if they were still to commute, Wayne would figure out where they could stay if the conditions became too terrible for them to return home.

"So here we go," Wayne said, and continued to pass out our assignments. As always, I hoped everyone would remember the procedure and learn what they needed to, then recycle the paper. I still thought it would be better for our director to email everything to us, but I knew this was easier for him.

I put out my hand for my page, while Sasha looked up at Wayne and wagged her tail. She got a pat on the head before he continued on.

I glanced down and was a bit surprised to see that I'd been assigned to work with Marnie in food preparation. If I got out into the field later, which I hoped I would, it would be for fun, not as part of my job.

I needed to learn about food preparation anyway.

And I also wanted to talk to Marnie.

"So, what did you get?" Lettie had been talking with Larraine, but she came over to us. "Can we go out on some of the trails together?"

"Not officially," I said, and let her know I'd been assigned food prep.

"Wow. Sounds good. You'll have to tell me about it later. I plan to stay here tonight, and I assume you do too."

"Most likely," I said. Even if the roads were passable, I'd brought a lot of food, after all. And I really didn't have much reason to return to my apartment tonight, then maneuver the whole way here again tomorrow.

I wouldn't be getting together with Liam, after all. Would I talk with him? Who knew? At least my cell phone seemed to work out here, unlike some of the areas I traversed on my boat tours.

"Everyone got their instructions? And you're all okay with them?" Wayne now stood one step up from the bottom and looked around at all of us.

"Fine with me," I said when our eyes met. I'd already looked around the room. Marnie was near the door that led to the kitchen area, and she was watching me. She apparently knew I was her assistant today.

With Sasha beside me, I headed her direction, exchanging greetings with some of the others.

"You're in charge of me today," I said when we caught up with her.

"Hmm. Putting it that way gives me lots of bad ideas." Marnie laughed. She wore a peach-colored, long-sleeved T-shirt today, and her blond hair was puffed around her face as usual.

"Maybe I should rephrase it," I said as Sasha and I followed her.

In the hallway, she went to the door that led to the kitchen. I had a thought, though. I'd popped in very briefly yesterday to see how Tikaani was doing, but never long enough to really observe him.

Last time I'd checked, he was still in the enclosed area Dr. Skip had placed him in after treating him. Since he was sometimes pacing, I assumed he was okay. I wondered when he would be well enough to be released back into the wild.

"I'll be right there," I told Marnie. "I want to check on Tikaani."

"Fine," she said, "although I thought I heard Dr. Skip go in there a while ago."

Really? Another early person.

Or maybe the vet was checking on his patient while he could, while the weather allowed him to drive here. I wasn't sure what his vehicle looked like, so it could have been in the front. But he was also able to enter the clinic area through the back, so maybe he'd parked there.

I tied Sasha's leash to the doorknob, then went inside.

Sure enough, Dr. Skip was in the clinic area, dressed in his blue scrubs, leaning into the enclosure where Tikaani was located and using a stethoscope. To check the wolf's heart rate, I assumed.

"How's he doing?" I asked, then worried if I should have waited. I certainly didn't want to startle the vet.

But Dr. Skip didn't turn to look at me. Instead, he continued checking Tikaani, including the still-bandaged area where the wolf had been injured. Fortunately, the wolf must have realized he wasn't under attack, since he remained calm. He'd probably learned he was okay during his prior exams.

The vet removed the bandage, then said to me, still without turning, "Looks like he's healing okay."

"Really glad to hear it," I said. "Just wanted to check on him. I'll leave now."

Dr. Skip backed out of the enclosure before I moved. "Glad you're concerned about him," he said, looking at me with his stern, dark eyes. "Most of the people around here are, I think. They seem to care about the wolves like all the other animals— even now, when they may be considered suspects in what happened to Oliver."

I didn't believe Dr. Skip had been here at any of the times Oliver might have been killed, so he wasn't one of my suspects. But I still had a good opportunity now to quiz him. "Fortunately for the wolves, and for my dog, I'm fairly sure the authorities are convinced a person did it. But—well, I wish they'd figure out who."

Those eyes of his narrowed as he continued to look hard at me. "I assume, from your saying that, that it wasn't you. Or that's what you want everyone to think."

"It's the truth," I said. "And I'm serious when I say I hope the troopers solve the thing fast. Without narrowing in on someone innocent, of course, like me."

Dr. Skip laughed then, lighting up his not-bad-looking face. "I'll take your word for it, at least for now."

I had to ask. "Do you have any suspicions about who did it?"

"Other than you?" When I glared at him, he laughed again. "No, I don't especially suspect you, but I don't know who had it in for Oliver." Before I could respond, he continued, "Anyway, from what I know about you, you're a true animal lover. Glad you came in here. I'll need to leave soon, though I'll report to Wayne that this wolf is improving. You can let the others know too."

"Will do," I said. "And now I'd better get to work. Drive carefully on your way back to town." I knew that was unnecessary, but it indicated to him that I gave a damn about his safety.

He did, after all, provide veterinary care for the wildlife here who needed it.

"Of course," he said. "And you be careful too."

He didn't mention my driving home or anything else.

Maybe he considered me to be in danger here, if I was innocent of killing Oliver. Which I definitely was.

I went outside the clinic door. Sasha must have heard me, since she was sitting up, looking at the door as I closed it, wagging her tail.

"Okay, girl," I said. "Let's go to the kitchen. Don't count on any snacks, but I'll bet it will smell interesting there."

Which turned out to be right. Even though my sense of smell wasn't nearly as acute as my dog's, I detected a scent as we entered, something grainy, so I figured Sasha sensed a lot.

Marnie must have heard us, since she turned and said, "Welcome. Ready to learn something here?"

I laughed. "I'm always ready to learn something. And learning more about food preparation for the wildlife I adore sounds good. Although, do you really feed all the animals every day now?"

I'd already helped a little with food preparation in the past. I knew that, through the same months I tended to give tours, the animals could probably survive pretty well on what was in their habitats, although since the carnivores weren't given free rein to go visit other areas, they had limitations on how much meat they could find on their own.

I also knew Marnie remained flexible in what was provided for them and when by observing their eating habits.

"Not hardly," she said with a laugh, as if she realized I was joking. "Let me remind you that, in addition to having a nice, big veterinary area at the back of this building in case we have to shelter large animals as they're being treated, we also have some big refrigeration and freezing units. Although I do take food out to animals all times of the year, we bring in a lot of frozen supplies from various sources, partly thanks to our donors. After we put our own spin on some of it, we keep it refrigerated or frozen till we need to get it out in the fields."

"Oh, yes," I said. "Sounds familiar. And I look forward to learning more."

About food preparation.

And anything Marnie knew, or suspected, about what had happened to Oliver.

For now, Marnie indicated she wouldn't get into anything too complicated, but she did take me to see the various supplies the sanctuary received. They got a lot of food of various types delivered to them at different times, from meats to breads, grains and cereal, fruits, vegetables, and even some pasta.

"Fortunately, despite the huge size of our sanctuary, the actual number of animals isn't too large, so though I'm always busy sorting through food and getting it ready for our residents, especially the carnivores, we don't put huge volumes of food out there for them. It'll definitely increase soon, though, as we really get into winter, even for the grazers, since plant growth is minimized, plus it'll be harder for them to reach what they need under the snow, even if it's there."

"Makes sense," I said, realizing this had to be part of her current initial spiel to new helpers. I was quite happy when she took me into the refrigerated areas to show me what was there.

I tied Sasha outside, though. No need for her to get cold too.

It seemed Marnie already had what she needed for the day pretty much prepared, since she didn't have me do anything but watch as she divided up some of the already packaged stuff into smaller parcels that she said would be delivered out into the fields soon.

That gave me time to think at first. And then talk.

"I know a lot of the others who work or volunteer here these days help you, right?" I asked, knowing the answer.

"Yes. It's part of what Wayne wants everyone to at least learn. I usually have it covered, but I like showing others what to do. I do get days off now and then, after all." She chuckled and looked at me, as if she half expected me to object.

"Makes sense to me," I said. "And I hope everyone does a good job helping you . . ." I made it clear I was hesitating, then said, "I gathered that even Oliver helped you, right?"

She had returned to sorting things on the wide counter but stopped now without looking at me. "He tried," she said. "A lot, in fact. Maybe more than I needed, but he seemed so nice at times."

I'd noticed that he had appeared to want to join Marnie in the kitchen more than he'd apparently been assigned there. "I kind of thought he wanted to help you more. And I wish now that he had."

"Because he bothered you about Sasha?" Marnie asked, looking at me this time.

"Well, yes. He seemed to be pushier with me out in the fields. And maybe if he'd been here, he'd . . . have been okay." And I had to ask. "But in here—did you and he get along?"

As if she'd admit it if they hadn't.

"Well, yes. Mostly. But—well, he was a bit pushy with me in a different way than with you." She hesitated, but I didn't have to prod before she continued. "The thing was, I gathered he wanted to get to know me a lot better. But that wasn't for me, not the way I believed he wanted. I liked him but definitely didn't want anything more." Now she took her hands out of the food and packaging and turned to look at me where I stood on the tile floor behind her. "And in case you're wondering, I didn't kill him. I had no reason to. He came on a bit strong but never stepped out of line, like touching me or worse."

"Got it," I said. "And in case you're also wondering—"

Marnie interrupted. "You didn't kill him either. Yes, I know you're a suspect, but I believe you're innocent too."

Which made me smile inside. I liked this lady.

I figured others around here did too.

In fact, I asked her who she thought helped her the most.

"Well, maybe volunteers Larraine and Bill, and even our new employee Carlo."

Made sense. But before we got away from chatting and really dived into food preparation, I asked, "It's stupid of me to ask, probably, but I'd like to know. You knew Oliver a bit and he annoyed you, though not enough to hurt him. But who do you think might have—"

"Killed him? I've pondered that," she said. "I never thought it was you, but I also haven't any real idea who it was. It'll be interesting to see who it is when the cops figure it out. And since the possibilities around here are somewhat limited, I have to assume they'll solve poor Oliver's murder."

"I hope so," I said fervently, then added, "As long as they get it right."

Chapter Fourteen

It was fun hanging out with Marnie and seeing what she did with the variety of foods she dug into and organized into meals for the various types and sizes of animals, then put back into cold storage. I helped as she directed, not minding getting my hands full of meats and vegetables and grains at various times.

"Are we taking any of this out to some of the residents today?" I asked her at one point.

"Probably not. I took quite a bit out yesterday, with Bill's help, so I think I can wait another day or two, even though it's snowing."

Which it was.

I was just as glad about not going out to place the food in whatever locations were appropriate without necessarily meeting up with whoever would eventually eat it, and Marnie seemed to recognize that without my saying so.

"I've been appreciating your help and your company," she said, "but I suspect you're happier out there observing our animals than hanging out in here and playing with food, the way I enjoy."

I laughed. "I think you're right, but I'm really glad to learn more about how it's done. And I'd be happy to do whatever you need me to, whenever you need it, including later today." I definitely didn't want her to tell Wayne that I was uncooperative. And I genuinely hoped to be of some assistance.

"Got it. But I think it may be time for Sasha and you to head outside and have some fun in the freezing weather and snow."

I silently agreed, especially since I'd already accomplished what I'd wanted to in my discussion with Marnie. I'd no reason before to think she'd killed Oliver and still didn't think she had. I wasn't surprised that the guy had attempted to flirt with her, since I thought I'd witnessed a hint of it, or that he'd been unsuccessful. But that would have been a more typical motive for him to hurt her than vice versa. Even though that still would have been absurd.

I had an urge, before leaving, to check again on Tikaani. Was Dr. Skip still here? As far as I knew, there were no other animals currently under his care.

Sasha and I slipped down the hall, and I opened the door to the vet clinic, holding my dog behind me. I didn't see a person there, and when I fastened Sasha to the door and walked in, it appeared that Tikaani was sleeping peacefully inside his enclosure.

I felt glad I'd looked in again, even though I'd no reason to believe the injured wolf was any worse than he'd been a few hours ago when I'd visited.

And now it was time to go outside.

We now headed back down the hall and into the lobby, which was empty. Presumably, everyone was working on their assignments of the day.

It was close enough to lunchtime, though, that I figured Sasha and I should go to the nearby building with its vending machines. I wasn't too hungry, but a snack sounded good. Plus it would be fun to see who was back from the fields and mountain areas and ready to eat.

But before I left the lobby, my phone rang. I pulled it from my pocket as Sasha and I stood near the door to outside. The number didn't look familiar.

"Hello?" I said, a little impatiently, since I wasn't thrilled about the interruption.

"Hello, Ms. Calder?" said a woman's voice. "This is Detective Lillian Christopher."

I froze, waiting for her to continue. Surely, if she was about to arrest me, she wouldn't be calling. Although, as an outside detective, she wouldn't be the one to bring me in—would she?

She didn't wait for me to respond. "Ms. Calder, we have some additional questions for you, but we may not be visiting the Juneau Wildlife World for another couple of days."

I was glad to hear the last part but not the first. I still said nothing.

"I expect that's where you are now, right?"

Okay, an answer was anticipated. "That's correct," I said, attempting to sound firm and not rattled at all.

"Will you be returning to your home in Juneau later today?"

Obviously, she hoped so. And I was glad to say, "No, my plans are to stay here for long periods now that the weather is starting to get worse. I've been assigned an apartment for the winter."

So come and get me here, my mind shouted, and I reeled at the thought. I didn't want them to come and get me anywhere.

"Okay, maybe we'll head there sooner than anticipated, depending on how bad the weather gets."

I'd not wanted winter to jump on us too quickly . . . before. Now I hoped the roads became totally impassable.

Still, if they were about to arrest me, wouldn't they come no matter what the drive was like?

She didn't wait for a response but said good-bye and hung up.

And I just stood there leaning on the door to the outside of the building, trying to catch my breath.

"Are you okay, Stacie?" It was Larraine. I hadn't noticed her before in the lobby or elsewhere in the welcome building, so I didn't know which room she'd come from. Not that it mattered.

But what mattered was that I must appear as distraught as I felt.

I made myself straighten and smile. "I'm fine, thanks. Just considering what Sasha and I will get from the vending machines. That's where we're heading now."

"Me too. Let's eat together, okay?"

"Sure." In fact, it would feel good to spend some time in the company of someone as nice as Larraine while I settled down.

But how much could I settle down when I knew those detectives were going to burst back into my life and ask questions undoubtedly designed to get me to admit something they could claim as evidence against me?

I had to get answers to save myself, even faster than I'd figured.

But how?

I hadn't gotten together with Larraine yet to question her about Oliver. But we'd be in public at one of the tables in the building with vending machines, so that wouldn't be the place to do it.

I'd gone out in the field with her before. Maybe it was time to do it again this afternoon.

For now, we both grabbed our parkas off the racks in the lobby, put them on over our sweatshirts, then went out into the yard. Sasha came as well, raising her nose as the wind blew snow at us, as if she was reveling in it somehow.

Well, it could be a lot worse than the minor skift we were getting now. It *would* be a lot worse as we really got into winter.

But for now, it was livable, and somewhat enjoyable to my husky.

The walk next door to the food building didn't take long, even in the worsening weather. I wondered why it hadn't been built as part of the main building, or at least attached to it with some kind of hallway. But whatever the reason, it was separate, and we had to go outside to reach it.

I didn't see as many cars in the lot now. Maybe any investigators who'd been here had been out in the field this morning—and had left.

We hurried as much as we could without slipping on the short, slick sidewalk. Sasha didn't seem to mind at all.

There were a few other people inside, including Wayne and Jesse and Bobbie and Bill. Must have been lunchtime for all of us.

But Lettie wasn't there, unfortunately. I'd really appreciate spending some time with her now, maybe even hiking with her later.

And sharing with her the phone call I'd received. My assistant, and friend, would undoubtedly be sympathetic, and I needed a friendly ear.

I'd have to wait, though. She was probably still on the grounds observing our residents. I also hoped I'd be able to discuss that with her later, including which wildlife she'd seen and where.

For now, I grabbed an egg salad sandwich and a bottle of water from a couple of machines and sat down beside Larraine, who'd already joined Bill and Bobbie.

"Were any of you out on the grounds before?" she asked them.

They all had been, though none had gone very far.

Which meant the best I could do for the sanctuary today would be to head way out there to get at least some view of the farthest wildlife.

Maybe it was the best I could do for me too.

Which I soon told Larraine. "Sounds good to me," she said. "Will we take one of the ATVs?"

I knew to do the best job, I'd eventually need to do that. But only when the weather got really bad. "Not today," I told her.

"Good! I know we won't have a choice one of these days if we really want to get out there, but hiking is always best to me."

And so, after we finished eating and I'd given Sasha a snack of treats and water, we began to hike. I zipped up my parka and put on my gloves. Among the few things I'd picked up at our downtown apartment that were now in our place here were some warm clothes for both Sasha and me. I'd stuck warm doggy boots into my parka pockets, and I figured it wouldn't hurt to put them on her. I wasn't sure how much she liked them, but she didn't seem to mind them.

We slogged slowly, watching the world beyond the nearest chain-link fences to the road leading from the visitor center parking lot, the way we observers headed most often. Cold, yes. My nose felt as if it was icing up, but I never put scarves over my face.

And I always did fairly well dealing with the cold as long as I was dressed appropriately, like now.

We decided not to go too far, at least not at first. The snow had fortunately eased up, but there was still plenty on the ground.

It would be fun to see whatever wildlife we could against the white backdrop of rolling hills and mountains before it melted.

Of course, it was always fun to see whatever wildlife was out there, regardless of what the natural environment looked like.

And even though Larraine wasn't Lettie, she and I had become friends. I considered letting her know that my mind wasn't entirely on what we were doing and who we were likely to see.

It kept rolling over and over my brief earlier conversation with Detective Christopher . . .

Well, no. I wouldn't mention it to Larraine. I didn't think she figured I was the killer, but I didn't actually know what she believed.

And like everyone else who had been around that day, she was a possible suspect too.

"Do you see any animals yet?" Larraine asked after a while, as we both kept staring through the fence. Sasha was sniffing at the snow a lot, but I didn't think many animals, even small ones, had been out here, so she must just be taking in all she could with her very special canine senses.

"Unfortunately, no. Even if these guys were species who hibernate, which most aren't, it's too early for them to do that anyway. But I don't imagine anyone around here knows what's on their minds, why they head into certain parts of their terrain at which times." I didn't even know for certain why the animals I pointed out on my summer tours—sea creatures, like seals and whales, and wildlife near the shores, like bears and wolves—chose to be where they were at any given time, but those who liked to hang out in or near the water seemed to be mostly visible when I wanted them to be. A good thing.

I'd hoped to see wildlife out and be able to do a suitable report, although maybe a report that no wildlife had been visible in the usual hangouts was of some use to those who monitored what went on at Juneau Wildlife World.

"Well, if the weather continues to get worse, which it will, I think I'll try driving one of those special ATVs out here one of these days," Larraine said from beside me.

"Really? Your thoughts are similar to mine. I figure I can learn how to drive one when I have to, but do you know how?"

"Wayne has been very encouraging," Larraine said. "He let me and some other volunteers know he would give us lessons when the time came. And I made it clear I couldn't wait."

"Oh, I can," I said with a laugh. "But that'll be very helpful."

We walked for a while longer, still viewing no wildlife, which made me feel sad. And my mind still never completely left what had been eating at me since that phone call I'd received before.

I needed to take control of what I could. And I didn't have to remind myself that Larraine was one of those I hadn't yet questioned about Oliver.

This would be a good time for that.

"So," I said, "how do you feel being out here alone with me?" I bent slightly to give my dog a small pat on the head. "Well, not completely alone."

"Why? Because some people suspect you of killing Oliver?"

"Well, yes," I said with a small laugh, standing up and walking again. "But, of course, I'm innocent."

"Of course," she repeated, but then said nothing else. What was she thinking?

I didn't want to ask directly, so I said, "It's a bit scary to be working with our colleagues thinking one of them could be a killer, don't you think?"

"Oh, yeah. I can't help being worried too."

"And it was such a shame," I continued. Maybe I could at least determine what she'd thought of the man who'd been murdered. "Oliver and I were far from best of friends, but I admired how much he thought of Juneau Wildlife World and wanted to protect it." I made myself laugh. "Even from my dog." I patted Sasha, this time on her back. My pup looked up at me and wiggled against my hand.

"Admired him? I thought you knew better. He was . . . he may have had a few good points, but he was a horrible person."

What? Now that was totally unexpected.

Could Larraine have disliked him enough to . . .

I had to find out.

And be careful as I did, since we were alone and I hadn't even brought my pepper spray. Yes, I knew my defender Sasha would protect me, but who knew what Larraine might try?

If she tried anything.

"In what way?" I managed softly.

Hey. There. We'd gone out quite a distance, which under other circumstances would be a really good thing.

Especially since I now saw some movement on a mountainside that wasn't too far from us.

They were mountain goats, a little hard to see with their white coats in the snow, but they had black horns.

I decided to wait for Larraine's response before I pointed them out to her.

But she said, "I shouldn't have said that. We just had a small falling-out like you did, I guess. Not about a dog, though."

"What was it about?" She probably didn't want me to ask more, but I did anyway.

She looked at me. I'd estimated her to be in her forties before and still thought so, but her face beneath her dark hair, now in a gray knit cap, looked really pained. She shrugged slightly, then smiled—sort of. "I don't know if he was lonely or what. Or maybe he just wanted to make a fool of me. But he came onto me as if he was attracted." She smiled but looked anything but happy. "I ignored him at first, but then—well, I kind of played along. And when I did, he just laughed at me, as if I was stupid and he'd just been testing to see if I had any brains."

"Oh, Larraine, I'm so sorry. That was just another way Oliver was apparently so . . . so difficult." She looked so distressed that I hugged her despite our thick outfits.

And wondered at the same time if she'd felt humiliated enough to want revenge. Real revenge . . .

"I shouldn't have told you," she said into my ear as she hugged me back. "Especially since . . . well, just in case you're wondering, I didn't kill him. I just started teasing him now and then, sort of, making it clear that he was not an appealing kind of guy on any level. Not nice. Not sexy. Not someone a woman would ever want a relationship with."

Interesting. Maybe he would be more inclined to do something to her after that, instead of her—

"Oh, look!" Larraine was now pointing in the direction I'd been looking before. "Mountain goats?"

I turned as if it was something new and stared that way too. "Wow! I think so."

We both began watching and making notes, taking pictures with our phones and talking in low tones, as if they could hear us. Doing what we were expected to here at Juneau Wildlife World.

Even as my mind determined not only to keep Larraine on my suspect list but to stick her near, or at, the top.

We remained there a while longer. The wind started gusting, though, and despite the fact that no more snow seemed to be falling, the wind was enough to make it feel as if we were in a minor blizzard.

"Time to go back," I said as I bent to hug Sasha. She was shivering a bit, and I regretted that I hadn't decided to use one of those ATVs and drive out here so I could get her out of this a lot quicker. And though some of the vehicles were open, a few were enclosed—a much better way to transport my pup, as well as myself, around here in bad weather.

Larraine too. Maybe. I still wasn't quite certain what to think of my companion out here.

At least she hadn't attacked me.

Maybe that was because I hadn't rejected her. Nor had my dog attacked her.

"I agree," Larraine said, but she sounded sad. "I just wish we could have seen more wildlife, or even seen those mountain goats a bit closer."

"Let's hope we do next time," I said.

And wondered inside if I'd want to go out on the grounds alone with Larraine again.

No matter that she'd said she hadn't killed Oliver.

Was she, like me, innocent and upset about what had happened?

Or could she, unlike me, be guilty?

Chapter Fifteen

O ur hike back to the welcome area took longer than usual thanks to the snowy, slick path, but we made it.

Our discussion while we walked was more sanctuary oriented, and we talked about where the wildlife might be in this area.

"I love going out and looking at the resident animals from a distance," Larraine said. "And I figure that's okay with you too, since you also give tours from a boat. But I've talked to some of our volunteers who would love to go out and meet some of the animals up close and personal."

"Like wolves?" I asked ironically. We both knew Oliver hadn't been killed by a wolf, but someone had intended to make it look that way.

"Well, yes. And I wasn't thinking about it, but you did meet one of them up close and personal, the one who was injured and is now in the infirmary getting better."

"That's right." I didn't mention I thought of him as Tikaani. That didn't matter. "And I know our vet Dr. Skip has met quite a few of our residents. The reason at least some of them wind up living here is because they needed to be moved from wherever they'd been located before, whether or not they're native to this area. Some of them were even injured."

"That's what I understand."

"I wonder when we'll get our next animal brought in like that." And I actually did wonder. Even though I hoped we never would, since that would indicate an abandoned or orphaned or injured animal had been found.

Well, better that they be found and brought in than left on their own in such difficult conditions. And our observation was partly to ensure newer residents were accepted into herds or other groups, or at least not harmed, without any of us getting too close except in unusual circumstances.

We reached the parking area at the end of our trail. "Time to go inside," I told Sasha, and Larraine too.

The humans removed their parkas, and I took off Sasha's boots. I'd go to our apartment soon and exchange my boots for the shoes I'd brought, but for now they worked just fine.

With Sasha, we both headed for the office, where we could enter our reports. We weren't alone. I was delighted to see that Lettie was there on one of the computers. She was with Bobbie, who was also sitting on one of the desk chairs typing away.

So the young volunteer college student was also coming here for the winter. Didn't she have classes?

Or was she planning on working around them?

I didn't have to ask.

"Hi, Stacie," Lettie called when she noticed me, looking up from her chair. "I hope you had as wonderful an afternoon as we did. Bobbie and I went out beyond where Larraine and you were—we saw you looking onto the landscape but didn't want to stop. And good thing we didn't. We saw some wolves beyond the area where . . . where you'd seen them before." And around where Oliver had been found, but she didn't have to say that.

"Didn't get to meet any like you did," Bobbie said, also still sitting there. "But I'll bet you also don't get college credit for seeing a big variety of animals like I do. I'm able to take time off from some of my classes for my volunteer work, as long as I hand in reports and tell my fellow classmates about what I saw."

"That's great," I said, meaning it. She might not get paid as an employee like me, but she did derive a benefit from being here beyond what a lot of the other volunteers received.

I hoped to hear more about her classes, but I didn't want to invite her, or anyone else, to my apartment for dinner, and dinner was what would come next—although I did plan one more stop first.

And as it turned out, Lettie mentioned that the two of them were going to the other building to buy their evening meal from the machines and would then go to Lettie's new unit to eat.

"I don't have an assigned apartment," Bobbie said. "Not yet, at least. But Lettie was sweet enough to say I could stay with her tonight, since the roads won't be fun to travel."

"Sounds good to me," I said, and it did. I hoped. I'd no reason to think Bobbie could be a real suspect in what had happened to Oliver. She'd only just started coming here, and although I figured she'd met him, I doubted there'd been time for them to start disliking each other much.

Although what if I was wrong?

Well, surely nothing would happen to Lettie tonight. After all, I'd heard the two of them would be together, so it would be too obvious who was involved if anything happened to my wonderful assistant.

That was when Wayne came into the office and said, "I heard what you were saying, and that's fine. But as with everyone else, Bobbie, I've got a unit you can stay in if it's late, or the weather tells you to stay here, or both."

I half hoped Bobbie would jump at the idea and ask to see her very own apartment, but she didn't.

And so I listened to Wayne's questions directed at the two at the computers first, then at Larraine and me. The others had seen more wildlife, but Larraine and I were the only ones to report seeing the remote mountain goats.

"Maybe tomorrow," Wayne said, and that made me glad. Maybe he figured I was better off out there observing than helping with food preparation.

Speaking of which, after Wayne told us all to have a good evening, I returned to the kitchen with Sasha to see if Marnie was still working.

She was. Didn't she ever do anything but try to help our resident wildlife by making sure there was adequate food for them?

Apparently, that was who she was, just like I was a wildlife watcher and aficionado.

She wasn't alone now either. I knew she tended to have assistants like me helping and learning and maybe even distributing at times.

Right now, the nice-looking volunteer Bill was with her, wearing a heavy black sweatshirt. What were the hours he worked at the restaurant he'd mentioned?

Would he continue to work through the winter and not come here much, if at all?

He'd told me once that he'd moved to Alaska because it was more frontierlike than where he'd come from. Would he hang out in this area that was more frontierlike than Juneau when driving became difficult?

Marnie and Bill were leaning over one of the counters, close together, and as far as I could tell from behind them, they were blending and kneading together grains from one of the large containers.

Bill must have heard me. He was the first to turn. "Hi, Stacie," he said. "Marnie said you were in here earlier helping her.

Care to join in?" Interesting that he was the one to invite me, not Marnie. "We're nearly done, but we want to fill a few more of the packets to refrigerate so they're ready when the time comes to get them out there. Which could be soon, considering the weather."

"Hey, I gather you know what you're doing, unlike me. Marnie was doing a great job teaching me before."

"So I gathered, from the way she described having to show you the ABCs—animal basic chews."

Marnie laughed, and so did I.

Just for the fun of it, I did join them for a short while. But then Marnie said, "I think that's it for today. More to come tomorrow, in case either of you are interested, although I'm not sure who Wayne may have in mind as my assistant then."

"Don't you get any say in that?" I had to ask. I figured she must, since there had to be some people who just weren't cut out to be a lot of help in the kitchen, even though the same people might be perfect at going out and leaving the prepared food at times and places appropriate for preventing the wildlife from getting too hungry.

"Yes, I do," she said. "But I've learned to be flexible, since sometimes people I figure won't be too helpful turn out to be really great."

Had she just aimed a glance toward Bill? I wasn't sure, but maybe he was one of those she'd been referring to.

Bill. He seemed like a nice enough guy, but I hadn't had a chance to talk with him yet. During the few times I'd seen him around Oliver, I didn't think they'd acted like friends, but they hadn't come across as enemies either.

I needed to know more.

Not now, though. He was clearly busy. Tomorrow, maybe?

"So I figure I know what you'll be up to tomorrow, Marnie, but will you be helping out here again too, Bill?"

"I'll have to see, though I certainly wouldn't mind."

Or maybe he could join me out in the boonies so we could talk? I'd have to figure something out.

For now, though, I finished with the packet I'd been working on, then said, "I think it's time for Sasha and me to go." My pup had just been lying on the floor near the wall, her head up a lot of the time as she watched us and took in the interesting scents.

"That's fine," Marnie said. "Thanks for helping out again."

"Like I told you, anytime." Well, not really. But I figured she understood that I wanted to be useful when she needed me, not constantly.

And not if I had a choice between staying in the food prep area or going out to observe wildlife at this amazing sanctuary.

Even when the weather got worse.

I'd already clocked out with Wayne when he saw me doing my computer report earlier.

I was done for the day.

Sasha and I walked outside the welcome building, which at the moment had no visitors except those of us who were committed to being here.

The weather had eased up. It was cold out, but there was no precipitation.

I wondered what the roads back to Juneau would be like tonight, but also tomorrow morning. Should Sasha and I go home?

And then what had been constantly in my mind, but not at the forefront, started scratching at it.

No. I'd told that detective I was staying here. And I'd better—

"Hey, Stacie." It was Bill, and he'd caught up with us from the building entry.

I turned to face him and smiled. I'd put on my parka, but he was still just in his sweatshirt. If he was chilly, he wasn't shivering or hugging himself.

"I thought you were still busy food prepping," I said.

"I am, even though we're wrapping up. I need to go back inside to help Marnie in a minute. But—well, I wanted to check on how you're doing."

I felt a little puzzled about why he'd ask. "Fine, thanks. How are you doing?"

"Okay. But what I meant was . . . I figure you didn't do anything to Oliver, even though you weren't the best of friends, but rumor around here has it that you're . . ."

At his hesitation, I finished, "I recognize that I'm a suspect, but I figure others around here are too." I didn't get into the fact that I appeared to be number one.

He might already know that, thanks to those rumors.

Still, this was kind of an opportunity. I'd wanted to talk to everyone. "Anyway," I continued, "in case you're wondering, I didn't do it. But who else do you think—"

Before I could finish or get an answer, we both heard Marnie call from the doorway, "Hey, Bill, are you coming back? There are a couple more things I want to finish tonight with your help."

He turned to her and said, "Absolutely. Be right there." He did turn back to me, though, and said, "I've been wondering about that too. But I really don't have any idea." He then hurried back to the doorway.

And as I began walking Sasha around a bit in case she had anything she needed to do, I mused that I'd most likely gotten my answer from Bill, even though I hadn't directly asked if he'd been the one to murder Oliver.

Because if he was the guilty one, he'd definitely have an idea who'd done it.

Not that he would necessarily admit it to me if he was the killer. He most likely wouldn't.

Why would he?

Why would anyone?

And now my mind was back on the phone call, where it had been before Bill had called out to me.

Slowly, I walked Sasha around, and then we headed into the apartment building. Yes, we were definitely staying here tonight. We walked up the steps to the unit that was now ours, and I swiped the key card at the door.

"Let's get dinner," I said as brightly as I could to my eager pup, who pranced a little and gave a soft whine. She recognized the word *dinner*, as she did many others.

I got some healthy kibble and canned food from the things I'd bought and combined them in a dog bowl. As Sasha ate, appearing happy about it, I put out some water for her.

Then it was my turn. Not that I was particularly hungry, but I had bought some prepackaged salads as well as packets of complete meals that required just adding water and microwaving—and fortunately this small apartment did contain a microwave oven. Wayne had thought of everything. The small unit I'd stayed in a couple of times last winter had been similarly equipped.

As I sat down at the small table with a salad and a meal of meatballs and pasta and veggies along with a fork—the place also came with flatware—as well as a bottle of water, I wished I'd brought a bottle of wine. Not that I'd drink much, but a little sip of something that might muddle my mind sounded good.

And what would I toast? I'd toasted a lot of silly things with Liam when we'd gotten together for dinner, mostly connected with Sasha or my having an exciting tour coming up.

Liam. Did he know I was back on the burner, that those detectives wanted to talk to me again?

Not that he'd admit it if he did know, but I hoped the sound of his voice might calm me a bit.

And so, when I was done eating, I called him, still sitting at the table and ready to sip from my water bottle, continuing to wish that it was something stronger.

"Stacie! I was going to call you later."

Yeah, right, I thought. Only . . . the idea that he again had been considering disobeying his orders to stay in touch with me made me smile.

True or not.

"Great," I said. We chatted for a little while. He let me know he was at his home but had to dash out soon on an assignment. I told him I'd moved into my designated apartment here at the sanctuary, anticipating how bad driving would soon get. "Not sure it would have been impossible to get home tonight, but I didn't want to worry about returning here tomorrow."

"Sounds appropriate," he said. "And I'm fairly busy, so I'm not sure we'd have been able to get together for a while anyway."

Which made me feel bad, even though it was probably better that way.

Was he planning to avoid me because he was supposed to? Did it really matter?

We talked a while longer, and I told him how I'd started learning more about food preparation and how I'd also gone out onto the grounds to see some of the wildlife.

I didn't mention that now and then I still saw troopers and other investigators, presumably still conducting their investigation. Usually at a distance, sometimes inside the welcome building and sometimes out in the field. But I tried not to pay a lot of attention to them. Fortunately, none of them had talked to me . . . yet.

Still, just talking to Liam did cheer me a bit.

But at the back of my mind—no, closer to the front—remained that phone call.

I liked Liam. Trusted him. Figured he'd shut me up if he really wasn't going to talk about the situation.

And so I said, as brightly as I was able, "By the way, one of those detectives called me today. She said they want to talk to me again."

Did you know about that? I thought. *Can you help me at all?*

"That's what I heard, Stacie," he responded, his voice soft. And caring? "I'm not sure what's going on, and shouldn't tell you even if I did. But I don't really know how the investigation is going, except that I've heard about some frustration. Under the circumstances, they thought they'd have brought in a suspect by now."

Me? I wondered, but didn't ask.

"In any case, I won't ask how your own inquiries are going. I shouldn't ask. But what I can tell you, again, is to be damned careful. I just wish I could be there with you . . ."

Sure he did.

"So do I," I responded. "And yes, I'm being careful."

Maybe I needed to be less so, though.

The troopers weren't the only ones who wanted the detectives to bring in not only a suspect, but the actual killer.

I certainly hoped they would soon.

After we said our good-byes a short time later, I felt bereft. I missed seeing Liam in person.

And I wished he really could help me.

What was I going to do next?

Well, first thing was to get back in charge of my mood and my mind. Since there was a TV in the small living room, I figured I might be able to watch some for a while, maybe a talk show starring a comedian I liked, with guests who would also be amusing.

That would be good for the rest of the evening.

Although knowing me, I'd have to keep a pen and paper beside me. I might decide to jot down notes about the people here I'd already talked to, and about the few I hadn't and wanted most to get together with next. I would continue to try to figure out who really was guilty of the crime I remained a suspect for.

If I had to talk to that lady detective again . . . there likely was no *if*. It was *when*. I figured I really had no choice about anything except the timing. The when. Maybe.

Anyway, I'd want to plan for it. I didn't know what she would ask, but I could guess.

If there was anything I could tell her first, like who I really thought had done it and why, especially if I could throw in some meaningful evidence, that was what I would do.

I sat on the small, comfortable beige sofa and took the TV remote from the table between the couch and a lounge chair.

Before I turned it on, I closed my eyes and pretended I was talking to Liam. I imagined I could talk to him the way we had when we were closer in both proximity—and relationship.

"I know you said I should do my own snooping and figure this one out," I told him. "And I've been trying. But if you could, and would, talk to me, what would you tell me to do next?"

He didn't talk back, even in my head.

And so the best I could do was hope something really helpful would come to me in my dreams.

Chapter Sixteen

I went to bed, Sasha on the floor next to me as usual. I'd brought in a blanket for her to sleep on.

As I lay there, not even close to sleeping, I thought about Liam and what he would tell me if he were permitted to tell me anything.

And how I was angry with him that he hadn't been more helpful, no matter what his orders were.

Except to tell me I should investigate on my own.

I *was* on my own, even more than when I'd wound up solving the other murder that had intruded into my life.

I burrowed under the warm comforter, moving my head back and forth on the pillows. And stewed. And worried.

One day very soon I'd be questioned again by those detectives, unless the weather made it impossible.

I'd seen enough troopers and snoopers doing their investigation at the sanctuary to figure that the Alaskan authorities could handle bad weather when they needed to. They had to. It was their job.

It was a good thing, after all, that I was at Juneau Wildlife World. So were all the other suspects in Oliver's murder—unless somehow someone had sneaked in under the disguise of a wolf and taken care of him. Or maybe a delivery person who'd brought in food to Marnie. Or a visitor who'd come to look around, though I hadn't seen any.

I had to assume it was one of the people here.

Someone I'd spoken with.

But who?

I'd questioned nearly everyone. The only ones who remained were Jesse and Shawna, and I didn't really suspect either of them, but who knew? I did recall that Jesse and Bobbie had been arguing with Bill a bit a while back, with Oliver trying to calm them. I never had learned what that was about, and it didn't mean any of them had killed him.

Or maybe Dr. Skip, but he hadn't been around when Oliver must have been killed. And getting rid of Oliver wouldn't have saved any animal lives.

And of those I'd talked with, none had stood out as clearly being Oliver's killer. At least not to me.

Probably because I hadn't really figured out any plausible motives.

Could it be Neil, because they were competing professionally? But they were already both managers.

Or maybe Wayne, because Oliver had done something wrong? If so, why not just fire him?

Who else? And why?

I wished, as I was lying there, that I could just trek into the outback area of the sanctuary with Sasha and do nothing but hang out with the wildlife.

Rarely, if ever, did the animals kill one of their own packmates or herd members. Unlike humans. But I was a human. I thought like a human. Acted like a human—although not one who killed another human.

I was nevertheless a person of interest, and more. I had to protect myself. Save myself by determining and proving who actually was the killer.

If only I could somehow communicate with Oliver. But considering the kind of person he'd been, I doubted he would give a damn about saving me.

Enough. I needed some sleep.

Also, I needed a plan.

So what was I going to do to save myself? Because that's what I was determined to do.

Somehow.

I'd already questioned a lot of people—but gee, I hadn't really *confronted* most of them. I'd been a nice buddy, a cohort in a bunch of suspects. I'd asked a lot of questions, including who most of them thought was the actual killer, and hadn't really gotten any helpful answers.

So . . .

Okay. The thought had lingered in my mind, but now it felt more urgent.

Next time around, I wouldn't just be a buddy and ask their opinions.

Starting tomorrow, I'd be asking the people around me some hard, maybe even accusatory, questions. And I'd see which ones started to squirm the most.

I must have made a noise as I made that determination, since Sasha startled beside me and stood up.

"It's okay, girl," I told her. But because she was awake, I knew I had to take her outside.

Leaving my pj's on, I bundled up with my parka and long pants over top and my boots. I put Sasha's boots on and took her outside, and we walked around near the apartment building, dealing with the growing cold.

I watched around us, just in case someone dangerous also happened to be out there. But it remained quiet, and we remained alone.

And as Sasha did her thing, I stared at the nearby welcome building and the parking lot filled with the cars of those of us staying there. No cop cars were parked at this hour, at least not any recognizable ones.

I looked back at the apartment building. Most of the lights were out. It was late.

I wondered who else, if anyone, was awake now. If whoever had killed Oliver was able to sleep. Or maybe that person was delighted that they hadn't been discovered and assumed they never would be, so they slept well.

Maybe.

When Sasha and I went back inside, I confirmed in my mind what I'd be doing tomorrow.

It might be even more dangerous if I did what I planned while alone with individual people out observing the wildlife.

I'd merely asked fairly innocent questions up to this point.

But starting tomorrow, as difficult as it would be for me, I intended to make some really nasty accusations.

And see which ones stuck. If any.

I actually slept that night after returning to my bed, Sasha again beside me on the floor.

I woke early, which was how I'd planned it.

I was planning a lot for this Saturday. I didn't assume I'd get many days off while working here at the sanctuary, weekends or not, though I'd take some relaxation time now and then when it seemed appropriate.

Not that I'd necessarily get to talk to everyone as quickly as I wanted, but I had to take advantage of whatever opportunities arose.

I would talk with everyone. Alone, yet not far from help if anything went wrong.

Would I actually figure it out by accusing people?

Would the detective arrive and delay my dangerous, but hopefully ultimately successful, undertaking?

Maybe the timing would be perfect. I'd no idea when Detective Christopher would arrive. Or if any other authorities would be around doing their investigative tasks.

But ideally, I'd figure out whodunit at a time some official was there to help me.

I shoved back the sorrow and irritation in my mind over the fact that the person who helped me definitely wouldn't be Liam.

In any case, I'd be able to stop overthinking this and actually do something.

Hopefully successfully.

And come out of it alive, with my name cleared.

But if the worst happened?

I didn't want to be pessimistic. But I did write a note and leave it in the kitchen, where I figured someone would find it if I didn't survive.

In that case, I wanted someone who cared to wind up with my wonderful Sasha.

And I knew that in no way could Lettie be guilty of killing Oliver. Plus she knew what an asset my pup could be on tour boats in the summer. So, if my wishes were followed—and I certainly hoped no one would have to determine yes or no—Lettie would inherit Sasha.

Okay. Enough of that.

I stuck the pepper spray into one of my pockets, just in case. Then I took Sasha out in the cold Alaskan air. There was more snow on the ground this morning, plus some still flaking down, and we came back inside and ate our canine and human breakfasts.

"Let's go into the welcome area," I told Sasha. Wayne was likely to be ready with our assignments of the day.

My intent was that our director would be my first target, even though I felt fairly certain he wasn't the one I was after, especially after the discussion we'd already had.

Still, when we got inside, the lobby had a few folks in it, including those I might like to confront later today. Manager Neil? Sure. Wayne, yes, to get him out of my mind as any possibility. Carlo? He was another one I doubted was guilty, but what did I know . . . yet?

Was my current plan stupid? Maybe. If nothing else, it could be repetitive, since I'd already asked my targets some similar, though not as accusatory, questions. Still, if it was successful, my life would definitely change for the better.

And even if Oliver hadn't been my favorite person, his death would potentially be avenged.

As I waited and said good morning to each of those who entered, I saw Bill exit the hallway with Marnie. They'd already been doing food prep? Maybe. Theoretically, it could be worked on all night.

I wasn't sure how much Marnie intended to get out on the grounds today, if any, but since the weather was worsening, it could be a lot more than she'd been doing.

I saw Wayne standing a few steps up on the stairway, passing out our assignment pages. I'd been doing as I should and sticking my instructions in the recycle bins sometime during each day, but I wondered if everyone else was as diligent.

I supposed the few pages didn't matter a lot.

Wayne soon waved a paper in my direction, and I scooted through the group, leaving Sasha where we'd been standing, to get my assignment. When I glanced at it, I was both pleased and sorry. I was going out on the grounds again, possibly far out, to do some observation.

But that wouldn't allow me to work on what I'd determined would be the next step in my investigation. At least not as much as I'd have liked.

On the other hand, it just might make it a little easier, if I was careful. I could accuse, then run if things got messy.

"Looks good," I said to my winter boss. "I do have a few questions, though, and would like to go somewhere quiet to ask them."

The large director of the sanctuary stared at me with his brown eyes narrowed, as if attempting to read my thoughts. Conversely, I wished I could read his. No, I really didn't suspect him—much—especially since we'd talked about this before. But he might know which of his employees or volunteers was guilty and be attempting to protect them.

"Fine," he finally said. "My office in a few minutes, once I'm done here, and then I'll want you to get out on the grounds. I took a quick look myself early this morning way out there and saw moose walking in the direction of the trail fence. Not sure they continued or if they'll be easily visible, but you seem the right person to go check them out."

Which made my heart soar. Wildlife. Moose. Viewing them in their habitat in the wild.

The only thing that would make me happier would be being able to show them off to some tourists.

Assuming I even got a glimpse of them later. And assuming they were still where Wayne had suggested.

"Sounds great!" I said, and I meant it.

I waited till he'd had a couple of conversations with others, including Bill, who wanted to stay and help with food preparation more, but he was also directed to go out on the trails.

And manager Neil, who had a brief, quiet discussion with his boss, then went to take his parka off the hook, as several of the others were doing.

Then it was finally time to join Wayne in his office, Sasha at my side.

I hadn't been there since the first day I'd arrived, but it was the same as I recalled it: cluttered, with a shiny wood floor. I sat in the same chair facing his desk that I had before, and as always, Sasha sat beside me.

"So," Wayne said, after he'd settled into his desk chair, leaning forward slightly over his messy desk toward me. "What is it? You don't like your apartment. You don't want to stay here over the winter and figure you'll do something else in Juneau. You—"

Okay, I'd made the decision last night, and I jumped in to interrupt him. "I just want to know why you killed Oliver."

There. The first of what I figured would be several accusations, but also a test, since I didn't mean it.

He moved back in his seat and stared. "We already talked about what happened to Oliver. You know I didn't do it. I didn't want him dead, even if he wasn't the best manager. But you're aware of that. What's really going on?" Those brown eyes of his narrowed shrewdly. "I can guess. You're panicking, so you're starting to do more than ask questions. You're making accusations to get people focused on possible suspects other than you."

Smart man, but I'd known that.

"I'm not panicking," I said, without addressing the rest of what he'd said. "I just had some thoughts about what happened and why and who and . . . well, for now at least, you're at the top of my list." Not for long, I felt fairly certain. But this time I was the one to lean forward and continue, "I'd like to learn if I'm right. What was your real motive?"

190

He laughed. "Okay, say and do what you want. But let's go back to our prior conversation. Like you, I wasn't Oliver's best friend. But I didn't kill him. I'd like to know why you think I did, though."

"Did you try to fire him? Or—"

"I don't want to start a guessing game, especially when you're just fishing. And I don't think that's what you do on your tour boats in the summer—fish."

"True," I said. "You've reacted sort of like I figured you would. I won't ask you any more right now. But—"

"But you'll keep me at the top of your list. Oh, sure."

He stood and leaned toward me again, this time looking like the big-bear-ish person I considered him. If I'd really mistrusted him, I would have felt even better that we were here in his office and other people were around. Assuming someone would react if I screamed.

But I felt certain I wouldn't have to.

Wayne's movement caused Sasha to stand too, but she remained by my side, watching Wayne and gazing back toward me.

"I killed Oliver," Wayne continued, "and I'm admitting it to you right now, because I was peeved with the guy, and now I'm peeved with you." He paused. "Not. Or at least I didn't kill Oliver. I sometimes got peeved with him, and I'm definitely peeved with you because of this conversation. But I'm not about to kill you, and I didn't do him in either. Got it?" Before I replied, he said, "I hope so, but in any event it's time for you to start your work of the day and go observe some wildlife instead of making bizarre accusations." He pointed toward the door. "Outa here. And since I gather you were questioning a lot of people around here before, or so I heard, I assume now that you're going to start doing more to get a reaction. Accusing them."

Oh yes, he was wise. I just said, "I'm hoping things finally get resolved."

"Well, you just be damned careful. See you later." He sat back down and grabbed some of the messy papers in front of him. I'd definitely been dismissed.

By a guy I really didn't consider much of a suspect.

But I'd at least begun the next round in my investigation.

Who'd be next?

I gently tugged Sasha's leash as I stood, and we left the office. I closed the door behind me.

I'd be glad to get out on the trails and do some animal watching.

But I also wanted to do some more questioning today. More accusing.

Before the detectives actually appeared for the next round of *my* interrogation.

I saw Lettie in the lobby talking with Larraine. As much as I enjoyed my assistant's company, I didn't want to go out on the trails with her now.

With Larraine? She'd be one of those I'd try accusing to see her reaction. But I still hoped to do most of that in the main sanctuary area, where I could get help more easily if I needed it.

Carlo came in then. A fellow employee rather than a volunteer or administrator.

He hadn't been around the day Oliver was killed. Or at least that was the way it seemed.

But the idea of his being my number-two accusee seemed okay. As another test, at least.

"So, fellow employee," I said, walking up to him with Sasha beside me. "What are you up to today?"

"Wildlife observation," he replied in his slight Spanish accent. The dark-haired guy was wearing the beige jacket I'd seen him in before and appeared ready to go out in the cold, although the jacket remained unzipped. "Not sure which trail I'll be taking, but I'll be delighted to see whatever's out there."

That's right, he'd told me he'd moved to Alaska after falling in love with watching wildlife. He seemed like my kind of person, and he hadn't been here the day Oliver was killed.

Still, I'd try my new approach with him, again more for practice than because I considered him one of the most viable suspects.

"First, though," he continued, "I want to look in on that wolf you helped to save a few days ago. I think he's still here, isn't he?"

"Yes, as far as I know."

And his going in the clinic might be a good thing. I could accuse him right here in the welcome building with others nearby, just in case he did turn violent.

"In fact," I added, "I'd like to check on him too. I'll go with you. Dr. Skip isn't here, right?"

"I don't know."

We both went into the main hallway together, Sasha at my side.

"Is it wise to bring your dog there?" Carlo didn't sound thrilled about the idea.

"I always tie her leash on one of the door handles outside. Sasha's a good girl and will just stay there, out of sight of the wolf."

"That's fine, then," Carlo said, "even though the wolf will probably smell her."

That was what I believed too. But I was ready to do something I was sure Carlo wouldn't consider fine.

Even though I thought it was unlikely that he'd been involved in Oliver's death.

But he was an employee, and he'd been here before. On the off chance he'd had it in for Oliver, why not sneak in here and kill him when Carlo theoretically wasn't around?

And so, before we opened the door to the infirmary area, I placed myself in front of Carlo without tying Sasha to any door, just in case I needed my pup's help.

"Okay, Carlo," I said in a stern and angry voice. "Tell me right now and right here why you killed Oliver."

His smooth features grew rough, and his dark eyes narrowed. "I didn't kill him. You know I wasn't even here. Why would you accuse me like that?"

I saw his hands tighten into fists at his side.

Had I made a mistake getting this far away from other people, even with Sasha around to defend me? My dog clearly knew something was wrong, since she came over and stood at my side, looking up at Carlo, who glanced down at her.

Okay, there was always the pepper spray, but—

"I'm accusing you because I have reason to believe that you and Oliver disliked each other and that you were arguing." Since Oliver argued with everyone, I figured that was a safe assumption. "I don't know the details of why you disliked him that much. Why don't you tell me?"

Carlo stood still for a minute glaring at me, his fists opening and closing. "Look," he finally said. "You're right that Oliver and I weren't friends. He was a manager—he was brought in for the position I thought I was going to be promoted to. So he was my boss, and he liked telling me what to do. Often in a nasty, critical way. Never mind that I liked our wildlife here a lot more than he seemed to. He claimed now and then that I was scaring them when I went out to observe them."

Really? This was new information. I'd have to keep an eye out to make sure that wasn't true in the future.

"So that's why you killed him?"

"Not hardly." Carlo appeared to relax just a little. "He kind of threatened me once or twice, but I gathered it was just because he felt I knew more than he did about the wildlife. I can't say I'm happy about the way he left this place, but I'm glad he's gone. But look, Stacie. I don't know where you got the idea I could have killed him. I'm an animal lover too. I don't like the idea of killing anything or anyone. I told the cops who questioned me that. I'm well aware you're considered to be more of a suspect than I am. Is that why you're accusing me, to try to find someone you can point the authorities to go after instead of you?"

I relaxed a little. He'd figured it out, as Wayne had, not that it was so unclear. Maybe I was being too obvious. I'd have to keep that in mind.

"No," I said, figuring I'd lie again so we could both calm down a little more. "I am in touch with some of the authorities, though, so if I can, I want to help them." *And protect myself,* I thought, though I didn't confirm that this was the basis of my lies. My difficult lies, even though I'd started using them for a good reason. "I'd heard some things about how Oliver and you didn't get along, and, well—"

"You decided to accuse me before I accused you any further. I get it. But you can be absolutely, positively sure I didn't do anything to hurt Oliver. In fact, you know I love animals enough that if I did hurt Oliver, which I didn't, I certainly wouldn't attempt to make it look like one of our residents did it. Now let's go in and see how our injured wolf is doing, okay?"

"Okay," I said. I wanted to tell him I was glad he hadn't done it, but under my current method of investigation, I still wanted to seem aggressive and angry. I hung Sasha's leash on a doorknob, edged my way around Carlo, and opened the door to go peek in on Tikaani.

Who was standing there in his enclosure, pacing and limping a little but appearing better than I'd seen him before.

"Hey," I whispered to Carlo. "He looks good!"

"I'm so glad," Carlo responded, again making me feel fairly sure he was innocent.

Unless Oliver had somehow harmed Tikaani. But that didn't appear to be the case.

Chapter Seventeen

S o what was next today? Maybe I could actually start doing my job here at the sanctuary and go out and observe animals again.

Hopefully the herd of moose Wayne had mentioned. And more.

It was Saturday, but I hadn't seen any tourists or others who might want to be shown around the park, which was only going to become more of the norm as the winter progressed. Much as I'd like to do my tour guide thing, it wasn't going to happen, and certainly not today, assuming it ever became my assignment, which was highly unlikely. That wasn't why I was here.

But as Sasha and I headed down the hall, Carlo behind us, I let my mind wander back to my tour guiding.

Instead of veering again into what I really needed to do: confront more people, especially anyone I thought could have been the one to kill Oliver.

And who was that?

I only wished I knew.

As we passed the door leading to the kitchen area, I saw it was ajar, and heard voices. I peeked inside.

Surprise, surprise. Marnie was in there, and Bill was with her.

So he was continuing to help with food preparation. He must really enjoy it. Presumably, Wayne wouldn't assign him to be here if he hated it.

I'd even seen him doing it when Oliver was around. And I'd have to do my accusation thing with him, and with Marnie, to keep my plan going.

Even though I had no reason to believe either of them had harmed Oliver either.

In fact, though they had griped a bit with him, I'd thought they were friends.

Even so—

"I think I'll pop in here before going out onto the grounds," I said as I turned back to Carlo. "See if there's any help needed, including taking some of the animals' foods out there."

"Good idea," Carlo said, and he also stopped. "Me too."

I opened the door and walked in, Sasha behind me. I was surprised to see Marnie and Bill heading our direction with large boxes in their arms.

"Hi," Marnie said. "This could be really good timing. Were you coming in to help?"

"Well . . . yes," I said. Even if that wasn't why I was here, I was always glad to be of assistance.

"Good." She thrust the boxes in her arms at me, and I took them. They were as heavy as they appeared, but manageable. Marnie said, "Please go with Bill to take these out and load them into one of the ATVs. I have a few more things to get before going out there. And since you're here too, Carlo, you can help me in the kitchen for a minute."

She turned her back again. Carlo glanced at me as he passed to join her, as if questioning whether I was okay with this. And I was.

I was always glad to do something to help our wildlife in any way possible.

And this would give me a few minutes to confront another suspect. In fact, I hadn't talked directly to Bill before about Oliver. I knew the two of them had snapped at each other now and then, though I didn't know of any reason Bill would have been the killer.

But now I could hopefully learn more.

"Let's go on out there," he said now. "You okay with it? I can manage to get the doors. Will Sasha walk along with us, or will she make it harder for you to carry those boxes?"

"We'll be fine," I said, and as we walked into, then through, the lobby, I saw others looking at us. "Guess we won't be out there long, so no need for our jackets for now." We both wore sweatshirts, after all.

"Exactly."

Lettie was there, and she scooted ahead to open the doors for us. "Are you okay?" she asked. "Do you need any more help?"

"Not now, but thanks for asking," I said. As Bill and I walked along the slick pavement toward the garage where the vehicles were kept, balancing boxes as Sasha stayed with us, I asked, "Where will Marnie be taking these? Which animals are they for?" I suspected the boxes contained meats. Although Marnie was getting grains and growing items prepared for when the foragers couldn't get anything from the ground or trees, she hadn't been taking that stuff out much yet, as far as I knew. The carnivores were separated enough by species not to be able to hunt much, and Marnie had been taking supplies to them more often.

"I think these are for your friends the wolves," Bill said as we reached the door to the garage. "It's some of the frozen raw meats that are sent in bulk, now thawed and kneaded and combined with nutritional stuff, ready for them to eat."

"Got it," I said. "Maybe I'll get to see some of that later, since I'm supposed to be going onto the grounds now, though I'm assigned to watch some moose." I hesitated. It was time. I could do with Bill what I'd begun to do with the others who at least theoretically could have been Oliver's attackers.

But first I waited till Bill put his packages on the ground and opened the rear of one of the large ATVs with sturdy wheels. He bent down again, then stacked his boxes inside and reached for mine, which I handed him.

Okay, now it really was time, I figured as he grabbed the raised hatch door and brought it down.

When he'd finished, I stood staring at him, Sasha standing beside me. My husky sensed my tension and reacted accordingly. Protectively.

"Before we go back," I said, "I'd like to know why you killed Oliver."

His brown eyes widened as his brows, which weren't quite as gray as his hair, furrowed. His scowl looked more than angry. It looked . . . well, a little scary.

Had I gotten it right this time?

If I yelled out, would anyone hear me besides Sasha? My dog was definitely on alert.

"Why on earth would you ask that?" Bill's voice came out as an angry growl as he took a step toward me, causing Sasha to make a small noise in her throat like the beginnings of her own growl, though she didn't move.

Bill didn't deny it, though.

Did that mean . . . ?

"Because I want to know the answer." I managed to make myself sound forceful and accusative, or at least I hoped so despite the way my insides were churning with fright.

"I. Didn't. Kill. Him." Bill's words came out individually, as if that made them true.

But were they?

They did constitute his denial.

"Why would I?" he continued, backing down a bit both in his tone and in his stance, even though his hands were now in fists. He'd taken a step back, though Sasha didn't relax beside me. "I didn't know the guy well. I've been volunteering here longer than he'd worked here, and I definitely didn't like his attitude about some things, including how he acted with you and your dog. But kill him? No way."

I considered beefing up my accusations, thinking about how I could ascribe a motive to him that he could deny—and maybe then he'd come up with something different. But before I did, I heard a noise behind me. The door into the garage opened then, and Marnie and Carlo walked in, also holding large boxes.

Good thing Bill hadn't attacked me, or he'd have been caught.

And I figured I'd have to add him to my list of people I'd accused who'd told me where to go without admitting anything.

Maybe this way of investigating wasn't such a good idea after all.

So far, I hadn't figured out who was actually guilty. And could I be sure the few people I'd already confronted were really innocent?

I wasn't certain.

Not even now, when Bill ran over to take the boxes from Marnie and help her get them in the back of the large all-terrain vehicle where our boxes now were.

She thanked him, and the smile he gave her was an entirely different expression from the furious scowl he'd leveled at me.

She then helped get the boxes Carlo had carried into the ATV too.

"Thank you all so much," she said. "And I'm sure there are wolves out there, and hopefully some bears if we get out far enough. Some of this food would be okay for them, even though they're omnivores and are also happy with plants, and it's too soon for any to hibernate. The weather so far may let us go as far as we want."

"We'll give it a try," Bill said, and I had a passing thought that I wished I could go with them. I'd seen many different forms of wildlife in the few days I'd been officially working at Juneau Wildlife World, but I hadn't seen a lot of bears.

For now, though, I exited the garage along with Sasha and Carlo as we watched Bill drive the ATV away, heading toward one of the major pathways into the sanctuary.

It was finally time for me to go out too, to see any of the moose Wayne had set me up to observe.

On my own, except for Sasha.

I wasn't sure where Carlo would go, and as far as I knew, all the others set to observe had already headed to their lookouts.

The idea of having a while when I wasn't with anyone, wasn't accusing anyone, sounded good. Especially since my latest idea hadn't provided me with any new clues.

Of course, there were several others I could accuse, and I figured some of them had more potential to be the real killer than those I'd already questioned.

I probably wouldn't find out more today, though. At least not till Sasha and I returned to the welcome building later and I could determine if there was anyone else I could drag off—figuratively—and accuse.

Or maybe that was enough for my first day of accusations.

Tomorrow would be another day.

For now, I hurried back inside the main building to get my parka. I'd be going out into the wild, where it was cold.

And I figured I'd enjoy it a lot, especially if I was bundled up enough not to freeze.

Soon Sasha and I were back out. I'd put her boots on to keep her paws warm, and we headed in the direction we most often took on starting out, through the parking lot and onto the trail that would take us far into the sanctuary if we wanted.

Cold, yes. With some snow flurries in the air and a skift on the ground, even on the roadway, which I knew had been cleared earlier by whoever Wayne had directed to do it.

But yes, winter was definitely approaching.

Even so, I enjoyed our afternoon. I did see Bill driving the ATV past us a while later and wasn't sure where in the sanctuary they'd go first, but the wolves were probably on the agenda now, as well as possibly the bears.

I didn't take Sasha far enough to see the wolves, though. I soon discovered the area where the moose ranged partway between the trail and the mountains in the distance.

I got to observe a small herd. They were far enough away that I couldn't see them well, even with my binoculars, but I could tell they were foraging in an attempt to get whatever dead leaves or twigs or other growth remained on the ground beneath the snow, since I saw their jaws moving as they lifted their heads.

I made physical and mental notes for my report later. I removed my gloves temporarily to make it easier to write, flexing my fingers a lot so they didn't freeze.

And I smiled a lot. This was why I was here.

And what happened anywhere else, including my need to investigate a murder to save myself, was put on hold for a happy while.

I even told Sasha how delighted I was, keeping my voice nice and low, though we were far enough away I doubted the moose paid attention, even if they could hear something from this direction. Which they probably could. Moose were known for their keen hearing, which to some extent was attributed to their antlers.

I was cold but was more concerned about how Sasha felt. But she seemed happy enough to be with me, to walk around in her doggy boots and sniff the air, as if she could catch the smell of the distant wildlife, which I believed she often did.

I loved it out here with just the two of us. And I managed not to think too much about what I'd been doing back at the welcome building. And what I intended to continue to do, right or wrong, until Oliver's killer was determined.

Whether or not it was me who discovered them. I hoped the authorities would be the ones to solve the mystery.

Still, it was hard to get it out of my mind.

I stayed out there for quite a while with Sasha. And eventually, we weren't alone.

Lettie and Larraine joined us.

Drat. Much as I really liked my wonderful assistant, I kind of wished only Larraine was there. She was one person I hadn't yet accused and noted a reaction from.

And I wouldn't do that with Lettie around, even though I knew she would understand what I was doing and why. Or at least I could explain it to her afterward if she didn't.

Yes, I considered it. But Lettie and Larraine soon moved on, apparently toward the area where the wolves were and maybe beyond, though they indicated they wouldn't stay too long and would return to the welcome building soon.

Which made me figure it was time for Sasha and me to do the same. It was too late for us to grab lunch with the group, but it wouldn't hurt to get something to eat before dinnertime.

Still, I was thrilled on our walk back to see a few Sitka deer in the distance, though the moose were no longer visible. More wildlife. More reason for me to be out here.

I would soon be off this path. What would I see, and learn, the rest of this day?

Nothing, as it turned out. Or nothing important.

Or useful.

I first went in to file my report. No one else was there at the time.

Then we headed for the food machine building. A few people, including Neil, Shawna, and Carlo, were sitting together at a table and engaged in a conversation, so I grabbed a seat at a different place to eat and give Sasha a little bit of my sandwich.

They all aimed glances toward us now and then. Were they talking about my accusations? I hadn't spoken to Shawna or Neil yet, but Carlo might have told them about my nasty conversation with him and said he denied everything.

It might be harder if the others knew. Would they assume from Carlo that I might accuse them too?

Maybe Carlo would be too embarrassed to mention it, but I couldn't count on it. And if rumors had started spreading around here, I probably wouldn't get anywhere accusing anyone else. They'd be prepared. Maybe even laugh at me for even trying this way.

And who knew if I'd ever get the truth from whoever actually killed Oliver anyway?

Maybe my latest cycle of blame to hopefully get answers was over. I certainly hadn't received any answers so far.

And I still didn't know who to point my fingers at next.

Okay, it wasn't like I was a real detective. The fact that I'd actually succeeded in solving one murder didn't mean I had any real experience to solve another.

Even when I appeared to be the main suspect.

So, what should I do next?

I had no idea. But maybe standing down till something dawned on me, or a person started really standing out as the killer, was the way to go.

And right now, being friendly with people I'd be hanging out with here at the sanctuary as the weather got worse probably wasn't a bad idea.

I rose, and holding my food and moving with Sasha, I approached the table. It was large enough that there were a couple of additional seats.

"Mind if I join you?"

"Sure, go ahead," Carlo said. The others didn't object. In fact, they both seemed to watch me as if they were waiting for me to say something interesting.

I didn't stay long, but everyone was cordial, even Carlo. We talked about the wildlife we'd seen today. Others had seen mostly moose too.

Soon I left with Sasha and took another hike, this time from the back area of the sanctuary. There I observed just a few mountain goats in the distance.

And pondered as I walked. What next? Did I want to try accusing anyone else? Did I dare?

Would it be useful if I did?

I had no idea. And that was bad. I always liked to take charge of things in my life, like studying, then taking on a career devoted to something I loved: wildlife. Coming to Alaska. Getting what seemed like a perfect job—providing tours.

And working at a very special wildlife sanctuary in winter?

Oh yes.

But . . . what was going to happen to me now? Would the right person be found and convicted of Oliver's murder?

Would the wrong person—me—be arrested?

I realized it was getting late. Despite my earlier thoughts about hanging out with people, I wished I'd figured out a way to hike this afternoon with Lettie. It would have been good to have someone friendly by my side.

"Along with you," I said to my wonderful companion, bending down to hug Sasha.

There wasn't anything more I could do at the moment but continue to worry, so I went back to the welcome building. A good thing, not only because of the cold. It was snowing again, but lightly, fortunately.

As I arrived, I saw Dr. Skip leave in his vehicle. He must have come to check on Tikaani and to see if any other animals needed attention, which thankfully didn't seem to be the case.

I did my report and walked Sasha again for a short while. I saw Wayne in the computer room, but he was looking over Larraine's shoulder as she typed her report too.

I waved good-night to both of them, then took Sasha to our apartment, where, after feeding my dog, I put together one of the dinner packets I'd brought.

I made myself watch TV that night. We didn't get a lot of channels, but I found another sitcom that I could stand to watch.

And then the news, but nothing was mentioned about any murder investigations—or the cops zeroing in and arresting Oliver's killer.

Bedtime soon after that.

Without much sleep.

I woke early, as usual, and took Sasha for a walk without seeing anyone else. I'd look forward to getting my instructions of the day from Wayne—which hopefully would involve going out there to view more wildlife.

That was who I was. Where I was. What I really wanted to do here.

And I wanted to continue that way through the winter, talking to other people but without accusations, unless my mind-set changed again and I decided once more that it would help.

I fed Sasha, then headed back downstairs. It was still early. I considered taking a quick walk before I got my instructions but decided to eat first.

I got a breakfast sandwich from one of the machines and a small cup of coffee and finished them quickly. Then I started bundling up again, including putting warm socks on Sasha.

But before I got anywhere, my phone rang. I took it from my pocket and froze—and not because of the weather.

I recognized the number. Unfortunately.

"Hello?"

"Hello, Stacie. I assume you're already at Juneau Wildlife World today," Detective Lillian Christopher said.

"That's right." I wished I could lie about it, but to what avail? She'd probably just ask where I was anyway.

Although I hoped she didn't really give a damn.

I wasn't that lucky. "Good," she said. "I'll be there in about an hour, road conditions permitting. We need to talk."

Chapter Eighteen

What?

My mind raced. Maybe I could tell her I had to be out on the trails working with the wildlife here.

Maybe I could tell her I misspoke, that I wasn't at the sanctuary after all.

But lying now, or even running away, wouldn't make her intention to talk to me again disappear.

I searched for something to say. The best I could come up with was, "I've already told you all I know about the situation regarding Oliver Brownling. I assume that's what you want to talk about, right?"

"That's right. And I have just a few more questions for you."

"You could ask me right now, over the phone," I blurted. Seeing her in person, letting her accuse me face-to-face, had to be a whole lot worse than sitting here and doing it at a distance.

"No," she said firmly, though she sounded a whole lot calmer than I felt. "It'll be better if we talk in person. See you soon."

I half expected her to say I'd better be here. That she'd already sent some of the troopers who had been here before investigating the premises and surroundings, so I'd better not run.

She didn't add any of that. But that was the way my mind went anyway.

I pressed the button to end my side of the conversation without saying good-bye. Why bother?

But I kept my phone in my hand as I stared at the wall in front of me. I'd gotten closer to it as I'd spoken, my back to the rest of the room and the people in it. I had a frantic urge to call Liam, but what could I say? What could *he* say? Even if he knew this latest interrogation of me was pending, he hadn't done anything about it, and undoubtedly couldn't.

"Hey, Stacie, are you okay?" Larraine's voice startled me. I turned toward her. She was near where I stood just off to the side of one of the food machines. A lot of other people were near us too, though I didn't think any were looking at me, fortunately, except maybe Lettie.

Sasha, though, moved slightly at my feet, recognizing my anxiety.

My first reaction to Larraine's question was to consider letting myself burst into tears and reveal who I'd heard from and why, and how scared I was.

But my self-preservation, and wisdom, somehow took over. Maybe I could use this upcoming situation to my advantage. To figure out who really was guilty.

To take some pressure off me.

Right.

How?

I made myself respond with as much of a smile as I could manage. Hey, I was a strong person. I'd take care of myself.

"Oh, I just got a call from one of those detectives." So how could I use this information to my advantage? I didn't know . . . yet. But I still tried. At least I'd kept my voice low, so I could claim anything I wanted about the call. "We decided she should come here to talk more. I've got some ideas to run by her." Yeah, like *Look at everyone else around here and leave me alone.* "She'll be here soon."

I didn't hear a lot of conversation around us, so I figured at least some of the others had heard what I'd said too. Fine. None approached. None asked any questions or offered any sympathy— or further accusations.

I was on my own in many ways. Which probably was a good thing.

Or at least I'd try to make it come out as well as possible.

Without getting taken into custody for something I definitely didn't do. Definitely hadn't wanted, no matter what I'd thought about Oliver.

"You asked to talk to her?" That was Lettie, the only one who'd joined us, which didn't surprise me.

Not at all, my mind screamed, but I needed to continue my optimistic attitude. My in-charge attitude, especially around these actual suspects who'd been around when Oliver was killed: Larraine, Neil, Wayne, and Bill. Carlo was here now and it was harder to consider him a suspect, since he hadn't been at the sanctuary then, but who knew? And not everyone who'd been around then was hanging out just now in the vending machine building.

My response to Lettie? "Sure. You know I've been asking a lot of questions around here, and they've resulted in some ideas I can run by her. I'm fully aware I'm still a suspect, but you know I didn't do it."

And so did at least one person who'd been at the sanctuary at the time, whether or not they happened to be in this room right now. But hopefully, since I was being blunt, everyone would wind up hearing that I theoretically had requested the detective to come and talk to me and hear my ideas.

Yes, I'd have to be careful. But I'd tried to be careful during my own amateur interrogations—and accusations—anyway. And I could always hope that whoever had really killed Oliver would be so nonplussed by this surprise aspect, if they weren't already, that they would do something to give themselves away.

"Absolutely," my dear buddy Lettie said.

Without referring to anything I'd said, Wayne handed me my instructions for the day, before doing the same for the others present rather than waiting till we all showed up. He looked at me long and hard as he gave me mine but didn't comment.

And I didn't mention I had an upcoming commitment, though I figured he'd heard what I'd discussed with Lettie.

Her instructions were apparently similar to mine again today. "So, are you going out onto a trail for now?" Lettie asked. "Would love to go with you."

"For a few minutes," I said. I didn't know how long it would take the detective to get here, especially since I wasn't aware of the current road conditions, but it should take her a minimum of forty minutes.

Which meant I couldn't go far, but a walk, and a view of any wildlife that might be nearby, might help calm my nerves.

Might being the operative word.

And any little bit would be better than the tension I was currently feeling.

Sasha and I walked with Lettie for a short while along the trail right off the parking lot. Sure enough, we saw wildlife in the far distance on the mountainside, a couple of moose.

And with that to boost my mood, my dog and I said a temporary good-bye to my tour assistant, who was going much farther, or so she said, without us.

I tried not to feel sad about that as Sasha and I turned back toward the welcome building. I'd miss seeing more.

And could only hope I'd be around to go out again later. And tomorrow. And the next day.

I checked as we reached the parking lot but didn't see any cars I didn't recognize.

When Sasha and I returned to the lobby, I looked around. No one was there. Presumably all those who worked here, officially or as volunteers, were off doing what they were supposed to.

I didn't want to just wait around for the detective, and I didn't particularly want to interrupt Wayne from whatever he was involved with. I hadn't done enough to file a report yet, so there was really nothing I needed to discuss with him.

I figured I could go to my apartment or back to the vending machine building, but neither sounded appealing.

I decided to go to the food preparation area. I couldn't really get involved with the work, but I could let Marnie know I might be able to help later.

Sasha and I went through the doorway and into the hall leading to the kitchen.

I wasn't particularly surprised to see that Marnie wasn't alone as she stood working with food along the wide counter. Nor was I surprised that the person with her was Bill. The guy appeared to enjoy food prep, and I figured that Wayne was okay with assigning him here a lot.

"Hi," I said. "Just wanted to let you know that even though my assignment for the day is out in the field as usual, I'll be glad to help out later, if I can."

"Thanks," Marnie said. She seemed to hesitate. "Have you had your . . . discussion with the detective yet?"

Obviously, Bill had heard my conversation with Lettie and had passed it along to Marnie, who hadn't been in the vending machine area at the time.

"Not yet," I said, as cheerfully as I could manage. "But it should be interesting."

Oh yeah, I thought. And no need to mention my bright idea of claiming I'd triggered the discussion to let the detective know my latest ideas. Or suspicions.

"Anyhow," I continued, "Guess I'd better go wait for her."

Where, I wasn't sure. But I didn't think I'd accomplish any more here—especially since both Marnie and Bill were regarding me with expressions I couldn't quite read. Were they suspicious? Angry? Sympathetic?

All of them, or none of the above?

I watched for a short while as they continued their work but couldn't really get my mind into learning anything. No, I supposed it would be better if I returned to the lobby to wait.

Wayne was there as Sasha and I returned. "I just got a call. The detective is almost here, so I need to go let her in the front gate. She wants to meet with you in the same office where she interviewed people before, which works fine. Do you want to wait for her there?"

No, I want to run, my mind hollered, but I knew better than to say it—or run. "Sure," I said. "Sasha and I will go up now."

Which we did. As I'd assumed, the office wasn't locked. I sat down not at the desk, which was where I'd been situated before during my interrogation, but on one of the chairs facing it, Sasha at my side. Detective Christopher could decide where she wanted to sit as she bombarded me this time.

Or . . . I still hoped to turn this into not only an interrogation, as she wanted, but also a discussion. A sort-of-friendly discussion. One that could have at least some good results for me.

Well, probably not really friendly. But calm and mutually informative could be good.

I looked around the office. Nothing had changed from before. It was small, unoccupied, with skimpy chairs in front of the desk. I thought about pulling out my phone to take up the time as I waited, but I figured it wouldn't be long. And to preoccupy my mind that way wouldn't help anything.

I needed to think. And worry. I couldn't really plan anything, since I didn't know what her questions would be this time.

So, yes, worry was the dominant thing I dealt with.

It was only a few minutes later when a brief knock sounded on the door and it was pushed open. Wayne popped his head in first and looked at me, then down at Sasha, who had stood up at the sound.

"Good. You're here."

He disappeared, and Detective Lillian Christopher entered.

"Hello, Stacie," she said, her tone calm. She too glanced at Sasha but didn't draw closer to pat her either.

"Hello, Detective," I responded. I'd stood up, and now I waited to see what she would do.

She didn't offer to shake my hand, which was fine with me. Neither did she head for the other chair on this side of the desk, which was where she had sat last time with Detective John Daniels. Instead, she went behind the desk, where I'd sat the last time. She gestured for me to sit, and I did.

She looked similar to last time, wearing a dark suit with slacks. Her dark hair framed her face, and her hazel eyes seemed planted on me, as if she hoped to read what was inside my head.

That wasn't going to happen. Not if I could help it.

But I wished I could see inside hers.

She remained quiet for a minute as she looked at me, and I had an urge to scream out *Why are you here?* But I figured it would be better for me to stay silent and let her run things . . . at least at first.

Eventually, she said, "As I said on the phone, I have some questions for you."

Oh yeah, as if I didn't recall that. "What questions are those?" I figured I didn't really have to ask. She'd let me know in her own good time.

But starting a conversation, rather than just waiting, seemed like a better idea if she didn't start soon.

But she did. She leaned over the desk a bit, her gaze not wavering from mine. "I'd like some further information from you."

I waited, figuring she would let me know what information she was talking about. Like, maybe, how had it felt to kill Oliver? Ha!

My tension grew as she didn't say anything for another few seconds. But I attempted to appear interested and unruffled and potentially willing to respond, depending on what she asked.

She sighed, then, and sat back. "Look, Stacie," she said. "We still don't have enough evidence to have you taken into custody for Mr. Brownling's homicide. But neither have you been exonerated."

I was glad to hear the first part. They could have theoretically found some false evidence, after all, and decided to arrest me. But the second part made me shudder.

Still, that was enough to prod me to talk. "You won't find any evidence like that, at least nothing real. I didn't do it. And I should be exonerated. Period."

She snorted a brief laugh. "Okay, let me get to the point. We've still been questioning other people who were here at the time of Mr. Brownling's death and haven't determined anyone more likely to have done it than you. But some of them have informed us about what you've been doing: questioning them too. Even accusing them of his murder—to see their reactions, I assume."

Yes, I felt proud of that. And nervous, especially with the detective. And scared now, since she'd discussed hoping to find enough evidence to take me into custody.

And it was interesting that anyone I'd questioned would have let the detectives know. I supposed they could have phrased things to make it clear that what they'd told me was about their perfect innocence.

But their even mentioning it might have given the detectives an indication of my innocence. If I'd been guilty, why would I have mentioned the situation to anyone else, let alone conducted my own inquisition? And accusations?

"That's true," I said to Detective Christopher.

"You were potentially putting yourself in danger," the detective said. "Assuming your innocence."

As if I didn't know.

Her expression didn't appear concerned. Maybe accusative. Again. This wasn't about protecting me.

"But since you've been doing it, to best conduct our investigation now," she continued, "I'd like you to let me know everyone you talked to and what they said."

I hesitated. What should I respond? Was it time for me to hire a lawyer?

"I've spoken with almost everyone who was here that day, I think, and a couple who weren't," I said. "I'm still working on it, but so far I can't point you to someone and say they did it, here's what I've learned, and here's the proof you're looking for."

"I assumed that would be the case, or you'd have let us know," she said, leaning back and appearing frustrated.

As was I.

But no one had manufactured and handed over anything that seemed like genuine evidence against me either.

Yet.

"Look," I said, "as you've no doubt learned, Oliver wasn't exactly the friendliest person here. Or the one everybody liked best. He irritated me because of his attitude against my Sasha, as I've said." I considered running down the list of those I'd talked to who'd admitted not being best buddies with the guy who'd been murdered. I'd also been making a list in my head, but I'd hesitated to write anything down in case this detective, or other authorities, got a warrant and started going through my possessions.

On the other hand, my thoughts didn't prove anything, unfortunately. And who'd come after me because of my unexpressed accusations? No one. Not yet, at least.

But I hadn't given up trying to find the truth. I couldn't. Not until I was cleared.

"Why don't we go over everyone you're aware of who was here that day, and you can tell me which of them you consider the most likely suspects and why."

Apparently, they didn't have real evidence against any of us.

That wasn't necessarily a good thing for me.

"Okay," I said hesitantly, then decided to do as much as I could to help myself. "I assume you've already considered all of us. And you've questioned all of us—including those I already accused, just to see their reactions. Fortunately, no one tried to kill me, but the bad thing about that is that I don't really know who's guilty. The only physical evidence I've heard about is that there has to be something that was used to pull open Oliver's throat, since it wasn't canine teeth. Have you figured out what was used?"

And will you tell little amateur me? I figured I already knew the answer to my unspoken question.

"The investigators appear to have a good idea what it was," she said, "but so far haven't found it. And they haven't determined who might have created it. They apparently did a good job, though, since the similarity to wolf bites was quite good."

Okay, nothing helpful there. Except that the detectives did, fortunately, realize the weapon had been manufactured in some way and that the wolves here were not genuine suspects.

Wildlife lover me was glad about that, at least.

"So now, let's go over the people here," she said. She appeared to wait for me to begin.

And so I did, starting with Wayne and continuing with manager Neil, then Larraine, Marnie, Bill, Carlo, and yes, even my buddy Lettie, and also Jesse, Bobbie, and Shawna, whom I hadn't questioned yet.

I mentioned those who'd appeared not to be best friends with Oliver and who'd admitted irritation with him. That included quite a few, though I admitted to myself that the causes of their irritation didn't seem a big deal. There was that slight altercation I'd seen between him and Bill. And Larraine had appeared to feel rejected, and Marnie had rejected Oliver's interest, and Neil seemed to dislike him as an alternate manager, and Carlo appeared unhappy that Oliver had gotten the manager job instead of him and had also pushed him about how he treated wildlife . . . Well, I supposed that any of them could have done it.

None of those reasons seemed serious enough to murder him over, though.

Of course, neither did his pushing me so much about keeping Sasha away, but that was apparently enough for the authorities to keep me at the top of their suspect list.

Fortunately, it hadn't led to their arresting me, and from what this detective had indicated, they were still trying to solve the murder.

Under the circumstances, so was I.

"That's it?" she asked when I was done.

Lark O. Jensen

I pondered for a few seconds but couldn't come up with any-one else to add. Dr. Skip? But he hadn't been around that day, as far as I knew. Of course, I hadn't confronted him.

And I'd no idea what he'd thought about Oliver, if anything.

I mentioned him to the detective, though, and indicated I hadn't spoken with him.

"Okay," she said. She didn't look happy. "I guess we're done here. I've got some more people to talk to while I'm around, but I assume you've been open with me about all this. As I said, I heard you'd been accusing people and I wanted to know more. I need to keep on with our investigation." She stood and headed toward the door.

I stood too, Sasha beside me, wanting to sigh in relief, but I didn't really feel relieved.

What would come next?

Detective Christopher put her hand on the doorknob, then turned back toward me. "Let me know if you learn anything use-ful. And—" She actually smiled. Sort of. "Assuming you actually are innocent, please be careful."

Chapter Nineteen

I hurried down the stairs in the welcome building with Sasha. It was late morning, and I didn't expect to see many, if any, people in the lobby.

I was right. It was empty.

My nerves were still shaky, and I wondered where the detective was heading. Who she would talk to next.

Whether she would accuse me of murder, even if it was to get whoever she spoke with to perhaps say something that would instead point fingers at them.

Ha. It hadn't happened yet, and it was unlikely to happen today.

The detective had seemed . . . not quite friendly. But certainly not as accusatory as before. She had asked questions that seemed pertinent to her supposed reason for talking to me again.

But had this been some kind of ploy with her? I'd hoped to learn something helpful in our conversation, but I hadn't learned much at all.

I was still a suspect. What had she been looking for?

Maybe she'd meant everything and was just seeking my help after hearing I'd been demanding answers from others.

Maybe.

And if so, I hadn't been able to tell her much.

I grabbed my parka from the rack, pulled Sasha's boots from the pocket, put them on her, and headed outside.

Into the cold. And onto the usual trail.

I had to think. Maybe I could use what had happened to my advantage. Somehow.

A lot of the people here had already known the detective was coming to this sanctuary to quiz me. She apparently was talking to others too, despite her having made it sound as if I were the only one she needed to speak with today. It made perfect sense for me to talk to a few others later too—ask about their conversations with her and tell them something about mine, though not everything.

And observe them. Their reactions. Anything that might give the killer away.

Right.

Nothing had before.

"Okay, Sasha, enough of this," I told my sweet dog, who'd easily kept up with my fast hiking along the main trail. So far, I figured, her thick coat was keeping her warm enough. Still, for what I had in mind for the moment, I might have been better off grabbing one of the ATVs to go way out there, but I really needed to walk off some of my sudden energy.

And let my mind continue racing.

Surely something useful would occur to me.

Yeah. As it had previously.

Right now, I needed to keep walking despite the cold. And walk some more. And see whatever wildlife I could.

Fortunately, there were some moose in the first area, not quite where I'd seen them before but not too far away. I slowed, and so did Sasha. I found myself grinning at them, wishing, as I often did with the wildlife I viewed, that I could communicate with them.

Which wasn't going to happen. They ignored us as usual.

Sasha and I soon passed the first set of fences, and I recognized I was sort of heading to where I'd seen the wolves. Where I'd helped with Tikaani.

Where Oliver had later died.

And realized I was, in some ways, trying to run away. That too wasn't going to happen.

I needed to rethink things. Rethink people.

Rethink how I might be able to use my session with Detective Christopher this morning to my advantage.

By becoming buddies with her?

No.

But maybe it would help me realize my goals if others believed I had.

I almost stopped. Almost. But I did want to go see the wolf area before I returned to the welcome building.

We kept going till we reached the area in the fence where the gate was. I had an urge to go through it again, but I just stopped.

I was thrilled to see a small pack of wolves not too far away. They appeared to be eating something. It certainly wasn't a person. And though it was possible their food consisted of something Marnie and company had prepared and brought out here, the weather was still manageable enough that they might have found game on their own.

Sasha, sweet and smart dog that she was, sat down, also staring but staying still, as if she knew better than to upset them.

She probably did.

"Good girl," I said, keeping my voice low and resting my hand briefly on her head between her raised and moving ears.

I made some mental notes, as I had regarding the moose before. I was still on duty, after all, and would need to file a report.

I had an urge to stay longer. Or even head farther out on the trails, as I'd considered before.

But as much as I might enjoy viewing more animals, I realized I needed to get back to the welcome building, whether I felt welcome or not.

And interact with my fellow workers there.

And utilize what had happened to me this morning, my latest meeting with a detective, in a way that somehow would help me. And hopefully even help in solving the mystery hanging over all of us.

I figured that planning what to say to each of the others didn't make sense right now. I'd wing it, as I usually did.

I didn't know whether it was a good thing or not, but because I kept us hurrying again rather than taking our time hiking, it was just a bit past the usual lunchtime when Sasha and I returned to the main area. The car I believed to be the detective's was still there.

I apparently wasn't the only one she was spending time with today. I wished I could be a fly on the wall during her other conversations. I knew she wouldn't tell me the results, and I couldn't be certain of the truth of any descriptions I got from anyone else either.

So how would I handle this?

The best way I could, as usual.

Sasha and I went straight into the building with the vending machines. Considering the time, I figured at least some of my coworkers would be there getting lunch, unless they'd headed to their assigned apartments to eat.

But I'd been right. Several were there, some at the machines and others at the tables eating already.

So now what? I almost wanted to stand in the doorway and state that I'd met with the detective earlier, which a lot of them knew, though they didn't know the details of what we'd said.

I was curious about what everyone's reactions would be, but I figured that wasn't a good way to learn what I wanted to hear.

Instead, Sasha and I headed to the first table, where Marnie, Neil, Bill, and Lettie sat. "Hi, gang. Can I join you to eat?"

"Of course," Marnie said, sweeping her hand in a welcoming gesture. Bill nodded, and so did Lettie, although her expression was full of concern.

She clearly wondered how my morning had gone so far.

Well, I'd find a way to mention it here, and with others, to see what the reactions were.

I told Sasha to sit near the chair I'd be taking, then went to get my food—a chicken salad sandwich today, plus a bottle of water. I'd give my pup a bit of my sandwich, mostly some chicken pieces.

Wayne was at the first of the machines. He looked at me and asked in a low voice, "How was your meeting today?"

"Oh, quite good." I didn't attempt to be as quiet. "I think the detective and I are somewhat in sync, maybe even coming to the same conclusion about . . . what happened to Oliver. We're at least going to attempt to work together a bit more."

Okay, it didn't hurt to try that out on the guy in charge, I figured. Not that I was sure it would get me anywhere with anyone.

He looked bemused but didn't say anything else. When I turned, I saw that Carlo and Larraine were now behind us. They might well have heard what I'd said.

And a minute after I'd sat down at the table, they joined us too, after pushing another table up to mine to add spaces.

"So, you and the detective know who killed Oliver?" Carlo said. "Right? If so, why hasn't she arrested someone, or gotten the troopers out here to do it? And why was she still talking to people? We had a short conversation just a little while ago where she asked me more questions, but she sounded as if things were coming together."

I just shrugged and said, "Sorry, but I agreed not to tell anyone specifics of what we discussed, though it was productive. And where she goes with it now is up to her, though I have a good idea what'll happen, hopefully soon." I looked from Carlo into the eyes of the others around us one by one, attempting to look a bit amused but also relieved and even a bit accusatory without obviously focusing on any of them.

I wasn't sure whether one of them was the killer, but they could be. Of course, so could others. But I wanted them each to feel the detective and I were now cohorts in the investigation and had a good idea about who was guilty, even if it wasn't conclusive enough for her to have anyone taken into custody.

Yet.

Even without everyone being here, I had to assume those who were would talk to the others about the situation and report what I'd said. So I decided to juice it up a bit.

"So are any of you going to admit right now to being the killer?" I said, laughing. "Of course, the person we started zeroing in on might not be with us at the moment. Or they might be. Either way, I'm not allowed to say. I wouldn't *want* to say. Not until it's time for the authorities to finally do something about it and arrest someone—and that someone won't be me. But one of you . . . ?"

"Why won't you tell us?" Marnie's voice was shrill. "We could all be in danger."

That could be true. But her reaction didn't necessarily mean she wasn't the guilty one, though she seemed to be one of the least likely.

Maybe.

"I understand," I said quietly. "I've thought about that constantly, especially since, to make my innocence clear by attempting to figure out who did it, I've potentially put myself in danger.

At least now I'm fairly confident the authorities believe what I've said, that it wasn't me, no matter how obvious my disagreement with Oliver had been. And—well, I really can't talk much more about it. The detective has to do what she needs to, and they will be the ones who'll ultimately determine when it's time to bring in the person that evidence demonstrates must be the killer."

"What evidence?" Bill demanded. "As Marnie said, we could all be in danger, and we don't know who to protect ourselves from."

I took a drink of water from my bottle with one hand while I petted Sasha's head with the other. My pup had stood up, as if sensing my discomfort, as she often did. I tried to communicate to her that things were okay.

Then I said, "As I indicated, I can't get into specifics. For my part, I'm just glad that the truth is likely to come out soon. And the best I can tell all of you now is to be careful. Till things are resolved, assume any one of you could be the guilty person. That doesn't necessarily mean you're all in danger, since the person had something against Oliver but probably doesn't have a grudge against anyone else. Of course, they might be after me for pushing this, so I'm the one who has to be most careful, I guess."

"Yeah," Carlo said, leaning over the next table down from where I sat. "We now all have a grudge against you, after all, for snooping around every one of us."

"Oh, she's not that bad," Larraine said, across from me but a couple of seats in Carlo's direction. She was facing Carlo, but then turned back toward me. "She just started on this to try to protect herself."

I nodded.

"By accusing everyone else!" Carlo shouted.

I took a deep breath and soaked in the fact that I had made Carlo, and maybe others, very angry with my accusations. Was it an indication of his guilt or an outburst of frustration?

"I apologize to those I've accused unjustly," I said softly. "Whoever is guilty—you know who you are . . . and like I indicated, I can't even say if you're in this room with us right now. But if you are, I'd suggest you be smart about this. Things will come to a conclusion soon, so it makes sense for you to turn yourself in to the authorities and maybe even negotiate what comes next for you."

I looked across the table from me, where Marnie was. Bill was on her right and Larraine on her left. I looked from one face to the next, then leaned so I could also glance at those on my side of the table, who included Neil and also Wayne now, who'd joined us.

When Wayne caught my glance, he smiled grimly but stayed quiet.

I said nothing more after that. My mind raced, as it so often did, attempting to determine if there was something I could say, something I could do, to help resolve the situation right now.

But I figured I'd done the best thing for the moment. Having the guilty party ponder what I'd said, then confess to the appropriate people, sounded like a good thing to me.

But would they do it?

I supposed we would ultimately find out.

For now, though, I decided I'd had enough. I gave Sasha some of my remaining sandwich, finished the rest along with my bottle of water, and rose.

"Time for me to do my report of the morning, then go out in the sanctuary again this afternoon." Was I goading whoever it was to follow me and attack? I hoped not. "See you all later."

With me healthy, alive, and kicking.

I hoped.

As Sasha and I headed to the office where I could create my report for today so far, I realized how awful I felt. Again. Still.

What was I doing at this sanctuary now?

I loved the wildlife, of course, as I always did, but I missed being able to give tours, and I doubted any tourists would return here this winter, even if they were permitted to. And not only because of the murder, though that was undoubtedly a factor. But just our small dash outside just now had been highly uncomfortable. There was more wind than earlier, and it swirled the snow around us.

But I knew it wasn't horrible enough to send me to my apartment for the rest of the day.

But what if I quit the Juneau Wildlife World, returned to town, and found some kind of blah but potentially safer job there?

Although . . . would I be truly safe till Oliver's killer was in custody? Especially now, when I'd indicated that the detective and I had pretty much zeroed in on who it was.

I wasn't a coward, though. And I wanted to view more wildlife, no matter how hard it was.

And no matter how careful I had to be with the people around me.

As I entered the welcome building, the detective was just coming out. "Hello, Stacie," she said. "And Sasha." My dog wagged her tail as her head got a pat. "I'm just leaving now."

"I don't suppose you're going to call for some trooper backup to arrive to make the arrest we've been hoping for, are you?"

She laughed. "Don't you wish?" But then she grew more serious. "Not sure when I'll get here next, or any of the troopers either. I've heard the weather's about to grow a whole lot worse, and till we have something else to go on, it's likely to be a while. So be careful, Stacie."

At least that seemed to indicate that she still considered me innocent.

"I will," I assured her. And myself.

"You've got my contact info," she continued. "Call me if you learn anything helpful. And don't hesitate to call the troopers right away if things go bad. They can use helicopters even in fairly bad weather if necessary to get here."

"Thanks," I said, and stood there in the wind and snow at the edge of the parking lot as she headed toward her vehicle. I wondered who she'd just been talking to, since even Wayne had been with us. And who her major suspect was now—assuming she hadn't just been fooling about taking me down a notch or two on her list.

I watched as she drove off, with Sasha moving back and forth at my side. My dog clearly wanted to go walking, for the exercise or to do necessities or both.

And I wanted to go walking to see wildlife and to clear my head—although the latter seemed impossible.

So maybe now I'd hike more slowly with my pup, out in the same areas we'd visited earlier but not as far. We'd likely see more of the others heading out that way as well.

A good thing?

Maybe not. But the idea of getting away from this area and from most of the people, whom I didn't know if I could trust, sounded appealing.

And so Sasha and I once more headed through the parking lot and onto the main trail, not walking nearly as fast as this morning. The weather seemed to have improved a bit, although there still were snow flurries, and of course it was cold. I didn't intend to go as far, though I still hoped I'd see some of the animals—most likely moose, at least.

We'd walked only a short while before I heard voices from behind us. No footsteps, since it was hard to hear anyone approaching on the snow, despite it being only a thin accumulation so far.

But when I turned, I saw Carlo and Neil approaching. What was their plan for the afternoon? How far out on the sanctuary terrain did they intend to go?

They drew up to Sasha and me quickly. "Hey, Stacie, can we talk?" Neil asked.

Heck, he was the remaining manager. If he wanted to talk, I couldn't exactly object.

"We want to hike with you this afternoon," Carlo added.

"Okay . . ." I realized I must sound hesitant. Despite what I'd told everyone before, I didn't really know yet who'd killed Oliver, so being alone with them with no one else around didn't sound appealing.

And even though there were two of them, that didn't necessarily mean I'd be safer.

Judging by the way Oliver had been killed, my assumption had been that there was one killer.

But what if there were two?

And what if my position of supposedly being allied with the detective and knowing whodunit had triggered their desire to get rid of me, since I'd be easier for them to deal with than Detective Christopher?

"You look a little scared." Neil's voice sounded almost sympathetic. "I get it. And we mostly just want to learn a little bit more information from you. We've talked about it before and trust each other as not being the person who killed Oliver. And if you really know who did it, then you should trust us too."

The older guy paused, looking at me with pale-brown eyes that appeared sympathetic somehow. Trustworthy? Maybe.

"Neil's got it," Carlo said, standing beside him and pulling his parka a little closer against himself. His dark beard had flecks of snow in it. "We're as innocent as you, but we want to get more information on what you and the authorities do and don't know.

We figure that at the moment, at least, you're the best possible source."

Maybe my paranoia was showing. In any case, I was glad that Sasha stood close to me, and I felt her against my leg, as if she was being the defender that she always was.

"Tell you what," Neil said. "We understand these days why it's hard to trust anyone, but I figure there's one person you'll most likely believe." He pulled his phone from his pocket and pressed a button. "Hi, Wayne," he said, when someone answered. "Carlo and I want to hike a bit with Stacie, but her information might not be correct. Just in case she suspects one of us, can you let her know how guilty we really are in Oliver's death?" He handed the phone to me.

The display did indicate Wayne's name. I held it to my ear. "Hi," I said.

"I gather that my assumptions are correct and you don't really know yet who's guilty in Oliver's death." He sounded sarcastic. "I've talked with both Neil and Carlo, together and separately. In my opinion, you'd be safe hiking with either of them. And both? You're in good company. So have fun."

Right. Would I have fun?

Well, I might have an interesting discussion. And most likely a safe one.

And that was what was important.

Chapter Twenty

As it turned out, my walk with them was almost enjoyable, since we did go far enough to see some mountain goats and reindeer.

And our discussion was pleasant too.

Not at first, though. They were friendly enough until they started to ask me what I'd talked to the detective about that morning.

"Who's her main suspect?" Neil asked. He walked on my right side, though not very close, fortunately. "Same as yours? Who's on the top of the list?"

"Neither of us, I hope," Carlo added. He was on my left, at Sasha's far side.

Despite Wayne's reassurances, I couldn't be certain of the innocence of either. And being out here alone with them, I especially hoped they hadn't worked together to dispose of Oliver—and somehow convinced Wayne of their innocence.

For now, I glanced first at Neil, then at Carlo, and said, "Hey, I already told you I can't talk about any results of the discussion with Detective Christopher. That's true even way out here, away from other suspects."

"*Other* suspects," Carlo growled. "Then you're not even suggesting that we're known to be innocent."

"Like I said—"

"You can't talk about it. Not even to give us any reassurances." Neil sounded perturbed.

But that was all I could do. Besides ramp up my suspicions of them a bit, but I wasn't about to tell them that.

We continued walking for a while, though, and I felt calmer as they too helped point out the wildlife we saw and seemed to enjoy the animals a lot, though I didn't think anyone could appreciate them to the extent I did.

We observed some Sitka deer for a while and watched their movements and interaction. I loved that part of our get-together.

We didn't hike for a long time, though, and I was sure it wasn't just because the weather was growing even worse. More cold. More snow.

The upcoming winter was starting to arrive, teasing us with what we would soon experience in the Alaskan wilderness.

The pace of our hike back was even faster than it had been coming out here. This would be my last visit to the far reaches of the sanctuary for today, and I just hoped it wouldn't be too bad tomorrow to even venture out for a while.

"Tell us more about the tours you give during the summer," Neil said as we walked, having to shout a bit over the snapping wind.

He was being nice. Nicer than he tended to be with me most of the time. To try to convince me of his innocence? Or because he really wasn't as bad a guy as he'd seemed before?

"Oh, they're fun," I said. "You'll have to come on one next season." And I started to describe some of the wildlife I pointed out there, with both him and Carlo asking questions.

Our walk back seemed to go fast, which wasn't surprising. Soon we'd passed all the fencing and were at the edge of the parking lot.

"Guess I'll go back to the welcome building," I said. "How about you two?"

"Oh, I'm going on another trail for a while," Carlo said.

"And I'm going into my office," was Neil's reply. Sasha and I accompanied him across the lot and into the lobby as Carlo began heading around the building.

I figured I could do my latest short report now and went into the computer room. It didn't take long to add in the wildlife I'd seen that afternoon—and I wished I'd seen more. Walked more. Done more.

Maybe learned more from my companions on that hike. I hadn't told them much, and they hadn't told me much.

Another dead end. I was experiencing a lot of those.

It really might be time to leave this sanctuary, at least for a while. Fortunately, I didn't think the detective was planning to have me arrested. But I also wasn't doing much good in determining who'd killed Oliver.

A bunch of people around here might not have liked him, but who had hated him that much?

I'd had enough.

But if I did leave, where would I go? What would I do?

I sat a while longer, pondering, with Sasha at my side. Maybe what I should do was just my job here at Juneau Wildlife World, observing and reporting on the animals as much as possible.

Ignoring the whole Oliver situation, as long as it didn't appear my freedom was in jeopardy.

For now, for the rest of the afternoon, I figured Sasha and I would just return to our apartment, where I could ponder some more. Maybe use my phone to get online and see what places I might be able to work if I did leave.

But more likely, I'd stay. Settle down more. Stop prodding people for answers. Stay as safe as I could.

And hope the detectives and other authorities did their jobs, solved Oliver's murder, and arrested the responsible person.

And made the rest of us safer to continue our work, protecting and observing and caring for the wonderful creatures at Juneau Wildlife World.

Yeah. I hoped. Sure. Believed? Not so much.

And I knew my mind wouldn't stop attempting to figure it out, whether or not I stayed.

Sasha must have realized my mind was doing its usual over-thinking. She stood up beside me and rubbed against my leg.

"Okay, girl," I said. "Let's get going." Most likely for a short walk, then to our apartment, where we'd stay and eat dinner.

And maybe watch a little television to give that mind of mine something else to concentrate on, at least for a while.

We walked downstairs from the office where the computer was and into the lobby, which was empty for the moment, thankfully. I'd had my sessions with people earlier. Some quiet would be helpful.

But as we neared the door to go outside, Marnie rushed in from the hallway where the kitchen was. "Oh, Stacie, you're still here. Good. I'd really like to talk to you. Could you come into the kitchen?"

"Do you need help with food preparation?" I asked.

Was that what she wanted to talk about? She wore her apron, after all. Her bright-blond hair swirled around her face, messier than usual. She remained pretty, of course, and yet there was something different about her expression. Remote, maybe. Or worried. Or . . . well, I didn't really know.

"Sure," she responded. "When don't I?"

But from what she'd said, I had the impression that wasn't the main reason she wanted me to join her.

Didn't matter. I was curious now, and if there was also something I could do to help, why not?

And so I joined her, Sasha at my side, as she entered the door to the kitchen. She headed to the main counter, as she usually did. There were wrapped containers on it, undoubtedly of food, though I couldn't tell what kind or for which animals.

"Are these ready to be taken out?" I asked. It was getting a bit late in the day, but I didn't know how Marnie scheduled her deliveries, even though I'd seen her out on the grounds sometimes.

"Tomorrow," she said. "I'll be placing them in the refrigeration room soon. But for now"—she gestured for me to sit on one of the stools facing the counter—"please sit down."

"Sure," I said, and walked over, Sasha beside me.

Marnie followed, and soon we faced each other.

"Okay," she finally said. "Here's what I wanted to tell you." She paused for a moment and looked away, then back at my face. Her lower lip stuck out a bit as she said, "I'm the one who killed Oliver."

"What?" I couldn't help exclaiming. Of all the people here, I'd considered her one of the least likely to be the murderer.

We'd talked about this previously. At least I'd told her I was innocent. And I hadn't believed she was guilty. Before.

Sure, she'd indicated she'd had a small tiff with Oliver, whom she'd said was coming on to her more than she'd liked.

And the few times I'd seen him try to help her with food preparation, I hadn't had the sense they were best buddies.

Still . . .

"I don't want to get into any details about why and how, although I'm sure you know the weapon that killed him was designed to make it appear that it could have been wolf fangs—and you can be sure some of my food preparation equipment can be modified that way."

"I get it," I lied. I didn't get it at all. Sure, she might have been able to put such a gadget together, but I just didn't see her using it.

But if not, why was she telling me this?

"Now, I'd really rather you not let the detectives know. If they start to arrest the wrong person, I'll of course step up and tell them the truth. But for now, I don't want to be interrogated further if I can avoid it, and I definitely don't want them to arrest me."

"I understand," I said. And I did understand that part.

Just not why she'd done it. Or, if she hadn't, why she was lying this way to me.

To protect someone? If so, who?

Wayne, maybe. He was her boss as well as mine. But I'd already stuck him way down on the list of suspects.

The most logical person, then, was Bill. He hung out with her a lot. Did they have something more between them than just a food prep relationship?

I did recall that Bill and Oliver hadn't seemed to be best buddies. Was that because Oliver had been coming on to Marnie and Bill hadn't liked it?

That seemed like a stretch to me.

Under these circumstances, though—with Marnie confessing despite, in my opinion so far, it being a lie—that was the best explanation I could come up with at the moment.

But I didn't just want things to stop there. "But what *do* you want me to do?" I asked her. "You've confessed to murder. You know I have the ear of one of the detectives, and I've been fighting to make it clear I'm not the guilty party. If you didn't want me to tell anyone, why did you confess to me?"

She had stopped looking directly at me and now stared down at the counter. From this angle, I could see tears at the edges of her eyes.

"I don't know. I shouldn't have, even though you seem to be the one around here who's been trying hardest to find Oliver's killer. Forget it."

"Are you trying to protect someone?" I demanded. *Like Bill? If not him, who?* But I didn't add that.

"No," she said, then, "Forget it." Then she added, "I'm just so confused and concerned about what might happen to Juneau Wildlife World if that murder isn't solved soon. I didn't want to think you'd killed Oliver, but it would have made things easier if the troopers believed you did and arrested you, so everyone could think all was now well here."

Nice. We weren't really friends, after all. Even so . . .

"But all wouldn't be well here. Not really. Not with the real killer still out there. Who knows why whoever it was did it, who they might go after next?" I paused. "Although it sounds as if you have the answers to that."

"Right, since it's me." But she was looking down toward the floor now, her expression miserable.

I had an urge to hug her. I also had an urge to dash out of the room with Sasha and call Detective Christopher and let her know this wonderful news of a confession.

But I didn't believe it.

"Look, Marnie," I said. "I can understand your stress. I think everyone here feels it at least somewhat, and I may genuinely still be near the top of that suspect list despite the fact I shouldn't be. But if you're trying to protect someone, just consider the potential consequences. I mean—" I hesitated, then said, "The person I see you with the most is Bill. Did he—?"

"Kill Oliver?" She appeared shocked. "No way. And there's nothing between us anyway, Stacie. I think he might like there to be, but though I like the guy, I don't like him that way. If I thought he was guilty, I'd say something."

Would she? Was this as much of an act as her confession? I wasn't sure what to think.

But I didn't get to continue asking questions, since the person I had a feeling she was trying to protect, despite her denial, came through the door into the kitchen just then.

Uh-oh. If he truly was the guilty party, what would he do if he thought she'd confessed? Did he care enough about her to protect her the way she might have tried to protect him and still tell the truth?

Or would he act as if he was shocked at this news but believed in her guilt?

Marnie slipped off the stool and took a few steps toward Bill. Her expression had changed completely, and she seemed to have regained her poise. She was smiling now. "Hey, assistant, how did you know I needed your help right now? Stacie's offered to help some too, but I want to get a couple more packages ready tonight so I can head out early tomorrow to one of the farthest areas, hopefully before the weather gets a lot worse."

"Sounds good. Let's get it together as soon as possible."

Would it be okay for them to be alone together now? Well, why not? They'd still be here in the kitchen, after all. They'd been alone in the wilds of the park before without any issues. And if they were protecting each other, why stop now?

And I still didn't know who Marnie had been attempting to protect, if anyone. She'd seemed to make it clear it wasn't Bill. I didn't understand why she'd confessed, and her reason of trying to protect Juneau Wildlife World made a teeny bit of sense, but not much.

I doubted either of them wanted my company any longer, which was a good thing. Even so, I said, "Guess you won't need my help now, since there are two of you." That gave Marnie—or even Bill—the opportunity to request that I stay for whatever reason, actual food preparation or additional company in case either of them felt discomfort.

"That's right," Marnie said. "Thanks for stopping in."

"We'll be fine," Bill added.

I certainly hoped so.

Pulling gently on Sasha's leash, I led my pup out the door, stopping just before leaving to glance toward Marnie. She was bending over the counter, Bill at her side. They were pulling things out of one of the now-opened plastic containers of food that I'd seen on the counter and apparently starting to combine them.

Hopefully that would be good for some of the animals, I thought, and we left.

I walked Sasha briefly in the increasing snow flurries, glad we weren't heading into the farther territories again today, a bit sympathetic that Marnie and Bill might be.

Or should I be sympathetic? I now figured that one or both of them had to be at the top of my suspect list in Oliver's death.

It made sense to put Marnie there, since she'd confessed, though I didn't really believe her words.

Should I believe her?

I was more inclined to suspect she was protecting someone, and notwithstanding her denial, the logical one seemed to be Bill.

Yes, I'd witnessed some interactions among Oliver and both of them, together and individually. Though I'd sensed they weren't great buddies, I hadn't figured they were enemies, especially not murderous ones.

Marnie had told me already that Oliver had hit on her but she'd rejected him. Had she done the same with Bill?

If she hadn't been lying in her confession, did that mean Bill was in danger?

Okay. Enough. I walked Sasha briefly, and then we returned to our apartment. I felt really confused. Upset.

As we entered, I made sure the door was locked behind me as I always did. There was a murderer around somewhere, after all, whether or not it was Marnie.

I went into the small kitchen with Sasha following me. Too bad I didn't have any wine or beer. A small drink sounded like a good idea.

But I figured I should just feed my dog and eat dinner myself while I thought about that day—and Marnie's sort-of confession.

And that's what I did, taking care of Sasha first. I hardly tasted the food I put together from the mixes I'd brought—a tuna casserole for now.

As I ate, I considered calling Detective Christopher. Maybe I should have done so right away after leaving the company of Marnie and Bill. I still might. I had her contact information, after all, and she'd figure it was something important if I tried to contact her.

But what good would it do? It was getting late in the day. I figured I could ponder it more tonight and call her in the morning. But what could I really tell her, with Marnie backing down that way and my feeling fairly certain that, whatever the reason she'd falsely confessed, I wasn't much closer to figuring out who'd killed Oliver?

Although my mind was now whirling around the possibility of Bill.

Hey, maybe I should call Lettie. My assistant was quite perceptive. Would she know if those two were, or were becoming, an item? That would give Bill a motive to kill Oliver, I supposed, since Oliver had apparently been attempting to cozy up to Marnie.

I hadn't seen her since this morning but figured she was enjoying herself out on the grounds, hiking the trails, viewing the hills and mountains and doing even more of what I loved.

It was late enough that she likely had returned. I called her as I sat at my small kitchen table, Sasha at my side.

"Hi, Stacie," she said almost immediately. "How are you? How are things at Juneau Wildlife World?"

"You're not here?"

"Unfortunately, no. I left this morning after my boss at the school asked me to come in for an important meeting early this afternoon, and Wayne was okay with me leaving. And now that the weather is acting up even more and is supposed to get worse, I don't know when I'll get back there." She hesitated, but before I could say anything, she asked, "Is everything okay? I mean— nothing bad has happened again, has it?"

Like another murder? Or how about a weird nonconfession? "No, everything's fine," I said. "I was just hoping we could get together for a beer or something this evening, but we'll do it another time."

No sense troubling her over what was going on in my mind. I had no answers, after all.

"Okay. But you sound a little strange, Stacie. You're sure everything's all right?"

"Yep. As I said, I was hoping for some friendly company besides Sasha, but now I'll just look forward to it whenever."

And look forward to having someone I trusted to talk to . . . Well, it all would have to wait.

"Okay. I'll come back as soon as I can."

"Fine," I said. "Have a good night, Lettie."

"You too."

I figured I would, I thought as I hung up. Even so, I considered again when I'd call the detective, but there was nothing really helpful I could tell her. Certainly nothing that couldn't wait until tomorrow. I knew she wouldn't hop in her car and drive here in a hurry if I told her Marnie had confessed and recanted.

That didn't exactly solve the crime. Although I recognized I had to let the detective know that, as absurd as it was.

I thought about who else I wanted to talk to as I sat down on the small sofa and prepared to turn on the television. Liam.

We didn't seem to be close buddies any longer, but I missed him.

I also missed the fact that he was a trooper who might be able to advise me. But did I really need any advice right now?

What could I say to him? That I was okay? Sure. That someone had confessed to me, maybe as a joke?

I figured he would be interested in that, at least. I gave in and called him as I sat a bit straighter on the cushions.

He answered immediately. "Stacie! Good to hear from you. Is everything okay?"

"Yes," I said, trying to sound upbeat. I pictured him: his short dark hair, handsome face, deep-brown eyes . . . and uniform, which I assumed he wasn't wearing now. "I haven't been arrested yet, although I figure you'd know it if I had been."

"Most likely. Are you at your home? Maybe I could come over now and—"

"No, I'm staying in an apartment at the sanctuary right now rather than commuting. But I've been having good meetings with Detective Christopher. She was here earlier today. She wanted to discuss my thoughts on suspects and indicated that, though

I'm not exonerated, there's no immediate likelihood of my being taken into custody."

"Glad to hear that." He seemed to pause, then said, "And who did you tell her you suspect?"

"Everyone," I said. "And no one. But—" Okay, should I tell him about this odd afternoon?

Why not? It wouldn't hurt to get his opinion.

"But what?"

"Well, I had an odd thing happen. I heard a confession."

"What? From who?"

"That's the odd thing. It was from one of the people here I suspect the least, and then she retracted it. Marnie, who's in charge of food preparation for the animals. I started to ask questions, assuming she was attempting to protect someone, and she said she'd given a false confession because she just wanted to try to do something to protect the whole sanctuary, which didn't make a lot of sense. I thought she might be attempting to protect one of the guys who's here a lot and helps her out quite a bit, but she claimed that wasn't the reason. Then that guy came in, so we stopped talking."

A pause. Then Liam said, "Even if it was false for some weird reason, I really don't like this. I'm going to give Lillian—Detective Christopher—a call. I'm still not supposed to be involved, but it's not like I'm on my way there . . . yet." He sounded concerned, which I appreciated. "We'll be in touch again tomorrow, believe me. And in the meantime, be damned careful."

Oh, I still cared for this guy, and he appeared to care for me too, at least in some ways.

"I will," I said. "Thanks, Liam. And—"

"And what, Stacie?" His voice was soft, and I had an urge to stroke his cheek, as if he were next to me.

"I miss you."

"I miss you too."

Then the call was over.

I watched TV for a couple of hours. When it was nearly time to go to bed, I knew I had to take Sasha out first. Remembering Liam's sweet warning—not that I wasn't planning on being careful anyway—I got the pepper spray from the drawer where I kept it when I wasn't carrying it and stuck it my pocket.

I looked around when I opened the door, and then we went downstairs. We walked around the main area of the apartment building to the side, in the cold and increasing snow.

Suddenly, Sasha stood at attention. "What's up, girl?" I asked.

And then I saw Bill walk from behind the building, coming toward us. That seemed strange. Why was he out here at this hour?

Just to get some air? Or was he heading toward the vending machine building for something to eat?

"Hi," I called out to him. "What brings you out here so late?"

It was probably no big deal, but I nevertheless let one hand drop to my side so I'd be able to grab my pepper spray if necessary.

"You do," he growled as he got a lot closer.

Sasha tensed, and I felt certain my dog, who was my defender, was ready to protect me if necessary.

I hoped it wasn't, but I didn't tell her to sit.

"What do you mean?" I asked, then gasped as he pulled a large kitchen knife from behind his back.

He swung it first at me, but immediately drew it down so it pointed at Sasha.

"Let's go inside and talk," he said, "and I'll tell you. But keep your dog away from me or I'll stab her."

No! I couldn't let him hurt my Sasha. But I was too far away to aim pepper spray at his face, and I'd no other way I could immediately think of to stop him.

246

Was he about to confess to Oliver's murder? Because he'd really done it, or to protect Marnie?

Or was he doing this for some other reason?

Didn't matter. I was going to defend my defender, no matter what.

"Okay," I said, trying to keep my voice from quivering. "Let's go talk."

Chapter
Twenty-One

What was I going to do now?

What else could I do? Holding Sasha's leash, I walked inside the now dimly lit welcome building with Bill—and it didn't feel so welcoming right now. Especially since Bill was at my side, the one opposite Sasha, much too close.

Certainly close enough to stab me if he chose.

He was wearing his black sweatshirt and dark pants, which would have made it hard for anyone outside to see him. Including me.

Until it was too late.

The lobby was empty. No lights were on upstairs to indicate anyone was in an office.

We headed down the hall to the kitchen. At this hour, Marnie most likely wasn't there, but I supposed it was the area here most familiar to the man who was now holding me hostage.

The man who'd killed Oliver? I definitely thought so now.

He wanted to talk. To confess? Something else? And now that he'd brandished a knife at me and my dog, what was going to happen? Did he intend to kill us too?

How could he let us go after this?

Once inside the kitchen, I wasn't sure what to do, where to go. Or how to save us.

I turned slowly in a way I hoped didn't appear threatening and saw him close the door behind him, still holding the knife in front of him. Unfortunately, I hadn't seen anyone else in the building who might have noticed what was going on and called the authorities.

"Where would you like me to go now?" I asked, just standing there.

He gestured to the stools facing the counter. "Sit down," he said, and I headed that way, Sasha at my side.

It felt familiar. That was what Marnie had had me do too.

But unlike Marnie, Bill didn't sit on the stool beside me, at least not immediately.

Instead, he edged backward to a cabinet with quite a few drawers in it and opened the bottom drawer, pulling out a large white plastic bag. "I'd hidden this under a lot of stuff in one of the refrigerator rooms before," he said, "but it's necessary now for me to use it." He joined me then at the counter, the knife pointing at me with one hand and the bag in the other.

I gestured carefully to Sasha to keep her sitting at my side. I knew she was uneasy and had the sense that things around her were bad. Maybe that her human was in big trouble.

But I definitely didn't want this guy to hurt her.

Not that I wanted him to hurt me either.

I could guess what was in the bag but waited for Bill to do whatever it was he'd planned, at least for now. I thought about the pepper spray in my pocket, but with the knife still aimed at me, I wasn't sure what he'd do if I attempted to spray him now, how I'd avoid getting stabbed, so I just sat there.

I thought I knew which drawers in the kitchen also contained knives, but I couldn't exactly dash over and grab one.

Not yet, at least.

And I felt as uneasy as my dog, or more so, as I continued to wait for whatever came next.

It didn't take long.

"I know you figured that Marnie was trying to protect someone when she confessed to you, right, and that the person might be me?" His brown eyes were narrowed as he glared at me. "Well, she was right to suspect me. And though I appreciate her attempting to help me that way, she only got herself into trouble. Maybe. But I give a damn about her too, and I'm going to change that."

I wasn't sure what kind of response he wanted from me, so I just waited and tried to keep my mind under control, which wasn't easy.

What was going to happen here? I figured he intended to kill me. Could I save myself?

Could I save Sasha?

Wouldn't his guilt be obvious now, and lead to his arrest for killing Oliver . . . and me?

How did he intend to handle this?

To handle me?

"So here's what we're going to do." He leaned forward on his stool, moving the knife, on the counter, closer to me. "You're going to open that bag."

I looked at the bag. That hopefully would be okay to do. I had an idea what was in it, right or wrong.

It turned out I was right. I carefully reached for what was inside, staying as far from Bill as I could, and pulled the plastic apart.

Inside was paper wrapped around something.

"Unwrap it," Bill growled.

Which I did.

And revealed a strange-looking thing made out of pieces of metal bound together with tape. It resembled a large kitchen whisk, only a whole lot more dangerous. There was a handle, and sticking out of it were very thick pieces of wire that seemed to form a . . . well, a claw with points at the end. Really sharp points.

Oh, yes. This could have been the weapon that killed Oliver. Those points could be used as the apparent teeth that had torn open his neck, as if done by a wolf.

I held it without looking at Bill, saying nothing.

But yes, I held a weapon. What if I used it on him, hopefully before he could stab me with his knife?

"I assume you can guess what that is," he said to me. "And what I did with it."

"Is it what was used to kill Oliver?" *How you ripped open his throat as if an animal, a wolf, had attacked him?*

And how fast could I use it now to attack Bill to save myself—and Sasha?

"Exactly. Now here's how things are going to go. You're going to attack me. I assume that's what you're thinking. Only I'm going to hold your hand so I can control the damage done to me—which won't be my death, as I'm sure you're hoping."

I stayed still, waiting. Thinking. Trying to figure out how to handle this.

Hurt him? I didn't like to hurt anyone or anything, but to save myself and my dog, sure.

But where was he going with this?

I could guess, which I did. "And then you're going to kill me, and tell the world you did it to protect yourself." I paused, but he didn't answer right away, so I continued, "And will you also claim I confessed to you that I'd killed Oliver this way, so you had to attack me in self-defense?"

It seemed so logical.

It seemed so scary.

What was I going to do?

Sasha moved at my feet.

I at least had to protect her. I held her leash even tighter.

"I always figured you were pretty smart," Bill said, "especially when you tried to save yourself by questioning everyone, accusing most people around here."

His grin now seemed evil, and I did have an urge to use the claw in my hand and slash it away.

But that would only do what he wanted. And give him an excuse to stab me now.

As if he needed one.

"Oh, and in case you're wondering," he added, "your damned dog will get out of this all just fine. You see, I'm going to open the door and get her out of here and hope she'll bark to get back inside—alerting people that something's wrong in here. They'll find me slashed and moaning and maybe even crying . . . since I had to kill you to save myself." He laughed.

I looked down at Sasha, feeling her try to move again. I saw she was reacting . . . but not to what was happening with me. She was glancing toward the area that opened into the freezer.

Was someone there? If so, I had to protect them as well as us. And not call any attention to whoever it was. I needed Bill's focus on me, at least for the moment.

"You've got this all figured out," I stated, letting my anger roll out. If there was someone there, how long had they been there? Had they heard what Bill said? Did they know what he was planning?

Was there anything they could do to stop him without getting hurt too?

Or was I just imagining this out of hope for my survival somehow?

"Yeah, I do." He got off the stool and moved his face in my direction. "Okay, go on. Do it. Attack me with that thing. You might even be able to stop me. After all, I did use it to kill Oliver."

Right or wrong, I gripped the weapon and even considered doing what he said—

But I stopped as Marnie dashed into the room, screaming. "What are you doing?"

Did she mean Bill or me or both of us?

"Marnie," Bill cried out. "What are you doing here?"

"I was worried . . . I have access to a sensor set up in here to let me know if there's any activity, not that I expect any. But this is my kitchen, and I want to make sure no one does anything nasty to the food I prepare. It let me know someone had come in here before, and because whoever it was left quickly, I didn't come . . . then." Maybe that was when Bill had gotten the knife. "But when the sensor said someone was here again, I decided to check it out. I sort of suspected who it was, but not why or what you're doing. Why did you kill Oliver, Bill? And why do you want to kill Stacie? This is horrible!"

She was crying, but she didn't get closer. She must have seen the knife in his hand—and the murder weapon in mine.

In my hand. Getting my prints all over it.

Well, if I survived this, I'd be able to explain to the authorities how they got there—and not because I'd killed Oliver with it.

Bill took a step closer to Marnie, but she moved farther from him.

Meanwhile, Sasha, standing at my side, started moving. She knew something was wrong. I held on to her harness to make sure she didn't attempt to jump on knife-armed Bill.

"Look," he said, "I did it for you, Marnie. For us. Oliver was trying to get closer to you. A lot closer. And you told me you were very much against that, but he didn't stop. I tried talking to him too, but he made it clear he had nothing to say to me, only you. Oh, except to tell me to lay off trying to win you over. I had to figure out how to keep him away from you."

"You didn't have to kill him!" she screamed. "You need to turn yourself in, Bill. It's only right."

His expression turned mournful. "I definitely need to do something now that you both know. I . . . I definitely don't want to hurt you, Marnie."

I noticed he didn't mention me. Not surprising. He'd clearly intended to kill me, but apparently he wouldn't do it right now, with Marnie aware and watching.

I felt slightly relieved. But I still needed to get the guy somehow, get him arrested.

But how?

He didn't exactly give me the opportunity to call the detective or any troopers. Or even use the murder weapon still in my hand on him, since he still held the knife up.

"I'm leaving," he said. "Right now. You two stay here. I'll get in my car and get out of here. And no one else will get hurt." He looked Marnie in the eyes. "I know you care about me. We worked so well together and seemed likely to get to know each other better. I just wish it had worked out."

She still said nothing, though he waited for a few seconds, as if he expected her to agree or throw herself into his arms for a final good-bye.

"I'll be in touch when I can," he told her. He yanked the murder weapon away from me and thrust it back into the bag, careful to wield the knife in my direction. Then he dashed out the door, still holding the knife in his right hand, the plastic bag in his left.

Sasha pulled toward him, but no way was I going to let her follow.

I grabbed my phone from my pocket, though, as I started after him, keeping my dog close at my side with her leash.

I debated calling 911 first or the detective and figured it was enough of a crisis to call the emergency number. I realized Marnie was following as Sasha and I dashed out the door into the hallway before I made the call.

Bill stood in the hall, not far from the door. His hands were in the air, the knife on the floor in front of him.

Liam was there, aiming a gun at him.

Behind him was Wayne.

My good friend the Alaska trooper glanced at me. "Our conversation yesterday worried me, so I figured I'd come. Good thing I did. Why does this guy have a knife?"

"Oh, Liam," I said, wishing I could run over and give him a hug. But he was doing his trooper thing highly appropriately. "His name is Bill Westerstein. He just threatened me with that knife. And he admitted to me that he was the one who killed Oliver."

Chapter
Twenty-Two

Things went pretty fast after that.

Liam said he had already called for backup and they were on their way. Not the outside detectives but the real thing, both the investigators and those who could—and did—officially take Bill into custody for the murder of Oliver Brownling.

They still had more investigation to conduct, but it didn't hurt that their suspect just happened to have the murder weapon in his possession.

I was safe. So were the rest of us.

Liam introduced me to the investigators who'd come, and I told my story to one of them, a tall, serious man named Trooper Jonaster, as we sat in the lobby of the welcome building—and these officials, two men and a woman, were definitely welcome, in my opinion.

Marnie was questioned by another trooper across the room, and Wayne by another one.

Despite how late it was getting, several others at the sanctuary appeared from their apartments but were told to leave. Wayne promised to let them in on what was going on in the morning.

Though it took a while, when Bill had been taken away and the troopers had left, Liam, Marnie, and I eventually sat in Wayne's office in chairs facing his desk.

Marnie was clearly devastated. She said to me, "You know I suspected Bill, but not for the reasons he said. I realize I should never have tried to protect him for any reason, but . . . well, I do—I did—care for him."

"I understand," I said, and I sort of did.

But there were other things I wanted to know right away—like how Liam happened to be here. Yes, he'd said he'd be in touch again after our conversation, but I thought more information was in order. Had he intended all along to visit me here? He'd said he wasn't on his way *yet*, after all. And I'd gotten the impression he was concerned about me.

Once we left Wayne's office and we walked down to the lobby, I asked him. We sat on a couple of chairs there and talked.

Turned out he had called the sanctuary to let Wayne know he was on his way, indicating who he was and his trooper credentials as well as his friendship with me. He'd said he had gotten some information about things he wanted to check on here, so Wayne had gone to the gate when Liam called to say he'd arrived and let him in.

With there being security cameras at various locations in Juneau Wildlife World, Marnie wasn't the only one with access to the gadgetry that let her know if someone was in the kitchen. Wayne, of course, could check the kitchen and all other locations here as well, and he'd been able to let Liam know where there appeared to be people within the welcome building.

They'd both waited outside without knowing exactly what was going on, but Liam had jumped in immediately when Bill emerged wielding a knife.

257

And saved my life.

Rather than heading back to Juneau in the increasingly bad weather, Liam spent that night with Sasha and me in our apartment.

I was glad that my defender dog hadn't really jumped in to try to protect me, not against a man who could have stabbed her.

I told Liam, as we settled down in my bed, Sasha on the floor at my side as usual, that she had clearly been uneasy, though, and might have attempted to do something if I hadn't kept her close against me.

"Good dog," he said. He moved over me to pat that good dog—and snuggle against me.

"Thanks so much," I told Liam again.

"Anytime," he said, taking me into his arms and holding me tight. "But don't ever get into a dangerous situation like that again, understand?"

"Of course," I said, and hoped it was true.

Liam and I remained close that night. But he had to go back to his job the next day, and he kept in touch with me so I knew he'd returned safely to Juneau.

I knew we wouldn't see each other often for the rest of the winter.

But of course I had even more reason now to stay in close touch with the man I cared about—and who'd saved my life.

Everyone who'd been at the sanctuary that night was full of questions the next morning—and some were even interrogated by the troopers who remained here.

Wayne helped with their anxieties by holding a brief meeting in the welcome building, standing on the stairway as he had when he let everyone know about Oliver's death. This time, he told everyone what had just happened. I hadn't let him know about Marnie's false confession, but he knew now that Bill had confronted me with the intent to kill me after making it appear that I'd attacked him because I'd supposedly killed Oliver.

"But Bill is the guilty person," Wayne said, looking down at me where I stood at the base of the steps, and I nodded.

"That's definitely the conclusion of my own investigation," I told all of those who were there. "And I'm just glad to still be alive."

I received a lot of sympathy and gratitude then. Everyone was glad to have the situation resolved. Were any upset that it had been Bill? If so, they didn't admit it.

And then we all went back to work, helping and observing the wildlife here at Juneau Wildlife World.

End of story. Sort of.

Weeks passed.

Bill remained incarcerated, and it was clear that he would face trial for murder.

Marnie remained sad but determined not to let what had happened deter her from continuing her food preparation for the wildlife at the sanctuary—a good thing, since the Alaska weather segued into winter.

Wayne was appreciative of me and all I'd gone through. And I appreciated his trust—and his having helped Liam when it was so necessary.

My assistant Lettie was amazed, said she wished she'd known what was going on and had been able to help. But I was just as glad she'd not been there—and not been someone else I had to worry about when I was trying to figure out how to save Sasha and me and then Marnie too.

I, of course, remained at Juneau Wildlife World, trekking out into the wilderness areas as far and as much as possible with the bad weather, Sasha at my side, to view the wonderful wildlife, although some had hibernated and fewer appeared in areas we could see. But that was life, and wildlife, and it was fine.

I remained in touch with Liam as much as I could, despite the distance between us, by emails, texts, and phone calls. And our communications were as warm and tender as I'd hoped.

Spring would be here eventually, and I'd be able to return to giving boat tours. I'd be able to return to Juneau. I'd be able to see, and point out, more wildlife, mostly closer to the animals.

I'd hopefully be able to see Liam more.

And thank heavens, the latest murder that had occurred around me was resolved.

No more!

I hoped.

Acknowledgments

Thanks to my publisher, Crooked Lane, for publishing this second Alaska Untamed mystery. As mentioned before, I, like Stacie Calder, adore Alaska and its wildlife, and I'm delighted to have the opportunity to tell another story that includes both—as well as a dog!

Another special thank-you to my wonderful agent, Paige Wheeler.

Thanks again to all the wonderful folks at Crooked Lane who have helped with this book, most especially publishing and production assistant Rebecca Nelson.

And all you readers who are enjoying my Alaska Untamed series—many thanks to you!